CHEEKIE

a novel

the Desire

by

Clarence Nero

COUNCIL OAK BOOKS
TULSA / SAN FRANCISCO

Council Oak Books, LLC, 1350 E. 15th St., Tulsa, OK 74120

First edition / First printing
02 01 00 99 98   5 4 3 2 1

The following have generously given permission to use extended quotations from copyrighted songs: From "Who's Lovin' You" by William Robinson, Jr., published by Jobete Music Co., Inc. "Shake Your Groove Thang" by Fekaris-Perren, published by Perren Vibes Music, Inc. "Everybody Plays the Fool" by Clark-Bailey-Williams, published by Alley and Trio. "Younger Man Older Woman Jack" by Gary Rose and Richard Rose, published by Perrace Entertainment Corporation. "I Ain't Gone Bump No More with that Big Fat Woman" by Joe Tex, published by Trio. "The Mardi Gras" by Rosie Ledet, published by Flat Town. "Mardi Gras Mambo" by Elliot-Adam-Welch, published by the Arc Music Group. "I'm Catching Hell" and "Our Love" by Jackson-Yancy, Capital Records; part of the Natalie Cole Collection. "Movin' On Up to the East Side" by Jeff Berry, performed by Janet Du Bois. "Good Times" by Marilyn and Alan Bergman and Dave Grusin.

Cover illustration, cover and text design by Carol Stanton

Library of Congress cataloging-in-publication data
Nero, Clarence, 1970-
    Cheekie : a child out of the desire : a novel / by Clarence Nero.
        p.   cm.
    ISBN 1-57178-063-7
    I. Title.
PS3564.E66C48   1998   98-12143
813'.54--dc21   CIP

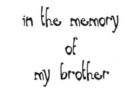

in the memory
of
my brother

D e n n e r e l l   W e b b

1974-1996

You ain't nothin' but ole cry baby,
been whining and crying ever since
you dropped forth from your
mama's gaping womb.

And ever since you were little
you been reaching for her bosom
sucking and milking her for
your own delight.

Just look at you with that pacifier
in your mouth, looking and peeping,
thinking 'bout what you gone cry 'bout next.

But you ain't no child now.
So take that thumb out your mouth
and hold your head up like you
got good sense.
'Cause you can cry
a pool full of tears
and ain't nobody gone mind you.
'Cause they already know
you ain't nothin' but ole cry baby.

That's why your grandmama
nicknamed you Cheekie in the first place.
She saw in you from the very beginning,
your cleverness and sneakiness
always trying to have your way.
But we own to you now,
so you stomp your feet,
and fall all over whining,
'cause ain't nobody gone mind you.
'Cause they already know
you ain't nothin' but ole cry baby.

— C. Nero
   "Cry Baby"

Contents

one
love don't live
here anymore
1

two
i'm catching hell
17

three
shake your
groove thang
29

four
ain't nothin' like the
real thing
47

five
the invisible man
59

six
my forest adventure
71

seven
tremors
81

eight
running away
89

nine
Jesus on
the main line
105

ten
bustin' loose
115

eleven
i'm deep!
123

twelve
the boogy man
139

thirteen
ain't nothin' goin' on
but the rent
151

fourteen
not the crazy lady
161

fifteen
everybody plays
the fool sometimes
171

sixteen
fighting back
185

seventeen
mardi gras mambo
191

eighteen
i can do bad
all by myself
205

nineteen
movin' on up
217

twenty
making the grades
231

twenty-one
amazing
grace
247

twenty-two
first born
261

acknowledgments

Giving honor to God, who is the center of my joy and the very reason why I exist, I thank my parents Katie and Clarence, Jr. for bringing me into the world, and my entire family for always believing in me, especially my grandmothers, Emelda, Rose, and Pat for their spiritual guidance. And everyone who once lived in the Desire from which this work was inspired.

There are so many people who guided me with this book that I would like to personally thank: Andre Hoyd, for being the first person to tell me that I have a story; Josephine Humphreys for taking the time out to guide me through rigorous rewrites; Roderick Terry, my attorney, for his legal advice and encouragement; Marie Brown, for reading and rereading my work and for her honesty in critiquing the work. My agents, Rhinold Ponder and Michelle Tuck Ponder, for coming aboard so quickly and doing the job that needed to be done. Renee Lapeyrolerie, for her prompt response to my request for pictures of the Desire; Dan Slater, for his constant encouragement and belief in the work; everyone at Pretrial Services who encouraged me as I wrote the novel especially Mr. Robinson, for giving me the room to grow; Jason Skerlov, for helping me with the editing and rewriting; Michelle, Daphne, Gorman and Mikal, for listening to me go on and on about the book even before I knew I really had a story to tell; Ms. Antoinette Williams, for reading the book and being so excited about it—it really meant a lot. And Ms. Carolyn Bowen, for giving a listening ear, always. You guys are the best!

I would like to express my gratitude and appreciation to the following people: Keith Boykins, Paul Butler, Mark Wallace, Mike Webster, Derrick Locker, Keith Magee, Ms. Chapman, Walter Pearson, Tanya Flowers, and Fred Harrison. A special thanks to Melinda Young, my fierce "diva" friend for being there and always standing by me no matter what other folks had to say; Dr. Augustus Valmond, a friend who has a heart of gold and continues to wish the best for me; Monique Kelly, for being that family member who believed in me, always; Rosalyn Andrews, my cousin, for her love and support; Dr. Dolly McPherson, a family member who has also been a role model in the literary world; Omar Tyree, a talented and gifted brother who read the work and inspired me to keep writing; Victor Haydel, my former roommate who listens to me even when he doesn't want to, and supports me anyway; Gregory Steven Small, my friend who passed away before he could see the work published but who I know continues to sing praises for me; Oprah Winfrey, who doesn't have a clue, but her show, her life and book club continues to inspire me every day. I thank her for what she is doing for writers. I thank James T. Cooper, for putting his own career goals on the side to help me with the editing and rewrites and the one person who stood by this project no matter what and who continues to support me in my writing endeavors. Dr. Maya Angelou, the most decorative poet of our times, for inspiring me through her own work, and for reading mine. And last but certainly not least, I thank Dr. Sally Dennison, Cindy McKee and the entire staff at Council Oak Books for giving me this chance and the positive energy that they bring to this project.

Love don't live here anymore

I thought Mama and Daddy had a good marriage. They seemed happy and in love while raising us three children — me, Torey, and Darrell. My name is Charles Webb III, but my nickname is Cheekie. Mama always say I'm too mannish for my age, 'cause I'm only nine years old-nappy-head Afro, sassy tongue, spoiled rotten, and the oldest of the three children.

Now, the reason why I say I thought they had a good marriage is because from what I've been told they been in love from the very first day they met. And their romance was almost like Romeo and Juliet. But that's no longer the case, 'cause now things seem to be getting worse and worse around here every day. But their story goes way back, and that's why it's so hard to believe things have suddenly changed between them.

Before I was even born, what happened was my daddy, Charles, met my mama, Faye, down in the Desire Project, in the Ninth Ward. They fell in love. Soon after Mama got pregnant with me, they moved into their very own place in the Desire.

You see, the reason why Mama and Daddy moved in the

Desire was because my Mama's whole family lived back there. My grandma, who we call Pam, threw me and Mama out her place. She threw us out because she never liked my daddy. She said he was too old for Mama, who was only thirteen years old when they first met. My daddy, he was twenty-one years old—barely an adult himself. But Daddy didn't let Pam stop him, because he loved Mama from the very day he laid eyes on her.

Back in 1966 was when Daddy and Mama first met. Even though Daddy lived over in the Seventh Ward, which is a distance from the Desire Project, he and his friends would hang out down in the Ninth Ward at a neighborhood sweet shop called Fletcher's.

Mama and her childhood girlfriend, Li'l Soul, were sitting in the sweet shop eating a bologna sandwich on french bread—a favorite at the sweet shop. Mama was a pretty, caramel brown, with big legs and big thighs. She wore her hair cut in a bob. Li'l Soul was an attractive girl, too. She was light-skinned, long haired, and turned all the boys' heads. Her real name was Wyona, but Mama called her "Li'l Soul" because she was light enough to pass for white, but had enough soul in her to be black.

Mama'nem were hanging out after school, listening to the tunes of the Supremes, the Temptations, and all the other Motown favorites. They were dancing, swinging, and bringing that shop down. And the fellows were either playing pinball or sitting around checking the girls out. Li'l Soul's boyfriend at the time, Fred Carrie, came over to the table, interrupted Mama'nem laughing and giggling like most girls their age who found just about everything funny.

Fred Carrie asked, "Wyona, who is your friend here?"

"Who wants to know, Fred?"

"My boy, Charles, over there wants to meet your friend here."

Daddy was sitting there trying not to look obvious and overly excited, even though he badly wanted her. He had seen Mama many times there in the sweet shop and that day he was going to make his move.

Mama giggled at the thought of meeting a man; she was kind of shy back then. They exchanged stares the whole time they were there, and then Daddy walked over and asked the question that Mama was afraid he wouldn't ask.

"So, can I come by and see you sometime, or get your number...?"

Daddy stopped in the middle of his question and waited for Mama to say what her name was.

"Faye," said Mama.

"OK, Faye, so will that be possible?" asked Daddy.

Mama knew there was no way in hell she could give that number out to no boy—her mama, Pam, would kill her.

Mama said, "Look, maybe I can get your number and call you sometime. My mama is kind of strict."

After that, Mama said, they met there every chance they got—sneaking and making sure Pam never found out.

Pam was a tall, strong woman, raising ten children alone in a four-bedroom apartment. She was strict on all her children—Bob, Trina, Dorothy, Annie Mae, Rodney, Charles, Toney, Florence, Coma Lee—all of them. She had moved in the Desire when it first opened back in the 1940s, before Mama was even born. Before the Desire became what it is today—a place of ongoing violence, homicides, and drug dealing—it was *the* place to live, if you lived in a New

Orleans housing project, that is. Named after the famous street in New Orleans called Desire, this project was the nicest and most respected of all. People stuck together, and everyone looked out for each other. They were proud of themselves and their homes. There were problems now and then with violence and drugs, but nothing really serious. People walked the streets at night and didn't have to be afraid. They could leave their doors unlocked and not have to worry about someone breaking in, stealing their stuff. The Desire was a community of people who respected one another. Mama has so many fine memories of her childhood growing up in the Desire project.

It was one of the biggest projects in New Orleans, with close to five thousand people. Mama'nem lived at the front of the project, right on Desire Street.

Anyway, Mama said two years had gone by, and Pam never knew nothing about her and my daddy seeing one another. Daddy would sneak by when Pam would be out—Mama would call and let him know. He didn't come inside, though. He would stand there under the window talking to Mama, who hung out the window from their second floor apartment, talking to him. He came often, standing under that window in the rain and sleet sometimes. My daddy's friends called them Romeo and Juliet because of how they had to hide their love for each other. And just like Romeo, he was determined not to let Pam stop them from seeing one another.

Mama's sisters and the neighbors gave him a nickname, too. They started calling him "Snowman," because he would stand out there in the rain so long that the top of his Afro would turn white like a snowman. When they saw him coming they shouted, "Here comes the snowman." They would even sneak and meet up over my daddy's friend's house. Everyone knew about their love for each other—everyone except Pam.

After two years of dating in secret, though, Mama got pregnant. She was some scared, too; she knew Pam would kill her if she found out. That's why she told Annie Mae and Dorothy first.

They explained, "Girl, you better tell Pam because in a couple of months she gonna know anyhow."

Finally, Mama got up the nerve to tell Pam. She found Pam in her bedroom, sitting on the bed. Mama sat in a chair next to the bed, shaking and trembling so bad that Pam shouted, "Girl what's wrong with you?"

Mama pretended like her stomach was hurting, trying to tell Pam she was pregnant. Pam knew already anyhow because Annie Mae'nem had done told her everything. She leaned over and grabbed Mama by the neck, "So, Annie Mae'nem told me you been sneaking around my back with that Charles, and now you done got yourself pregnant. How you gonna take care of a baby, Faye? You only fifteen years old. Tell me how, Faye?"

Mama cried, "I don't know, Pam, but me and Charles gonna work it out."

"Ya'll gonna work it out? Thanks to him you pregnant in the first place. Now I don't want that nigga around my house, you hear me?"

Mama shook her head in fear, because Pam had her hands around her neck so tight she thought she might choke and die.

Pam said, "I guess you gonna keep this baby. We'll figure somethin' out later."

Mama was terrified after facing Pam, but that still didn't stop her from seeing my daddy. They would sneak and meet up at Fletcher's until she had me. And that's when Pam really got hateful. She complained from one day to the next about "that baby."

"He is such a cheekie baby, always whining and crying, and never satisfied."

Pam said it so much that everyone started calling me "Cheekie." I was born on December 23, 1968, and was only one month old then—still a newborn—when Pam threw us out. Mama remembered how I was screaming, yelling, and cutting up somethin' trouble the day it happened.

Mama's sisters and brothers stood around looking shocked. They just couldn't believe Pam was throwing us out in the cold with no place to go. But she did. Threw all of Mama's things and her and the suitcase out the door.

Mama had me in her arms, patting my back, trying to stop me from crying. She thought me crying like that was making matters worse. But crying or not crying, Pam was not changing her mind. She threw us out that cold, December night.

Mama ran to a pay phone right across the street. She said her hands were so cold that she couldn't even feel them. And her lips were so chapped that she could barely open her mouth wide enough to tell my daddy what had happened.

My daddy's mama, Emelia, is a compassionate woman who loves to help people in need. When she found out what had happened, she said, "Charles, go and get that girl and your baby and bring them in out of the cold."

When Daddy found Mama, she was sitting outside on

Pam's front porch, shaking and crying. Mama wrapped me in a blanket to keep me warm in the freezing weather. As they walked away, Pam peeped between her curtains so that they could not see her watching from her living room window.

When we arrived at my Grandma Emelia's house, they were sitting around talking about how Pam threw us out into the cold. My grandma, Emelia, and her husband, Larry, Great-grandma Rose (who is blind), and my Auntie Sonya (who was just a little girl).

Larry had a good job, so they had a nice place. They all lived on Claiborne Street, which is just a li'l distance from the Ninth Ward. Now, Larry was not as understanding as my grandma, but he said nothing for the moment about Mama and me coming to stay with them. Everyone else was excited about Charles's new son. (Mama named me after my daddy, who was named after his daddy.) From the time we walked in everyone was playing with me and holding me. They loved me even though they had never met me.

My grandma said, "Faye, you are welcome to stay here with us until your project comes available." (Just before Mama was kicked out of Pam's house, she had applied for a project in the Desire.)

My blind great-grandma, Rose, who had heard how "fine" Mama was, wanted a chance to feel for herself.

She said, "Come here Faye, let me see why Charles is so crazy about you."

She touched Mama's face, thighs, and hips.

She said, "Girl you are a brick house!" Everyone laughed.

She was a brick house, big legs and big thighs.

7

Grandma Rose continued, "Girl, you better stay away from eating so much cornbread."

Mama was excited to be around a warm and loving family like Daddy's family. They made us feel welcome, and Grandma Emelia treated Mama like she was her very own daughter. My daddy's sisters, Debbie, Karen, Roxie, and Selena, would come over and take Mama out sometime. She became really close to my daddy's oldest sister, Selena.

Selena was a fair-skinned girl with long flowing hair and big full eyes. She was pretty and known for having a sassy tongue. She always spoke her mind. And Mama just loved hanging around with her, because like Li'l Soul, Selena was fun to be around.

Selena was raising two daughters herself, named Rachelle and Tanya. Rachelle was two years old, and Tanya was a newborn like me.

We stayed with Grandma Emelia for a couple of months when the old saying, "all good things must come to an end," came true. Larry finally spoke his piece to Grandma.

He complained, "Mella, your son, his girlfriend, and their baby have to find somewhere else to live. It's too crowded in here." (He would always call her Mella for short, rather than Emelia.)

Grandma just couldn't tell them they had to go, although she knew Larry would if she didn't. But it was only a few days later that they got word—their apartment in the Desire had come available.

Mama and Daddy were excited from the start. Now, even though they were young and in love, they did not marry until *after* I was born, which means I was born out of wedlock. It was when they moved into their new home that they decided to tie the knot.

Everyone was there for the wedding. All the neighbors, my aunts and uncles were all there. My Auntie Annie Mae was the maid of honor. She had a newborn named Chad (nicknamed Butterball because of his turkey-like shape), and a little girl named Donna, but we called her Woody because she was skinny and had two big front teeth like a woodpecker's beak. My Grandma Emelia, Auntie Selena, and her two daughters were there, too. Everyone was there—everyone except Pam. Mama invited her and wanted her to be there. She sat around waiting, praying, and hoping Pam would come, but she never showed up.

After hours of sitting and pacing, Daddy said, "Girl, your mama don't like me, and ain't no way in hell she is coming to our wedding."

Mama was disappointed, but still managed to say those magic words, "I do." And they did, and it was official. They were husband and wife. They were so in love that they went and got tattoos on their left arms.

We live way at the back of the project—right on Alvar Street. Our place is small, too: a li'l kitchen, living room, bathroom, and two bedrooms. My room is right across the hall from Mama and Daddy's room. The inside of our apartment is painted in off-white, and the floors made out of light brown wood—good cedar wood. Mama is on welfare and Daddy is always looking for work. We are poor, no doubt, but the Desire is our home, and we make the most of it.

The Desire is a beautiful place to live, too. Each building is made of red brick, with apartments laid out like town houses, stacked side by side, one behind the other, and catty-cornered. In each building there are two apartments upstairs and two apartments downstairs. We live at 3924 Alvar Street, upstairs on the left side.

There is a neighbor across the hall named Ms. Johnson who lives with her boyfriend, Sly. They are raising four teenage sons—Perry, Stan, Raymond, and George—and a daughter named Annette. Sly is not their real daddy, but he is hard on all of them. He makes them run errands, take care of chores around the house, and keep the neighborhood clean. One of Ms. Johnson's sons, Raymond, has a glass eye and is kind of slow—you know, retardy. He is twenty-some-thin' years old, but acts like a much younger child.

Downstairs is a lady named Ms. Saphena. She is raising three girls and two sons—Sharrel, Daphne, Possie, Toney, and Reggie. Her youngest son, Toney, is also retardy.

Across the hall from Ms. Saphena is a lady named Gwen, and she is raising one son named Ronnie. Mama is very close to Gwen, Ms. Saphena, and Ms. Johnson. In fact, they became real good friends. During the bad times—they are always there for Mama.

They were married only a month before Mama got pregnant with Torey. He is a dark-skinned baby with curly hair. A year after having Torey, she got pregnant with Darrell. Darrell is a red, fat baby. Mama nicknamed him "Chub."

Me, Darrell, and Torey share one room with bunk beds. I have my own bed on top, and they share the bottom bunk. Mama decorated our room with blue and white Super Friends sheets, curtains, and posters. Boy, we love all the Super Friends: Wonder Woman, Superman, The Wonder Twins, all of them!

We were a happy family when we first moved into the Desire Project. Daddy and Mama took us to movies, amusement parks, and stuff like that. Every time they went out for fun, they took us with them. They were just a young couple, trying to survive and raise three children at the same time. Mama spent most of her time keeping the house in order and minding us children. Daddy spent the days doing odd jobs around the house and looking for permanent work.

It was when Daddy found a job working for the project as a maintenance man that everything started to change. I don't know if it was because he was working all the time or because Mama was lonely. All I know is that the "perfect" family doesn't live here any more. The good times we used to have are gone, and things are starting to change for the worse.

Mama's old girlfriend, Li'l Soul, started coming around while Daddy was at work. Daddy doesn't like Mama hanging around with Li'l Soul because she has a bad reputation around the Desire—sleeping with other women's husbands. That's why she never comes around when Daddy is home. Soon as he leaves out for work, though, she shows up. I guess she knows Daddy doesn't care for the likes of her. After a while, Li'l Soul started trying to get Mama to go out with her. There is this "joint" called Maze not too far from our house where Li'l Soul hangs out all the time. Mama says she is a singer there, too.

I was sitting in the kitchen eating one day when I heard Li'l Soul say, "Faye, girl, you need to come out with me sometime and have some fun for a change. Charles is always working—as he claim—and you are always stuck in this house with these chil'rens."

She realized I was sitting there listening to the whole

conversation. She grabbed hold my chin and said, "Well, they're pretty chil'rens, but still you need to get out sometime."

Mama said, "Girl, Charles would kill me if he found out I was hanging out at some joint with you."

"Well, child, he work nights anyhow, and we could be back before he gets home."

Mama asked, "And what about the children?"

"Put them to sleep, lock the door, and there you have it."

Mama didn't go out with her that day, but she thought long and hard about it for weeks. And Li'l Soul begged and begged until Mama decided to go out one night.

It was right after Daddy left for work. Mama was in the bathroom curling her hair when I walked in.

"Mama, I'm scared if you go out," I said, rubbing that crabby stuff out the corners of my eyes.

Mama looked down at me as she curled her hair.

She said, "Cheekie, now don't you start. Mama just going out for a li'l while. I'll ask Ms. Johnson, across the hall, to look after ya'll. So get in the bed and go to sleep, and ya'll never know I'm gone. 'Cause I'll be home before you know it."

I went to my bed and pretended like I was sleeping, but I wasn't. I was peeping. I saw Mama in the bedroom putting her lipstick on and ironing her clothes. She was looking like a whole new person—hair nice and curly, short skirt on, and high heel pumps.

She came in our room, leaned over, and kissed Torey and Darrell. She rubbed my head and then kissed me, too. I was awake, but I still pretended to be sleep. Mama closed the bedroom door and left us all alone.

At first I was scared, but after a while I woke Torey'nem up and we were playing and watching TV. We were having so much fun that being alone didn't seem all that bad after all. But soon as we heard the door open downstairs, we ran to our room, turned the lights off, and pretended to be sleep.

Mama and Li'l Soul came in laughing and giggling. I guess they had a good time at the joint. I knew Mama was there dancing, drinking, and smoking reefer because they came home and talked about their night out. I sat up in bed listening to the whole conversation.

Li'l Soul said, "Girl, we had fun tonight didn't we? Dancing, drinking, and bringing that joint down. By the way, did I sing tonight or what?"

She started singing right there in the kitchen, "I've got love on my mind, 'cause love is soft, love is sweet, love is nice, love is gentle, love is joy, love is pain, love is nothing in the wind. I've got love on my mind, love is always right on time, love is you, and love is me, love is gonna set you freeeee, yeah, our Love."

Boy, she was singing and spinning around like she was on stage or something. Mama says that Li'l Soul loves Natalie Cole's singing. Li'l Soul is sure some sassy; she is the one who started Mama smoking reefer.

She said, "Girl, take a hit of this reefer I done rolled up."

"Well, I don't know. That stuff ain't no good for you, I hear." Mama sat, looking at it for a moment.

"Child, I don't know who you been talking to, 'cause this shit can't hurt a fly. Try it and see."

Mama held that reefer in her hand for a moment, then she took a puff or two. Mama coughed out loud.

"Damn, this shit is strong!"

Li'l Soul laughed, "Girl, take another hit."

Mama did, and she kept hitting it and hitting it, until she couldn't get enough of smoking reefer, so that Li'l Soul had to snatch it away from her.

"Damn, bitch. Give it back. You do catch on fast." They fell out laughing.

Mama was happy like never before, hanging out with Li'l Soul all the time. Daddy seemed to never be home, always working and hanging out. And Mama was always sneaking out behind his back. She and Li'l Soul sneaked out just about every other night. She always managed to get back before Daddy got home from work. She had his schedule down so good, he never knew she had been out.

But one night, Daddy got off a little early and found us hanging and swinging out of the window, clowning around. We could have easily fallen out of the window or something, if Daddy hadn't walked in to make us behave.

"Where's your Mama?" he asked.

I looked blank. And when he discovered she wasn't there, boy he was mad. He paced back and forth all night until Mama got home. She tip-toed in with Li'l Soul, laughing and drinking as usual. When Mama flipped the light switch on and saw Daddy sitting in the dark, waiting, boy was she stunned.

Li'l Soul made a sudden turn back and out the door before any fireworks exploded. She said, "Catch you later, Faye. Call me."

Mama couldn't get a word out before Daddy shouted, "Are you out of your mind, leaving these kids all alone? I found them about to fall out of the window when I got home!"

Mama's voice sounded real cracked. She was nervous and ashamed.

She said, "Look, Charles, I just wanted to have some fun for a change. You are never here, claiming you are always working, but Li'l Soul said she heard you were hanging out with Fred one night. I get tired of being in here all day doing nothin'."

"So, you go out and leave your children by themselves and run the streets with that whore?"

Mama cried, "Li'l Soul ain't no whore, and besides, we have been friends for years. You know that."

"Don't tell me what I know. All I know is that she ain't married, and you too damn stupid to see that you've got no business hanging out with her." Boy, Daddy was shouting at the top of his voice.

"You must be out of your fucking mind, acting like a child! Well, since you want to act like one, I am going to treat you like one."

Torey and Darrell were asleep, but I stood at the door, peeping and listening. I saw him knock her head up against the wall and drag her through the house. I was too scared to move and too frightened to cry out loud. I stood there crying quietly, tears pouring down, hoping he would stop. I saw the buckle of his belt hit her all over, all upside her head. I could not move. The noise finally woke Torey and Darrell who sat up in bed, crying and shaking, calling out loud for Mama. I covered my ears, trying to block the noise. My whole body was trembling as I watched Mama crawling around the house on hands and knees like a dog, begging and pleading out loud for mercy.

When it was all over, he shouted at us, demanding that

we go back to bed. He told us that Mama was all right. But Mama wasn't all right. I saw her lying on the bathroom floor, bruised, crying and screaming, hoping that night would be over soon—hoping that she would wake up from a bad, bad dream.

i'm catching hell

Days have gone by, and Daddy and Mama still have not talked about that night he beat her. In fact, they barely speak to each other at all. They live together, but still nobody says nothing about that night. It is like they are trying to forget it ever happened.

Me and Torey were sitting at the table eating cereal when Daddy walked in from work. Mama was standing next to the sink washing dishes. He came in, threw his pouch of tools on top the washing machine, sat in a chair next to the table, and kicked his shoes off. Mama said nothing as usual.

Daddy asked me and Torey, "So how my li'l men doing today?"

Torey smiled, "Fine, Daddy."

I said nothin'; just watched him while I ate my cereal. I just kept seeing his belt buckle hitting Mama all over. I couldn't forget it—I tried, but I couldn't.

Daddy got up, grabbed Mama around the waist, tried to give her a kiss. Mama pushed him away, but Daddy kept pulling and pulling, trying to get Mama to give him a kiss.

After a while, Daddy got serious. He asked, "Faye, how long this gone go on? We haven't spoken in days."

Mama stopped doing dishes for a minute and looked him straight in the eyes. "Well, you should have thought about that before you raised your hand to hit me."

"Look, I don't know what got into me. I mean, I had never hit a woman before, and I swear it won't happen again. But you don't understand. I've been under a lot of pressure, working all the time, trying to earn money for you and the kids. Come on now baby, give me a break."

Mama left the sink and started cleaning the kitchen table. And then she started sweeping and mopping the floor. She was mad, and Daddy knew it. He said, "Look, I'm trying to apologize. You need to forget about this, because you know my sister and her children are coming to visit us for the weekend."

Mama had nothing to say. After a while Daddy grabbed his pouch, put his shoes back on, and walked out the door. I sat watching Mama clean the whole house. I kept thinking, "I can't wait until Selena'nem come to visit us."

Selena lives uptown in the St. Bernard Project, right around the corner from my Grandma Emelia's house. She comes to visit us from time to time, because her former mother-in-law, Ms. Betty, lives right up the street from us. Selena was married to Ms. Betty's son, John Henry, when he got into a fight with some man there in Ms. Betty's building. John Henry was shot twice in the head. He was Rachelle's daddy, and she was just a baby when it happened. I feel sorry for her because she never really had the chance to know her daddy. Selena is now seeing a creole man (half black and half white). He is Tanya's daddy.

18

When they arrived, Mama and Daddy tried their hardest, pretending like everything was fine between them. Me, I was just excited to have Rachelle and Tanya to play with.

We played and got into all sorts of trouble together. They weren't there for a minute before we ran down to Ms. Betty's house to buy some frozen cups (huckabucks). Ms. Betty sells candy, cigarettes, pickles, just about everything right there from her apartment in the project. Another great thing about having Rachelle around is, we get our huckabucks for free.

Ms. Betty is a big, fat woman who sits right in the doorway of her apartment waiting on customers. She was glad to see Rachelle when we walked up. She shouted, "Oh, my grandbaby! Come here and give me a kiss."

Rachelle did. Me and Tanya stood there looking. She said, "Ya'll give Ms. Betty a kiss, too, sugar."

After all the kissing and hugging, she asked Rachelle, "So, where's your mama and how is she doing these days?"

"She's by Cheekie n'em house, and she said she's coming to visit you later on," Rachelle replied.

"You tell her to do just that. Now, y'all take care, you hear?" she said as she waved us goodby.

We ran home and sat on the front porch just licking and eating our juicy, icy, blue colored frozen cups. It was hot and humid outside that day, so that ice felt so good going down.

As we sat there licking and licking, we noticed a cab pull up in front the house. It was Ms. Saphena getting out that cab. We saw her pumps first, and then her big legs, her big breasts, and then that "Big Hair" she was wearing on top

of her head. I knew it wasn't her hair, because it was too big
to be hers.

Ms. Saphena is a mystery. She stays to herself all the
time, never comes outside that much. But there are these
few times when Ms. Saphena gets all dressed up, goes out,
and comes back the next day all happy, like she done been
out having the time of her life. We all just sat there looking,
and watching her coming.

Rachelle n'em asked, "Who's that?"
I said, "That's Ms. Saphena, that's who!"
She's coming, switching, and twitching
being sassy as usual
talking that talk
and walking that walk
who is she, they wondered
I say, that's Ms. Saphena, that's who.

Sassy, and tall, and black
with big legs, and big thighs
stacked like a brick house
and built like an amazon
Who is she they wondered
I say, that's Ms. Saphena, that's who.

She looks like a sunset high
a divinity in motion
a big wide ocean, moving and rolling
who is that woman, they wondered
I say, that's Ms. Saphena, that's who.

It's the motion of her hips
the fullness of her lips
and the grandness of her walk
that says she's a woman, a black woman
but who is she **really**, they still wondered
I just say, that's sweet, sassy Ms. Saphena, that's who!

When she finally got to the porch where we were sitting, she rubbed me on the top of my head, and said, "Hi, Cheekie."

I smiled. "Hi, Ms. Saphena. Can Daphne n'em come outside and play?"

"Yeah, now that I'm home."

"Thanks, Ms. Saphena."

I just sat there with Rachelle and Tanya, thinking how I couldn't wait until the next time, because I knew I wouldn't see Ms. Saphena for a while. She seldom comes out the house, it seems.

I was so glad at first when Daphne n'em came outside to play with us. Daphne and her sister, Sharell, are around my age. (I'm eight and a half years old.)

As usual we were downstairs in our front hallway playing, and Daphne wanted to fight. She always starts fights. Every time we play together, she wants to fight. Daphne can fight real good, too—but so can Rachelle.

Rachelle punched Daphne in the face, and they were there fighting, and pulling hair, and scratching each other up. I stood around enjoying every minute of it, because Rachelle was beating Daphne up.

Gwen opened her front door when she heard them fighting. She broke it up and told Aunt Selena and Mama what happened. And when the story got back to Mama n'em, they claimed I started the whole fight. I did in a way (just wanted someone to kick Daphne's butt). But Mama didn't believe Gwen, though.

She said, "Cheekie never starts trouble; it must have been Rachelle and those other bad-ass children who started the fight."

Selena got mad because Mama blamed Rachelle for starting the fight. After that, the tension in that house got worse.

After lunch, Selena gave all us children oranges for dessert. When I was done eating mine, I wanted another one.

Selena said, "No, I will give you another one after supper."

I was spoiled some rotten, and wanted mine then.

I cried, "I want another orange now!"

Selena shouted, "Well, that's too bad because you can't have it now!"

I went crying and whining to Mama.

I cried, "Mama, I want another orange, but Selena won't give it to me."

I knew Mama would do just about anything for me. She gave me that orange. I went to Selena, bragging and teasing. I was real sassy with her.

"Now, now, I have my orange." I turned it into a little song, and sang it loud enough for Selena to hear it.

Boy, she was mad; so mad she snatched that orange out of my hand and shouted, "Now tell your Mama that." And I did.

Mama was not having it. She said, "I gave it to him because what Cheekie wants, Cheekie gets."

I stood there holding Mama's leg, enjoying every minute of her going to battle for me.

Selena said, "Not in this life, he won't."

Mama told her if she had a problem with it, she could take her children and get the hell out. And so she did, but they didn't go far because they had no way of getting there. They were sitting out on the front porch with all their things when Daddy got home from work.

He asked, "What are you doing out here in this scorching heat with these kids?"

"Your bitch of a wife threw me out, that's what. I'm tired of her attitude. She been acting funny every since we got here."

Daddy was some mad; he couldn't believe Mama threw them out over no orange.

He shouted, "Faye, are you crazy, throwing my sister out in that heat with no place to go over some damn orange?"

"Yeah, I threw them out because she wouldn't give Cheekie another orange. This is my house and I can do what the hell I want."

Mama was determined to throw them out, and she was not going to change her mind. After begging, demanding, and begging some more, Daddy finally gave up and called them a cab.

When the cab arrived, I was in the front window eating oranges, feeling kind of bad they were leaving. It was after they left that I realized I started the whole mess. But I was like that sometimes, just always trying to have my way, "cheekie," just like Pam always said.

After that mess with Selena, things just kept getting worse between Mama and Daddy. He was never home, and Mama started going out with Li'l Soul again just about every other night. As usual, Mama and Daddy fought when she got in.

The beatings kept coming, and Mama kept going out with Li'l Soul at night.

One day, Mama decided that enough was enough. She was ironing our clothes when Daddy walked in from work.

He shouted, "Where's my dinner?"

Mama said nothing, she just kept ironing, and pressing our shirts.

He shouted again, "Girl, do you hear me? I'm talking to you! I said where's my damn dinner? And by the way, while you at it, you need to get up off your ass and clean this place."

Mama started humming and singing, ignoring Daddy. This made him even madder, because he is the kind of man who hates to be ignored, especially by his wife. He raised his hand and he slapped Mama across the face.

Mama stopped ironing and for a moment stood there holding the iron in her hand. She was trembling, trying to hold in her anger.

Daddy said again, "Now like I said, get my dinner and clean this fucking place up!"

Mama ran into the kitchen and grabbed a butcher's knife so big, I was even scared. My heart was racing and pumping so fast you would have thought Mama was after me with that big knife. Daddy made a run for the door, and Mama chased him out and down the stairs. All the neighbors were out that day, sitting on the front porch. Daddy was too fast for Mama to catch, so she threw the knife hoping that it would land straight in his back. I'm glad she missed, because Daddy would be dead, Mama would be in jail, and there's no telling what would happen to us children.

Mama shouted as he ran away, "And don't come back either, because I'm tired of this shit!"

Ms. Johnson and Gwen sat in shock as Mama chased Daddy a li'l ways up the street. Me, Torey, and Darrell were looking out of the window scared and ashamed by what we saw—Mama chasing Daddy up the street in front of all the neighbors. Mama cried all the way back up the street.

When she got back to the porch where everyone was sitting, Gwen asked, "Faye are you all right? Is there anything we can do, girl?"

Mama shook her head no, wiping the tears and snot that was running down her face. Mama didn't want to talk about it. She knew this was probably the end of their marriage. I just sat in the window, with both hands up against my face, crying with tears streaming down. I had this bad feeling that Daddy was never coming back.

Mama came in and put us to bed early. It was still daylight outside, but Mama put us to bed anyway.

She spent most of the night sitting there in the living room alone, slouched over the sofa, drinking her favorite drink (coke and brandy) and listening to slow music. She was just sitting there crying her eyes out, thinking we children were asleep. Torey and Darrell were asleep, but not me. I couldn't sleep after all that excitement—Mama chasing Daddy away like that.

When she played that song "I'm Catching Hell," by

Natalie Cole, Mama just lost it. The lyrics of that song seemed to be written just for Mama that night.

As it played, Mama cried and cried as she played it over and over:

"Tonight, I just want to talk to the ladies. Fellows you cool, but girls if you got a good man, you better keep'em. Oh, I know you saying, now, what does she know, who is she to tell me about my situation? Well, I don't know your situation, but whatever it is, try to stay together. You know that big argument that you had today, remember, well, tonight it's nothing. Just don't let him leave you honey, 'cause you'll find out that it wasn't those really big things you loved about'em, it was the real small things. Go on and laugh, but it's true. You know things that you seen a thousand times around the house, but never paid any attention to: like helping with the groceries, helping in the yard, painting and repairing, hah, paying the bills. But now, all you have is memories and regrets. You could have given ya'll love a chance to grow, but you had to challenge it and be heard. Let me tell you something, that female liberation stuff, I don't know, sometimes I don't think it's worth it. And I'm really feeling, feeling kind of bad ya'll."

I'm Catching Hell
Living here all alone
I've never realize
Oh, Lordy,
You mean so much to me.

If I could replay, if I could replay
that whole scene again
I would never say it again
And to tell you the truth
I'm going out of my mind.

Yeah, yeah
Lordy, Lordy, do you know
what it's like
catching hell.

Boy, Mama couldn't stop listening to that music, crying, and turning over and over on the couch. She was cracking up and breaking inside. I think she realizes how much she still loves Daddy. I laid in my bed crying, too. Just hated to see Mama like that, and missing Daddy already.

That's when I heard a glass break against the wall. I jumped up and ran into the living room. I shouted, "Mama are you all right?"

She was kneeling in the middle of the room with her hands up against her forehead, head bowed down, crying her eyes out. I looked down and saw the glass there on the floor. I figured she must have thrown her glass of brandy up against the wall.

She looked up and said, "Cheekie, I'm fine. Now go back to bed. Go ahead! Get back in the room."

I didn't want to go, but I could tell Mama just wanted to be alone.

After that night, Daddy called now and then to check on us, but those calls came fewer and fewer with every passing day. Daddy was long gone, and Mama was hurting for a while, but she eventually got over it. After a while, she picked up her old routine, hanging out with Li'l Soul and leaving us children alone at night.

shake your groove thang

"Shake your groove thang
Shake your groove thang,
Yeah! Yeah!
Show'em how to do it now
Show'em how to do it."

Boy, Mama was in the middle of our living room floor showing them how to do it, too! She was swinging and jamming to the sounds of Peaches-N-Herb, "Shake Your Groove Thang."

It was girls' night to have fun. Once a month, Mama and her closest girlfriends got together to have what they call a "Tupperware party." Last night was Mama's turn to play hostess. All her lady friends were there: Li'l Soul, Ms. Johnson from across the hall, Gwen, and even Ms. Saphena. They came with big fun in mind (and, by the way, to order the latest in Tupperware). Most of all, they came to cheer Mama up. Everyone in the neighborhood saw Mama chasing Daddy away, so it was no secret that Mama needed her lady friends.

Mama put me, Torey, and Darrell to bed early, and spent the next few hours preparing for the party. She cooked a pot of slamming red beans and rice, laid out the Tupperware on the living room table, and even cleaned the whole house spotless.

The guests arrived around 8:00 p.m. At first, they just talked about Tupperware. They placed orders for plates, spoons, forks, bowls, and whatever other stuff they needed. The hostess receives a little bit of money from each sale. So in a way, they are helping each other make a little money.

While Mama entertained her guests in the living room, I entertained myself in the bedroom trying on my new clothes for school. I was starting fourth grade the next day. I stayed up late last night, not only messing around with all my new clothes but peeping out the door at Mama's party as well. Boy, I swear I must have tried those clothes on fifty times! I am more excited about the new clothes than I am about going to school.

Torey and Darrell slept through the whole party. As for me, I couldn't sleep. Besides, Mama n'em were laughing and dancing and talking so loud that I couldn't sleep even if I wanted to! I cracked the door just a little. From time to time, I would tip-toe near the door so that I could see everything.

I saw Mama on the dance floor, just shaking and moving all over the place. I was surprised, because I had never seen Mama act like that. Ms. Johnson, who wears eye glasses and a short li'l Afro, was up doing the bump with Mama. They were bumping and swinging and singing right along with the song. Li'l Soul, Gwen, and Ms. Saphena sat around clapping and cheering them on. It was easy to see that they were having a good time. I was having a good time, too, just watching them act up!

When the song ended, Mama fell on the couch real hard, breathing and breathing real fast. She was out of breath!

Li'l Soul said, "Girl, you still know how to have a good time."

Mama laughed, "Child, everything I know, it comes from hanging with you."

Everybody laughed.

Gwen grabbed a bowl of chips and passed it around the room. She is the shortest of the four women and wears a nice, short Afro. Gwen is a pretty, fair-skinned woman. She was just glad to be having a little fun. She works during the day and attends nursing school at night. So, in between raising a child, working all the time, and going to school, she doesn't always have time for letting go like this.

As she munched on some chips, she said, "Child one thing I like about these Tupperware parties is that there are no men. Just a time for us women to make a little money and have some fun for a change. In fact, I look forward to this party every month."

They all nodded their heads in agreement. Even Ms. Saphena, who is the hardest to persuade to attend parties, agreed. She keeps to herself more than the others. That's why I was surprised to see her out and having so much fun. I had never seen her like this before. After laughing and drinking most of the night, they sat around and talked about their favorite subject—men. Mama brought the subject up first. She asked Gwen about this man she is seeing.

"So, Gwen, what about this man I saw sneaking into your house the other night?"

This question brought everyone to the edge of their

seats, waiting to hear something juicy. I cracked the door even wider, so I could hear, too.

Gwen looked real surprised that Mama knew she was seeing a new man, but when you live this close together, everybody sees and hears everybody's business.

Gwen smiled, "Well, child, I met him at the grocery store."

Li'l Soul interrupted, "Girl, that sounds hot already."

Gwen continued, "There I was, going about minding my own business, and suddenly I noticed someone following me."

"Girl, what did you do?" asked Ms. Saphena.

"Child, I stopped and asked the nigger if he had a problem!" She paused as everybody laughed out loud. "He came over smiling from ear to ear, and said he was only checking me out. He had seen me around the store and couldn't help hisself. After he thought he'd told me enough of what he thought I wanted to hear, he asked me for my number!"

Mama sighed, "Girl, you do work fast." More laughter.

"Girl, of course I do. Shit, if you don't scope it out, believe me, some other woman will."

"Well, I heard that," said Li'l Soul.

Gwen finished, "After all the eye-making and blushing, girl, I asked him the three most important questions that I can ask any man: Are you single? Do you have a job? And do you have you own place?"

They all nodded their heads in agreement.

Li'l Soul said, "Girl, the last thing a woman needs is a broke brother who can't even entertain you at his own place. 'Cause, child, I met this man—right?—who wanted to cook me dinner and wine and dine me all night. Child, he really had me going, but there was only one problem."

"Girl, tell us the problem, please," Mama begged.

"Child, the nigger didn't have a pot to piss in or a window to throw it out. Now tell me how in the world you gone cook somebody dinner when you don't have a place to cook it at?"

Ms. Saphena said, "Child, I don't know, but did you ask'em?"

"Did I ever! Faye will tell you I don't have no time for no man who can't satisfy my every need—sexually and financially. 'Cause you see Soul can do bad all by herself. Needless to say, I got rid of him, because I saw right away he was not the one. Like the old saying goes, 'Ain't nothin' going on but the rent.' "

Everybody was laughing so hard, I'm sure that the insides of their stomachs were hurting. I chuckled, too. Just found the whole thing real funny. Mama wanted more details about Gwen and her new man.

"So, Girl, don't keep us in the dark. What happened the other night when he came over?"

"Well, I put Ronnie to sleep, and, child, before I knew it I was on top of him in the living room, riding 'it' into the sunset."

Li'l Soul reached over Mama and gave Gwen a high five. She said, "Well, girl, I didn't know you had it in you."

Ms. Johnson, who is the oldest and the most old-fashioned of the group, didn't like the fact that Gwen slept with this man on the first date.

She complained, "Gwen, you make this mistake over and over again, sleeping with men on the first date. And you wonder why they don't respect you later. You can't go around sleeping with men too soon, because in the morning they won't have an ounce of respect for you."

Ms. Saphena agreed, but Mama and Li'l Soul didn't.

Mama said, "First of all, why do *we* have to always be so serious when it comes down to sex? Most *men* aren't. I say if you feel it, and you want it, go for it. 'Cause believe me, men don't like playing the waiting game. I believe that if a man wants you, he wants you. And it don't matter if you do it to'em the first night or a month later."

Li'l Soul nodded her head in agreement, and added, " 'Cause, child, when a man has to wait too long to get the stuff, he starts feeling like you playing the pussy game. So, while you waiting to give it up, he done already moved on to someone else. And when you come along like the virgin Mary to get with the program, oh, he takes it gladly; then kicks you to the curb. I've seen it time and time again. I think women need to stop using their pussies to trap men. Just have fun and let things happen naturally. I always say, don't go to the table with too many expectations. It turns men the fuck off."

Ms. Johnson was really bothered by what Li'l Soul was saying. I could tell by the wrinkles on her forehead. She got up suddenly and said, "Child, on that note I better be getting home. Sly's 'bout ready to come home from work. So, Faye, I'll pick my order up next week."

Li'l Soul said, jokingly, "I see that man has you on a leash."

Ms. Johnson rolled her eyes and said, "At least I have a man—my own man at that—and not somebody else's."

Li'l Soul moved her head all the way back, flipped her

hair under, and replied, "I thought you knew I was only kidding."

"Well, women like you bother me. You go around sleeping with every Tom, Dick, and everybody's man, and then wonder why black men don't respect black women. It's because women like you let them believe that we don't respect ourselves."

Mama noticed that the conversation was getting way too heated, and if she didn't stop it, Li'l Soul and Ms. Johnson might be rolling over fighting.

Mama said, "Look, let's call it a night. Shit, we are all tired, and all probably need some dick right about now."

Everyone looked at Mama, really surprised, and then broke out in loud laughter. Next thing I knew, they all were hugging and laughing like nothing ever happened—even Li'l Soul and Ms. Johnson.

After everyone left, Mama was up cleaning the living room and washing dishes. I had stayed up so long that now I was good and sleepy. But then I had to use the bathroom. "Gosh," I thought, "if I go to the bathroom now, Mama will know I was up listening." She knew how I was, always listening in on grown folks talking.

I tip-toed to the bathroom without making any noise, but when I opened the door to leave, Mama was standing right there with one hand on her hip. She looked at me as if to say, "I caught you."

Mama asked, "Cheekie, what are you still doing up? Don't you know you have to get up and go to school tomorrow?"

"Yeah, but I had to use the bathroom, so I woke up."

Mama looked at me like she didn't believe a word I was saying. She said, "Don't lie to me Cheekie. You were up all night listening to grown folks talk. You are too mannish for me! Now get back in that room and go to sleep."

I sighed a bit, and then began to walk to my room slowly.

Mama shouted, "Boy, you better put a move on it if you know what's best."

I picked up my pace real fast and closed the door shut. As I was about to climb up the ladder that led to my top bunk, I looked over to see if Torey and Darrell were still sleeping. After all that noise Mama n'em had made, I was surprised to find that they were still peacefully asleep.

I tried to open Torey's left eye and then the right eye, but still he was just snoring and sleeping.

I jumped up in my bed and rolled over smiling to myself. I felt like I had done something big, you know, listening to grown folks talk. It made me feel mannish when I heard grown-ups carry on. I guess I was mannish, just like Mama always said.

I finally drifted off to sleep, dreaming about wearing all my new clothes to school, especially my new All-Stars tennis shoes. I dreamt about the first day of school for the rest of the night.

Yesterday was the first day of school. Mama got me up early Monday morning just to make sure I was ready on time. I got all kinds of new clothes—a new outfit for every day of the week. Mama dressed me in a pair of Levis jeans, a 'gator shirt, and my All-Stars tennis shoes. Boy, was I looking sharp! I was so excited—not about going to school, of course—but about all the new clothes.

After getting dressed, I sat at the kitchen table eating some Apple Jacks and pretending like I was reading the back of the cereal box. And boy, I just love Apple Jacks, my favorite cereal.

As I sat there eating, Mama tried to comb my hair. She pulled and pulled.

I whined, "Mama it hurts, shu. It hurts."

But Mama just kept pulling and combing my hair, trying to get them naps out my head. I wear a short li'l Afro, and, boy, is it thick and nappy!

Mama shouted, "Boy, keep still. Hold your head straight, so I can get these naps out."

As Mama stood there combing my hair, I complained, "Mama, I don't want to go to school. Why I gotta go anyhow?"

"Because I said so, that's why. Besides, you need to get your education, so you can make somethin' out of your life."

I didn't care about making somethin' out my life; I felt like I always do on the first day of school—just didn't want to go.

Mama insisted, "You don't have no wants. Now let's go!"

I got up from the kitchen table pouting, my lips sticking out. That's when Mama took her hand and grabbed me by the jaw.

"Put your lips in, before I tear them off your face. Now, like I said, you don't have no fucking wants, 'cause you are going to school today."

And I did, too. But the whole time we were walking to school, I said nothing else.

Dunn Elementary is right around the corner from our house, so we got there in no time. Mama dropped me off, kissed me on the forehead, and said, "Go ahead, now. Be good for Mama. I'll pick you up later."

I held on to Mama's hand. I didn't want to go in. I was just too scared to go. I don't know why, but I found fourth grade just as frightening as the first day of kindergarten.

Mama said, "Now, go ahead Cheekie. You gettin' too old to be actin' like this."

Ms. Wilkins, my fourth grade teacher, heard Mama fussing at me in the hallway. She came out and tried to help.

She asked, "What's the problem here? You don't like me?"

"I don't know why he actin' like this," Mama said. She was embarrassed by my behavior.

"What's your name?" asked Ms. Wilkins.

I was still holding onto Mama's hand when I mumbled, "Cheekie."

Mama laughed, explaining, "That's what we call 'im, but his real name is Charles, ma'am."

"OK, Charles, come on inside. Don't be scared. I promise you I won't bite. I'll make a deal with you, OK? Let's say if you don't like my class after about an hour, you can go back home, if you like."

Ms. Wilkins is a pleasant, Creole woman, light-skinned and tall. She is very pretty, and is so charming that she persuaded me to stay with her all day. She even moved my desk right next to hers.

I guess I am spoiled rotten and I just can't help myself. Everyone says that I am a Mama's boy. And it's true, too. I am very close to Mama, and that's the reason why it was so hard for me to let go of her that first day of school.

Mama just waved me bye-bye as I sat next to Ms. Wilkins' desk with a very confused look on my face. I wasn't sure what would happen to me when Mama left. I smiled back though, and was all right after a li'l while, just like Ms. Wilkins said I would be.

I had some fun in class, too. After coloring most of the day, we watched *Sesame Street*. I sat there, feeling like I was too old to still be watching *Sesame Street*. Anyway though, I like Big Bird with his tall, yellow self. I also like Cookie Monster (I love cookies). I sat there laughing at *Sesame Street*, not knowing that I was suppose to get more than humor out of it. I sang along with the whole class, "Can you tell me how to get, how to get to *Sesame Street?*" Boy, I love that song!

When the program was over, Ms. Wilkins asked, "So class, what did we learn from *Sesame Street* today?"

Daphne, Ms. Saphena's daughter, raised her hand and shouted, "I know, I know!"

But instead of her picking one of the students who had raised their hands, she picked me. I was thinking to myself, "Shu, why she gonna pick on me?"

She asked, "Charles, do you know the answer?"

I was so embarrassed because I wasn't paying attention. I couldn't remember anything from *Sesame Street*. I sat in my chair looking stupid, hoping she would ask someone else.

After a while, she said, "Well, that's OK. I'll let you off the hook this time, but next time, you had better pay attention because I'm going to be asking ya'll questions about what we do in class."

"Yes, Ms. Wilkins," the whole class shouted.

I was relieved and so happy she didn't embarrass me any more than I had already embarrassed myself.

During lunch time we went outside on the playground. I stood around by myself watching all the other kids playing jump rope, football—just having so much fun. I wondered what Mama n'em were doing. I wished I was at home.

Daphne came over while I was sitting on the edge of the monkey bars. She asked, "Cheekie, you want to turn rope with us?"

I kind of wanted to, because it looked like fun. I know boys aren't supposed to play rope like no girl, but I still wanted to play. I didn't care to play football like the other boys—just wasn't interested. I played jump rope yesterday, and I found out I'm pretty good at it, too.

We played jump rope again after school. Daphne n'em turned rope and sung, "Oh King Kong was sitting on a fence, trying to make a dollar out of fifteen cents. He missed, he missed, he missed like this." They tried to make me mess up, but I just kept jumping higher and higher and never missed. After a while, I was jumping rope better than all the girls in the neighborhood.

Daphne is jealous of me because I can jump rope better than she. After all, this is a girl's game. I know she is jealous, because when we play "hots," she turns that rope so fast, trying to make me mess up. But the faster she turns, the faster I jump.

Saturday Daphne got so mad that she picked a fight with me. I was in front of the house jumping rope, as usual. Everyone was sitting outside on their porches, trying to find some relief from the humid, New Orleans heat. First, we played hopscotch—me, Daphne, her sister Sharell, and Booby, another girl in our neighborhood.

As I stood waiting for my turn to play, I looked over on our front porch and saw Raymond (Ms. Johnson's oldest son) looking at me. He was staring at me. I paid him no attention because I know he is kind of retarded. So I just kept on playing hop scotch. But there was something creepy about his stare that made me wonder what he was thinking. He is jet-black and has a glass eye, kind of creepy looking. I blocked it out of my mind then, telling myself that he's a bit crazy.

After we played hopscotch most of the morning, someone pulled out the jump rope. That's when me and Daphne got into it. She stood in front of me as I was jumping rope. She balled up her fist, patted her left eye, her right eye, and then her lips. I knew that was a sign that she wanted to fight, and I was scared.

She ran over and pushed me down for no reason. She shouted, "You ain't nothin' but a punk anyway. That's why you like to jump rope, like a girl."

I looked at her real funny, trying to understand why she called me a punk. That was the first time I heard someone call me that, but it wasn't the last. Once Daphne called me a punk, all the kids in the neighborhood started calling me that—mostly when they're mad at me or when they're making fun. I feel like something's wrong with me when they call me a punk. I'm not sure what a punk is, but I know it's something bad.

Anyway, I got up from the ground, and Daphne and I started fighting. I wanted to run away, but I was so mad that I fought. Usually, I would be too scared to fight, but this time I was mad because she called me a punk. I pulled, kicked, and scratched, just like a girl would. I didn't care though, just wasn't going to let her get the best of me.

Gwen saw us from her kitchen window, scratching and biting one another. She ran over and shouted, "Stop this! Break it up!"

All the other kids stood around in a circle watching the whole fight. I was crying when Gwen pulled us apart. Because I was crying, all the kids said Daphne beat me up. But she didn't beat me up. They took my crying as a sign of defeat. The truth is, I always cry when I fight or get upset. I get it from Mama. Mama cries at the drop of a dime, and I must get that emotion from her.

Gwen took me by the hand, dragged me in the building, and told Mama what happened. She explained, "Girl, he out there fighting—him and Daphne—but I broke it up."

Mama said, "Thanks, girl, for stopping it."

Then she grabbed me by the chin, and asked, "What's wrong with you fighting, Cheekie? You know I taught you better than that."

I started crying again, just screaming and crying out loud. I cried, "Daphne called me a punk, and I ain't no punk."

Mama sat me down in a chair next to the kitchen table, and said, "Here, wipe your nose and stop all this crying. You ain't no punk. Those children are just jealous of you because you are somethin' special."

I was really confused. "Somethin' special?"

Mama smiled and held my chin in her hand. "When you were a little baby you almost died."

My eyes got real big.

Mama continued, "It was one Christmas we spent with

your daddy's family in Morgan City, Louisiana. It was winter, but kinda warm outside. You were outside all day with your cousins, Rachelle and Tanya. Your Grandma Emelia noticed you were not wearing a shirt, so she told me that even though it was warm outside, you should be wearing a top. I didn't pay her no attention, because I thought you would be just fine.

"Later that night, your Grandma Rose noticed you were running a high fever. I gave you medicine, but you were still burning up hot, just burning and shaking. We rushed you to the local hospital. I thought you would die before I got there, because you were just shaking, eyes rolling back in your head, and going into convulsions. When we finally got you there, the doctors and nurses were running crazy, trying to save your life. I was some scared, 'cause I thought you were dying. And all I knew was that your Daddy was going to kill me. You see he wasn't there yet, was on a job interview, and was going to meet us later.

"We waited for an hour in the hospital, and the doctors came out and said that we arrived not a minute too soon, because if I had waited a couple of hours more, you would have died. Everyone sighed relief, but your daddy was some upset when he found out you almost died of pneumonia.

"I felt bad after the incident, and always said that you were a blessed child—somethin' special—because God spared your life when you could easily have died."

I was shocked to hear that I once almost died.

I said, "Wow, I had no idea! I mean, you never told me."

Mama smiled, leaned over, and kissed me on the forehead. "I don't like thinking about it."

Even though I found Mama's story interesting, I still

don't understand what a punk is. I know it has something to
do with a man acting like a woman, because that's what I see
on TV and hear folks say.

Like the other day, I heard Mama, Gwen, and Ms.
Johnson talking with this man named Tyrone. Tyrone lives
right up the street from us and comes over from time to
time. He is tall and slim and about Mama's age. Sometimes
he stands outside on the porch with them for hours.

I've seen him walking and switching down the streets.
The way he switches reminds me of how Ms. Saphena
walks.

I saw him yesterday when he came by. He was wearing
cut-off shorts. They were so short you could see the black
cheeks of his butt. He also wore a shirt tied up in the front
like a woman's blouse. His hair is long and he pulls it back
in a pony tail. He stood around for hours making Mama
n'em laugh, talking about "mens" and his problems with
them. I listened to the whole conversation.

He said, "Child, men are dogs, aren't they? I'm seeing
this married man, child, who has three li'l children. His
wife is so stupid she don't suspect a thing. But I tell you, he
is some fine, child, and got a big dick, too. His dick so big,
girl, that when we doing it, I have one feet on twelve
o'clock, and the other one way pass six, screaming and
yelling. That's how good it is, child! I call'em 'Big Dick
Joe.' "

They fell over laughing at his stories. I just found the
whole story nasty. When he ran out of stories, he switched
off, just like a woman. Mama n'em talked about him behind
his back. Gwen said, "Girl, you know that's a shame. He's
more woman than the three of us put together!"

"Ain't that's for true," Mama agreed.

That's what I thought a punk was, and I know I'm not no punk like Tyrone. Still wonder why Daphne n'em call me that? I just can't come up with an answer that makes sense to me. I like to jump rope, but so what?

ain't nothin'
like the real thing

Mama was getting lonely and started thinking that she needed a man to survive. That way of thinking led her into a pattern of taking whatever man she could get: married, no job, almost any kind of man.

The other day, I came home from school and heard Mama in her bedroom with a man I had never seen before. Torey and Darrell were in the other room watching TV. I heard strange sounds coming from Mama's room. I tip-toed next to the door so I could hear better. At first, I heard moaning and groaning. Then, I heard Mama scream, "Oh, Nathan, don't stop! Don't stop baby! Please don't stop!"

It sounded like he was killing her! My heart started pounding. Then he screamed, "Yeah! Yeah! Yeah, baby!"

At first I was afraid, but then I realized what was going on. "Oh, they in there gettin' booty," I thought to myself.

I wanted to see more, so I cracked the door just a little. Mama was on top of him, moving and moving back and forth. He was lying on his back, covered with sweat. He gripped the bed with both hands. Then he screamed again, "Yeah! Yeah! Yeah, baby!"

They were so into it, that they didn't even see me peeping. Boy, they were sweating like they had done been out-side in that humid New Orleans heat. I saw sweat dripping from Mama onto him, dripping like a leaky water faucet. I had never seen a man and woman like that before, so I stood there really enjoying myself, watching them going at it. Mama was screaming so much, I thought he was hurting her. But he wasn't, because she just kept moving on top of him. She was enjoying it! I thought back to that Tupperware Party, when Mama said, "If you feeling 'it,' and you want 'it,' then go for 'it.' " So, I guess Mama was going for hers. I stood there for a li'l while, and then I closed the door and tip-toed outside. I smiled as I left, just felt like I had done something bad but fun at the same time. I liked that feeling.

Nathan Junior is the name of that man that I heard in her bedroom that day. He is the first man Mama's dated since she chased Daddy away. He treats Mama well, and he always gives us children some money when he comes around. We think Nathan Junior is rich, because when he gives us money, he pulls out a roll so thick, I feel like I might choke just looking at it. He is a nice-looking man, too—fair-skinned, and a nice dresser. Nathan Junior also has a big yellow Cadillac.

Sometimes I'm outside playing in the court, right next to Dunn School, when I see that Cadillac coming. It is a big court, so big that we can play almost any game we want to play. It has a big play area, too, with big, green turtles, all kinds of swings, and monkey bars.

Anyway, I was out there the other day playing cops and robbers with the neighborhood kids. Instead of being a cop or robber, I wanted to be the doctor who helped the injured in battle. I always was the doctor no matter what—never a cop or a robber. I don't know why, but I always like being the doctor. I was kneeling on the ground, trying to bring one of my injured patients back to life, when I saw Nathan Junior coming from up the street. I jumped up from my patient, leaving him to die, and ran home. Boy, I was running and running, until I ended up in front our porch. I found Mama sitting outside with Gwen, talking about Nathan Junior. I interrupted them, breathing so fast my chest was hurting.

Mama shouted, "Boy, what's wrong with you?"

I managed to get the words out, "Nathan Junior. Here comes Nathan Junior, Mama. I saw his Cadillac!"

Boy, Mama jumped up off the porch and ran inside. She was running around trying to find something to wear. She even took those rollers out her head that she had been walking around in for days. When he knocked on the door, Mama checked herself in the living room mirror that hung on the wall. Mama smiled, "Hi, Nathan! I've missed you."

He handed her a dozen roses and smiled back, "So did I, baby."

Then they went into Mama's room, and I heard those noises all over again. They were in there going at it and bringing that room down. I heard noises come out of that room that I had never heard before.

Mama is very happy with her Prince Charming. She thinks he is the real thing. I heard her telling Gwen that he is good looking, he has money, and he treats her like a lady. He is everything she every wanted in a man except one thing—he is everything but a free man.

Nathan Junior is married and his wife is a bitch. She's no joke, according to him. I heard him telling Mama, "Faye, Beth is crazy. She is a big, fat, ugly woman who fights me and beats me as if I was a child."

I thought that was strange—a man gettin' beat by a woman. Mama just hopes and prays she never runs into that woman.

But she did run into that woman. One night last week Nathan Junior took us to Ponchartrain Lake. It is a big, beautiful lake. We sat on the shore and watched the waves come in. I especially liked how the waves rolled, leaped, and crept up like a thief tip-toeing into the night.

There is also a playground at the lake for children to play on. Me, Torey, and Darrell were playing and swinging on the swings. And Mama and Nathan Junior were kissing and holding each other under the beautiful moon and glittering stars that lit up the sky above us.

After leaving the lake, we pulled into a gas station. Nathan Junior got out of the car and, to his surprise, bumped into his wife, Beth. He was shaking like a leaf on a tree during a windy, stormy night.

Beth asked, "Who in the hell is in our car?"

Nathan Junior stuttered, "Look, B-Beth d-don't get upset. It's not what you th-thinking."

She shouted, "The hell it ain't!"

She pulled a big, black gun out of her purse. Boy, that gun was big! Then she walked over to the car. Nathan Junior was crying and trying to stop her. But he couldn't stop her, because she is so fat, she pushed him right out the way. I don't know if Mama was scared, but I sure was.

Torey, Darrell, and I were in the back seat. Boy, I was shaking so bad, I thought I would pee all over myself.

She came to the car and said, "Bitch, get your kids and get the fuck out of my car!"

Mama opened the car door as she stared down the gun that was in her face. She got us out the back seat. Mama kept her cool, but we were crying out loud.

Mama said, "Don't cry, everything is gonna be all right."

As Mama walked away, Beth said in a very angry voice, "Don't let Nathan get you in no trouble hear, 'cause you see, the next time I ain't gonna be so nice."

Mama said nothing, just kept on walking. We caught a bus home that night. Mama was sitting on that bus crying her eyes out. I felt sorry for Mama, losing her Prince Charming like that. I was embarrassed too, you know, Mama crying like that on the bus.

She was crying so much that the bus driver stopped the bus, turned around, and asked, "Ma'am, are you all right back there?"

Mama said, "Yeah, Mr. Bus Driver. I'm gonna be all right."

But for a long time now, Mama hasn't been all right. She is always depressed. She misses Nathan Junior, but she never takes none of his calls anymore. I guess I've seen the last of Nathan Junior.

But Nathan Junior, he came back. One day I came home from school, and I saw that yellow Cadillac sitting out front. That car was shining so that it gleamed in the sunset. Boy, I was so excited that I started running and jumping up and down and around. I just knew I was about to get hit with a stack of money.

As I ran upstairs to our apartment, I heard voices coming from the kitchen. But when I knocked on the door, everyone got silent.

My auntie Annie Mae asked, "Who wizit?"

I said, "Cheekie."

When she opened the door, everyone seemed to be holding their breath. They seemed relieved to see it was me. I walked in and found Mama, Nathan Junior, and Annie Mae sitting around eating crawfish, drinking, and listening to the sounds of Aretha Franklin. Nathan Junior was glad to see me.

He smiled, "Come here li'l man, and give Nate some five."

He pulled his right hand out, and when I shook his hand, he put a stack of ones in my hand—a stack so big that my eyes got real wide. I mean real, real wide. There must have been ten dollars in that stack.

I smiled and said, "Thanks, Nathan Junior."

Mama asked, "You want some crawfish?"

I took one of those li'l crawfish, peeled the skin off, ate the meat inside, and sucked the head dry. Boy, the juice from the head of that crawfish was hot! And good!

As I sat there sucking crawfish, Nathan Junior was hitting my chest lightly, boxing with me.

He asked, "So, what you gone buy with all that money?"

Mama said before I could answer, "He need to save it for school, 'cause he wants to go to City Park with his school on next week. And, shit, I can't afford to pay for no trip like that."

I looked at Mama as if to say, "I ain't spending my money on no trip." In fact, I couldn't wait to run down to Ms. Betty's house to buy me a huckabuck and some Mary Jane candy. Mama would have me spend the whole ten dollars before I even get to Ms. Betty's house.

I washed that nasty crawfish smell off my hands, ran outside and showed Torey and Darrell my money. They couldn't wait to run upstairs to get some for themselves. Me, I was running down the street to Ms. Betty's house.

After running all the way there, I stood in line in the hallway outside Ms. Betty's apartment, running out of patience, waiting to buy me some Mary Jane candy and a huckabuck. Her daughter, who we call "Mookie," was working the door and Ms. Betty was sitting at the kitchen table cutting up an onion. I knew it was an onion because I could see her eyes were running and running. Tears were streaming down her face. Ms. Betty looked up from chopping that onion, and was glad to see me.

Mookie smiled, "How you doing Cheekie?"

I handed her a one dollar bill, and said, "Fine. I want to buy me three Mary Janes and a blue frozen cup."

Ms. Betty said, "Is that Cheekie? Is Cheekie over there?"

"Yeah, Ma, that's him," said Mookie.

Ms. Betty asked, "What's up, Cheekie?"

"Nothin', just buying me some candy and a frozen cup."

"How's my granddaughter doing?"

"Fine."

"Tell her I asked about her."

I ran out so fast that I hardly said goodbye. I was so excited that I was skipping and running, holding on tight to my Mary Jane candy and sucking on my huckabuck.

I sat outside on our front porch. Daphne and Booby were playing out there. I made them so mad, because I was teasing them by sucking on that huckabuck like it was the last huckabuck in the world. Daphne rolled her eyes, but I kept sucking and chewing on that huckabuck.

I was almost finished when I noticed a big, fat, black woman moving towards our front porch. She wobbled so much, she looked like a big wave coming in to shore. She was so fat that when she walked, it looked as though she had to walk around herself, as her big, fat legs rubbed together. As she got closer, I realized that it was Nathan Junior's wife, Beth! She stopped and stood right in front of me. I was so scared, I dropped my huckabuck on the ground. Daphne n'em laughed out loud. They were glad I dropped my huckabuck.

Beth asked in a very deep voice, "Is Nathan Junior in ya'll house?" I shook my head no.

She said, "Well, he better not be."

She continued upstairs and knocked on the door real hard and loud. Bam! Bam! It sounded like Bam-Bam on the *Fred Flintstone* show. Maybe it sounded like the wolf threatening the three little pigs inside, yelling, "Open up or I'll huff and puff, and blow that damn door down."

Annie Mae opened the door, smoking a cigarette. Good thing for Mama that Annie Mae was there, because she is not scared of no one, not even a fat woman like Nathan Junior's wife.

I felt my stomach turning over and my heart pounding when she screamed, "Is my husband here?"

Annie Mae exhaled a puff of cigarette smoke in her face. She waited a while for the smoke to clear. Then she looked her dead in the eyes and said calmly, "No, he isn't."

"Well his car is sure out front, and there's nobody else he knows around here."

"Look, it's not *my* problem if you can't keep track of your man. But like I said before, he ain't here."

She wasn't buying what Annie Mae was saying. She had a feeling that Nathan Junior was there, and she was right. But I was thinking the whole time, "Where in the hell did he go?"

"Where's Faye?" Beth asked.

Mama peeped around the door, and said, "I'm right here, and like my sister said, Beth, he's not here."

Beth raised her voice, "Bitch, I don't believe you! His car is out front and I know he's in there. Now didn't I tell you once before about messing with my husband, slut?"

Annie Mae stepped between Mama and Beth and said in a very mean voice, "Look, miss, I don't know what the problem is, but my sista said your husband ain't here, and he ain't. Now, you best take that shit somewhere else, if you know what I mean."

Beth pointed her finger at Mama. "Look, this is between me and that bitch right here."

"And she ain't gone be too many of your bitches either," said Annie Mae.

All the neighbors were in the hallway listening to everything. I was feeling scared for Mama, because Beth was real, real mad. I thought she was going to take out that big, black gun of hers and shoot Mama.

Sly came from across the hall just in time and got between Beth and Annie Mae. They were close to fighting.

Sly said, "Look, ma'am, the ladies said your husband

ain't here, and I think it's best you leave before things get out of hand."

Beth looked at him and rolled her eyes. Then she clutched hold her purse real tight.

She said, "Oh, I'm leaving, but Faye, girl, if I find out my husband has still been sneaking around with you, it's gone be me and you. 'Cause a woman like you knows that Nathan is the real thing, and would do just about anything to trap him for yourself. But like I said before, if I find out that he is still messing around with you, the devil himself ain't gone be able to stop me from getting to you."

Mama waved her hand and said, "Whatever girl, just get on."

Beth turned around and wobbled on down the stairs. I was standing at the bottom of the stairs when she moved on by.

She stopped and said, "And here's fifty cents for that frozen cup you dropped."

I took that fifty cents and moved out of her way. Beth took one last look at Mama n'em standing at the top of the stairs. She rolled her eyes, and wobbled right on down the last flight of stairs.

Mama said, "Thanks, Sly, for helping out. I'm sorry for this mess."

"No problem, Faye. But a word of advice: leave that woman's husband alone."

Mama managed a smile and closed the door shut.

People had done come from across the other hallway and down the streets just to see what was going on.

Sly shouted, "OK, the show is over. Come on everybody. Go home, now."

I wiped my forehead and ran inside. Right away I noticed Nathan Junior's hat sitting on the living room sofa. After a while, Mama went to the back of the house and said, "She's gone. You can come out."

When he did, I couldn't believe my eyes. Nathan Junior had done peed all over himself. I swear he had pee running all down his leg. And sweat was running down his face. He was scared!

He asked, shaking and trembling, "Ya'll sure she's gone?"

Mama said, "Yeah, she's gone, and now it's time for you to go, Nathan. And don't come back either, because I'm tired of this shit. You keep telling me it's over between ya'll, and now this woman then come to my house."

Nathan Junior tried to calm Mama down. "Look baby, I know it's crazy, but I'm trying to break loose."

"Well, when you loose from the big fat goose, you know where to find me. But until then, it's over."

He grabbed his hat off the sofa, looking real sad after hearing what Mama said.

He asked, as he was walking out the door, "Look, is it all right if I wash my clothes right quick? 'Cause you know I kind of had an accident."

Mama held the door open, "Look, I think you should go Nathan. And go now."

As he drove off, I hung from the living room window. I was thinking how much I was going to miss Nathan Junior and all his money, too.

Annie Mae was on the floor laughing hard, thinking about how Nathan Junior let go all over himself when he heard Beth outside the door. She was hitting the wall and falling out laughing all over the place. Mama giggled a bit herself, because it *was* kind of funny.

Mama is serious, though, about not taking Nathan Junior's calls anymore. He keeps calling, begging, and pleading to come over. Mama isn't stupid. She loves living too much to risk Beth catching them together again and blowing her brains out.

Needless to say, her Prince Charming is history. Well, it was fun while it lasted, anyway.

the invisible man

Mama's been kind of down since her relationship with Nathan Junior ended. That's why she's started hanging around with Li'l Soul again. Li'l Soul came by and got Mama one day last week. She came in wearing all black, long hair flowing. She was pretty, as usual.

Mama was sitting on the living room sofa listening to slow music like she always do when she gets sad. Me, Torey, and Darrell were in our bedroom watching a Martin Luther King special on TV that Mama made us watch. She said we needed to know something about how it was back in the sixties before the civil rights movement. I couldn't believe that blacks couldn't eat in certain places, hang out where white people hung out, or even use the same bathrooms as whites. But what amazed me more was how Martin Luther King, Jr. changed the whole world with his nonviolent movement.

I was shocked by what I saw on TV. As I sat in my bed, I got scared, then mad when I saw police dogs attacking innocent people just because they wanted to be treated as equals. Torey and Darrell were laughing at the whole thing.

Torey said, "Man, look those dogs are eating those people."

I don't know why their laughing upset me so, but it did.

I said, "Don't laugh at that. It's not funny. It's not funny!"

Torey laughed, "Yes, it is!"

"No, it ain't!"

"Yes, it is!"

Before I knew it, we were about to fight. Mama came in just as I was about to swing and hit Torey in the head.

Mama asked, "What's going on in here?"

"Torey laughing at those people being attacked by police dogs."

Mama turned the TV off and then turned the light switch on.

She asked, "Torey is that true? Were you laughing at those people?"

Torey's head was bowed. He knew he was in big trouble.

He mumbled, "Yeah."

Mama said, "Speak up, I can't hear you."

"Yeah, Ma. I was laughing."

"Why, Torey?"

He moved his left shoulder up, indicating to Mama that he didn't know why he laughed.

Mama said, "Well, Torey this is nothing to laugh about. What happened back then was not funny. People died, just so ya'll wouldn't have to live like that. You understand me, Torey? So, I better not hear you laughing again."

Tears were streaming down his face. I just stood there grinning at the whole thing, glad he had got into trouble.

Mama then turned to me and grabbed hold of my ear real hard. I was moving and twitching because she was turning my ear and pulling on it real tight.

I whined, "Ouch Ma, you hurting me."

She said, "That's the point. Now, you listen to me. You are the oldest here, and you not supposed to be fighting your brothers when they don't understand something. If you learn anything from Martin Luther King, you should know that you can't solve problems with violence. You hear me, Cheekie?"

"Yeah, Ma."

Torey and Darrell were giggling as Mama held onto my right ear, hurting me.

"Now, it's time for ya'll to go to bed."

Mama turned the light switch off and cracked our bedroom door just a little. I jumped up in my bed and rolled over, turning my back towards the door. I was really mad. I didn't fall asleep right away, though. I wanted to hear what Mama and Li'l Soul were talking about.

Li'l Soul asked, "Girl, what's going on in there?"

Mama said, "Child, you know how it is. Boys will be boys. Torey and Cheekie in there fighting over Martin Luther King."

"What?" Li'l Soul asked in amazement.

"Yeah, child, can you believe it? Of all the things to fight about."

"I know what you mean. We've seen some rough times, haven't we? Child, I'm so glad things are different for blacks today."

"Girl, who you telling?" asked Mama.

"You remember the old days? Even Mardi Gras was caught up in that mess. Black folks couldn't even go to Canal Street to watch the parades. That space was reserved for white folks."

Mama said, "I sure do. We had to hang out under the Claiborne Bridge and imagine what was happening on Canal Street."

"But even though racism caused a lot of problems for black folks, we still had ourselves some good old times, didn't we?" asked Mama.

"We sure did. These kids today don't know nothing. Back in those days, black folks stuck together. We had no choice but to. But now it seems like everyone is out for themselves."

"Nevertheless, racism is still alive and well in New Orleans—on *both* sides of the color line," Mama added.

"You know *I* know, child. Just because I'm light-skinned and half white, some black folks turn their nose up at me. Say I'm too white. Shit, I can't help if my great-grandma fucked some white man."

Mama laughed, "Girl, you are crazy, but you done cheered me up all over again."

"Well, speaking of cheering you up, let's go out tonight."

"I don't know. I don't like leaving these children in here by themselves, you know. Things aren't as safe as they use to be."

"Girl, ask one of your neighbors if they can keep them, 'cause we going out tonight."

I heard Mama dialing the phone. Li'l Soul sat in the living room, rolling up a joint of reefer. That stuff looked like green grass from outside. I just thought it was strange for them to be smoking grass.

Mama called Ms. Johnson across the hall. I heard her asking, "You sure Ms. Johnson, it won't be a problem?"

Then, Mama hung up and gave Li'l Soul a high five. They were excited to be going out.

Li'l Soul handed Mama that reefer she rolled up. Mama took a puff or two.

Mama coughed out loud, "Child, let me get these children up before it gets too late."

Mama came in our room and turned the lights back on. She said, "Wake up! Ya'll going over to Ms. Johnson's next door because me and Li'l Soul going out for a li'l while.

Mama grabbed our tooth brushes and a few clothes, pushed us into the hall and knocked on Ms. Johnson's door.

Ms. Johnson was in her night clothes when she answered the door.

Mama said, "Hey, girl. Here they are. Thanks, again, for keeping them for me. I'll pick them up in the morning. Now you sure it ain't no problem, right?"

"Of course not. Besides, I have some room anyhow, 'cause Perry is staying over a friend's house tonight."

Mama and Li'l Soul waved us 'bye. I had a brown paper bag in my hand with a change of clothes. I stood in the door for a moment and watched Mama walking and switching down the stairs wearing a short dress and high heel pumps. She was so happy to be going out. You know, nobody can get her going like Li'l Soul can.

After Mama dropped us off, we didn't go to bed right away. We sat in the living room with Sly, watching *Charlie's Angels*, one of my favorite shows. Ms. Johnson was in her bedroom reading the paper. Raymond was in his room sleeping and Annette was in the kitchen washing dishes. It must have been her week to do the dishes. Boy, Sly is strict on them. He makes them take turns washing dishes. I know, because I saw a schedule posted on the refrigerator.

Sly, who reminds me of Mr. T., is a tall, stocky built man. He's also the most organized person I know. He keeps a schedule posted for everything. I like the way he helps to keep the neighborhood clean, always organizing things.

After *Charlie's Angels* went off, Sly said, "OK, fellahs, it's time to hit the sack. Torey and Darrell can sleep in Annette and George's room, and Cheekie, since Perry over his friend's tonight, you can sleep with Raymond."

I suddenly felt the insides of my stomach drop. I thought back to that day I was playing outside with Daphne n'em and saw Raymond staring at me. I didn't pay much attention to Raymond's behavior that day he was staring at me, but the idea of sleeping with him gave me the creeps. Remembering his stares terrified me. I could see him, with that false eye, staring me down. I wanted to go home soon as Sly closed the door and left me all alone with Raymond.

It was dark in that room. I mean real, real dark. I couldn't see a thing. I laid on the edge of that bed with my back towards him. He seemed to be 'sleep at first. Boy, my heart was pounding and my whole body was shaking. I was scared! Deep within me, I knew something was going to happen, and I was shaking and trembling, hoping someone would open the door and stop it. I felt my knees knocking together.

And then I felt him moving closer towards me. He took his thing out, and he rubbed it up and down my back. Then he pulled my pants down, and he tried to push his thing inside my butt. I kept shaking and tears were streaming down my face. It was like he was the invisible man. I couldn't see 'im but I could feel him touching me. He reached over and he played with my thing. Then he whispered in my ear, "Relax, I am not going to hurt you."

I laid in that bed crying and hoping and praying he would stop. I wanted to scream out loud, but I was too scared. I just wanted that nightmare to end.

After he finished fondling me, he demanded, "You better not tell nobody what happened or else." Then he rolled over and went straight to sleep. He never finished that sentence, but I knew by the sound of his voice and the way he grabbed hold my shoulder that he would hurt me if I ever told anyone about what had happened.

I wasn't going to tell a soul what he did to me. I just wanted to forget the whole nightmare ever happened, but as hard as I tried, I couldn't.

When Mama picked us up the next day, I ran in the house, straight to my bedroom, jumped into my bunk bed, and tried to forget last night.

Mama knew something was wrong by the way I ran out of Ms. Johnson's house. She came in and asked, "Cheekie, what's wrong with you, boy?"

I had nothing to say, just laid with my back facing Mama. Mama stood in the doorway with her hand on her hip, waiting for an answer.

I turned over and said, "Nothin' Mama, just wanted to get to my own bed."

But the truth was that I was scared to tell her. I didn't know how, really. I was afraid of what she might say or do to me. I was so confused, didn't know whether I should tell someone or just try to forget about it. I hated myself, and I couldn't understand why he did what he did to me. I was not only confused, but afraid—afraid of what Raymond would do to me if I told anyone. As a result, I've stopped wanting to go outside as much. I stay to myself. Nobody notices the change in my behavior, though. I do a good job at hiding it from Mama and everyone else.

A few days later, Raymond tried to do the same thing to me again at school. I was playing in an empty hallway by myself after school. I was playing with my red spinning top. I was getting ready to go home when Raymond showed up. He must have seen me go in that hallway. He stood in the doorway wearing a blue jean overall jump suit. Even though I was scared, I was not going to let him touch me again.

As he came closer, I backed up, trying to think what my next move was going to be. I thought if I screamed and someone heard me, I would have to explain why. Since I still didn't want anyone to know what he did to me that night, I didn't want to have to explain anything.

He asked, "You didn't tell anyone what happened the other night, did you?"

I shook my head no. He said, "Good. Now, I ain't going to hurt you, I promise."

I kept moving away, trying to think what I was going to do. When I ran out of room and couldn't move backwards anymore, I knew I had to get past him somehow. Before I knew what was happening, I kicked him in his thing and pushed him aside. Then I ran. I ran like a bat out of hell. I ran until I ended up on our front porch. I was out of breath and my heart was pounding. I walked upstairs to our apartment and knocked on the door.

Ms. Johnson was coming in from making grocery at

Schwegmann's supermarket. She asked, "Cheekie, have you seen Perry, George, or Raymond?"

I shook my head no. When Mama opened the door, I pushed my way in and ran inside.

I heard Mama say to Ms. Johnson, "Girl, I don't know what's wrong with him. He been acting strange for days now. Anyway, I'll bring them over around ten o'clock tonight. OK?"

Ms. Johnson said, "That will be fine, Faye."

Mama closed the door shut and came in my room. She asked, "What's wrong with you, Cheekie, breathing real fast like that and running like you crazy."

"Nothin' Ma. I was just running and playing with Daphne n'em that's all."

Mama stood in the doorway of our room looking at me funny, as if she didn't believe me.

She said, "You know, Cheekie, if something is wrong you know you can tell me, right?"

I looked Mama dead in her eyes. I wanted to tell her so bad, but I didn't.

I said, "I know, Ma, but there's nothin' to tell. I swear."

"OK, then. Well, dinner is ready, so come on and eat. Afterwards I want you to take a bath and get ready to go. Ya'll staying over Ms. Johnson's house tonight."

I thought to myself, "There is no way I'm staying over Ms. Johnson's house." I didn't know how I was going to get out of it, but all I knew was that I was not going to stay there.

Mama was going through her regular routine, curling her hair, putting make-up on, and ironing her clothes to go out.

She had already packed up our clothes to go over Ms. Johnson's house. After getting dressed, she took us across the hall and knocked on Ms. Johnson's door. As soon as she knocked on that door, I started screaming and yelling like I was crazy.

I yelled, "No, I ain't staying over there no more."

Mama was shocked. She couldn't believe I was shouting like that.

"Cheekie, what's wrong with you, boy?" she asked.

Mama took hold both my arms, and shook me real hard. She shouted, "You hear me talking to you? I said what's wrong with you?"

I wasn't saying nothin', head bowed, not saying a word. Ms. Johnson and Sly had done opened their door and was waiting for me to answer Mama's question. I looked up and saw Raymond standing behind his mother, staring at me. He was hoping, of course, that I wouldn't tell on him.

I yelled at Mama, "I don't want to go sleep there, and I'm not going to."

Mama shouted, "Cheekie, you don't have no wants. Now, Ms. Johnson was nice enough to let ya'll stay there. Don't you give her no trouble, now!"

Mama grabbed hold my arm, trying to pull me, but I wouldn't move. I am a stubborn child, and once I make up my mind, that's it.

I kept yelling and screaming, "No, I'm not going."

And Mama kept pulling and pulling until she gave up.

She said, "Well then, I'll go downstairs and ask Ms. Saphena if she would keep ya'll, 'cause I'm going out with Li'l Soul tonight and you're not going to stop me."

I thought, "She is more concerned about going out

shaking her butt, when obviously something is the matter with me." But in a way I was kind of glad to be going to Ms. Saphena's house. First, her life was a mystery, and I liked solving mysteries. Second, I had never been inside her house and I couldn't wait to see it.

Mama took us down to Ms. Saphena's apartment and knocked on the door. She opened the door wearing a short night gown that showed how big her legs and thighs really are. She was wearing "Big Hair" as usual. All I can say is that she is a brick house—thirty-six, twenty-four, thirty-six.

Mama said, "Hey, Girl, I'm sorry to disturb you, but I was wondering if you can mind my children for me tonight?"

"Yeah, that would be fine, girl. They can come right in here and go to sleep, 'cause my children are already in the bed."

"Thanks, Ms. Saphena," said Mama.

Mama waved us bye and couldn't wait to get out with Li'l Soul. She pulled off in a car full of people. I don't know who those people are, but it was a car load of them. I think Mama loves hanging out so much because she is still young, only twenty-one years old.

Well, I was finally inside of her house, and it was no longer a mystery. Daphne and Sharrell were in their room, sleeping. Torey and Darrell had already fallen asleep on the living room sofa. Me, I couldn't sleep. Her house was a mess! She had trash, dirt, and oily floors everywhere I looked. The house smelled bad, too. I couldn't even sleep if I wanted to. It smelt like week-old garbage or the inside of a baby's dirty clothes hamper. Well, she does have a li'l baby, and his pampers were thrown all over the house. I mean this woman must have taken the pamper right off the baby and left it right on the floor. I sat there on the couch, disgusted by what I saw and smelled. To make matters worse, her retardy son, Toney, was running back and forth, from one end of the house to the other. He was holding his thing and running around in circles.

Ms. Saphena finally came into the living room and put him to bed. Boy, when she came into the living room, I couldn't believe my eyes. That big hair she had a minute ago was gone, and all that was left was this li'l hair underneath a stocking cap. She was bald-headed!

She said, "Cheekie, lie down and go to sleep. Your Mama gonna come back and get you in the morning."

I managed a fake smile and laid down holding my stomach. I felt like I was about to throw up. I thought to myself, "I liked it better when she was a mystery, 'cause she looked much better when she was a mystery."

I was awake all night, nodding now and then, but never really to sleep. I just wanted that night to end so I could go to my own bed. Morning couldn't come fast enough.

my forest adventure

When morning came, I returned home, anxious to get into my own bed. To my surprise, I found that Mama was not alone. She had a strange man lying in bed next to her. I could see them, because her bedroom door was propped open. I had never seen him before. I was too sleepy to give it much thought at the time. I soon drifted off to sleep in my own comfortable bunk.

When I woke up, Mama was sitting in the kitchen with this stranger. He was eating when I walked in. Mama smiled, "This is my oldest son, Cheekie, Richard."

His name is Richard Cain, and he's Mama's new man. He is a tall, dark-skinned man, with long arms and long legs. His head is bald and shinning like Kojak. She found Richard at Maze nightclub and fell in love with him from the start. Mama doesn't know much about Richard, like where he's from, who his family is, basic information that she should know before allowing a stranger to move in with us. But after two failed relationships, Mama just wanted herself a man. Before I knew it, he was living with us.

Right away, Richard started making changes around the

house. He tore down that wall paper Mama and Daddy put up when we first moved in. He painted the walls black and white to match the one black and green plaid sofa we have sitting in the living room. Richard also waxed the floors, fixed the windows, and built new cabinets for the kitchen. He did all this in a week. On top of all that, he cooks dinner every day and waits on Mama hand and foot. Mama just loves all the attention she is getting. I think I'm starting to like Richard, too. He seems like a real family man— watches TV with us, helps me with my homework, and other neat stuff. He gives us more care and attention than Daddy ever did.

One day Richard took me, Torey, and Darrell fishing at Ponchartrain Lake. While we were there, he talked us to death. Richard loves to talk to us about making something of our lives. While we were fishing, he started asking us what we wanted to be when we grow up.

He asked Darrell first. "So, Darrell, what you gone be when you grow up?"

"A firemen," said Darrell.

Darrell was always fascinated with fire trucks. Last Christmas, he begged for a toy fire truck until he got one. Every time he hears a fire truck coming up the streets, he just about breaks his neck getting to the window. He shouts out loud when the fire trucks pass by, "Mama! There they go, Mama!" Boy, he sure loves fire trucks.

Torey wants to be a policeman. He loves wearing toy guns and fake police badges. Every time he sees policemen in the building or around the neighborhood, he follows them from a distance. He's observing their actions and admiring their guns. He loves guns.

Next, Richard turned his attention to me, just as I was about to haul one in on my fishing rod. He asked, "What about you, Cheekie? Do you know what you gone be when you grow up?"

Before I could answer, the fish on the end of my line started moving and jerking, trying to break loose. I fought back, trying not to lose it. Richard grabbed the rod from me and hauled that fish in. He smiled, "Now, that's how you do it."

It was a big, black fish with these nasty looking whiskers on it. I was shocked that we were going to eat fish that looked like that. At the end of the day, Richard took out a small butter knife and showed us how to scale a fish. He held the fish on the ground and started scraping the scales off. Scales were popping all over, everywhere. We had to jump back to get out of the way.

As he scaled the last fish, he asked me again. "So, Cheekie, you never answered me. What you gone be when you grow up?"

"I want to be a doctor."

His eyes got real big as he moved his head all the way back. He said, "Wow, that's something to want to be. We need more black doctors in the world."

I was just smiling, feeling like I really said something.

Richard said, jokingly, "Well we got it all right here with the three of ya'll. If we have a fire, we'll call li'l red right here, Darrell. And if we have trouble with the law, we'll call Torey. And if one us get sick, got damn it, we'll call Dr. Cheekie."

He laughed out loud. Richard has a real long laugh, one that lasts long after the laugh comes out. He is truly happy being a father to us, and we are happy having him around.

cheekie

When Christmas came around, Richard bought Torey, Darrell, and me everything we wanted: bicycles, Hot Wheels, and skates. My birthday is around Christmas, so Richard took me shopping for Christmas *and* birthday presents. Usually, people buy me one gift and pass it off like it's one big birthday and Christmas gift, but not Richard. I really think he is cool after buying me two separate gifts. He bought me a radio for my birthday and a plaid hat that matched his hat. I am thrilled to death. For the first time, I am opening up to someone, and starting to trust a male figure in my life. Until now, all the men in my life have disappointed me.

I think Richard understands that about me. One of the reasons why I like to be around Mama so much or play jump rope is because I don't have a man around to show me how to be a little boy. But Richard is changing all that. When he sees me outside playing jump rope, he gets after me right away.

He explained, "Boys aren't suppose to be playing rope. You need to be playing football and stuff like that."

Richard bought me a football, too. He even tries to show me how to play. I love all the attention Richard is giving me, but I'm still not interested in sports. I also like how Richard always persuades Mama to let me do adventurous stuff like other boys my age. I get to do stuff that she never would allow me to do.

Mama would never let me to go with Perry n'em to pick berries in the woods across the street. She always said it was too dangerous because she had heard there were snakes and all sorts of things running back there in those woods. It is a big forest, too. It runs from one end of the project to the

74

other. Before Richard moved in with us, Mama always said no when I begged to go pick berries.

Yesterday, Perry and some other boys in the neighborhood were going to pick berries. I ran inside and asked Mama if I could go. As usual, she said, "Hell, no." But Richard stood up for me right away.

He explained, "Faye, let that boy go. He's a boy and need to do stuff like this."

I whined, "Please, Mama. Please let me go."

"No, Cheekie. I heard some little boy got bit by a snake over there last week."

Richard said, "Look, why don't I take'em back there and prove to you once and for all that there ain't no damn snakes back there."

Mama still didn't want me to go, but because Richard had agreed to go with me, she allowed me to go pick berries with Perry n'em for the first time.

I was up early this morning, sitting at the table with my brown paper bag, just waiting for Richard to wake up. To me, this was an adventure that I'd waited for a long time. Mama came in as I was sitting at the kitchen table waiting for Richard.

She laughed and shook her head in disbelief. "Boy, you sure are serious about this, ain't you?"

I shook my head yes.

"Well, Richard is getting ready in there now, so you won't have to wait much longer."

Richard came in wearing green camouflage pants and shirt, with a rifle thrown over his back. He looked like he was going to war, rather than to pick berries.

Mama shook her head. "Ya'll are really taking this forest adventure too far. Now Richard, be careful with my baby over there."

Richard waved his hand, "Girl, stop worrying over nothin'. We just going right across the street."

Perry and his brother George knocked on the door as we sat in the kitchen eating breakfast. Mama answered the door.

Perry asked, "How you doing, Ms. Faye?"

"Fine, Perry. I see ya'll are ready, too."

"Yeah, we 'bout ready," said George.

Mama asked, "Now, Perry, ya'll sure everything is going to be okay over there?"

Perry smiled, "Yeah, Ms. Faye, it's safe to pick berries back there. We do it all the time."

Mama looked as if she still didn't believe him. As we left she admitted, "I just don't have a good feeling about this."

When we crossed the street and entered that forest, my heart raced with excitement, and my eyes lit up like never before. I couldn't believe it. This place looked like a forest I had seen on TV or something—big old trees, birds flying over high, crickets chirping, and little patches of swamp water.

When we reached the berries, I was the first to start picking. George and Perry went one way, and me and Richard, another. Boy, I was so excited, I was grabbing ten to twenty berries at a time. After a while, it seemed like I was far from home—not right across the street.

As I was going about picking berries, I saw squirrels running by and all sorts of bugs flying around. Some of those

bugs started biting me all over. I started scratching and rubbing, trying to stop the itching.

Richard asked, "You all right over there?"

"Yeah, except these bugs keep biting me."

He pulled out his bag some spray called "Off," and
sprayed it on my arms and legs.

He said, "That should stop them from biting for a
while."

It did too. I wondered what was in that stuff, because
after he sprayed me, the bugs stopped biting me.

My whole bag was filled with berries in no time, and
so was Richard's. We tried to catch up with Perry and
George, but they were nowhere to be found. So we headed
back towards the street when I suddenly had to use the
bathroom.

I said, "Richard, I have to pee, and I can't hold it."

Richard looked at me as if he didn't really want to stop.

He said, "Give me your bag, and go behind that tree
over there—and hurry up."

I ran over by that tree, pulled my thing out and peed all
over everywhere. It felt so good as that pee skeeted out all
over the tree.

Then, as I was standing there peeing, I heard a sound
I had never heard before. It was a hissing sound, not like
the sounds of crickets, and birds, and the other sounds that
I had heard. When I turned around, my eyes got real wide.
I saw this big, long, black snake moving towards me. I saw
its sharp fangs and skinny tongue licking out at me. My
heart started pounding, and sweat was streaming down my
face. I stood there, holding my thing, afraid to move an
inch. I had heard from somewhere not to move when a

snake was around—it's best to stay still. After a while, I found my breath.

I screamed out loud, "Richard! Richard!"

Richard came running over, and when he saw that snake in front of me, he started talking real slow. "Don't move, Cheekie, just don't move. Everything gone be all right."

I stood between the snake and the tree; sweat streaming down, and stomach turning over. Richard took his rifle from round his neck and aimed it right at that snake. Boy, I was so scared, and I was thinking that at any moment that snake was going to reach up and bite me on my thing, which was still out in the open. I felt my knees shaking as Richard tried to get his aim.

He said, again, "Don't move, Cheekie. Just stay still."

Suddenly, Richard fired one shot and then another one. That bang was real loud and strong. But when I opened my eyes, that snake was laid over dead. I took a deep breath and wiped the sweat off the top of my forehead.

He shouted, "Got that sneaky little mother fucker! Are you all right?"

I shook my head yes, but the truth was that I was still in shock—just couldn't believe that I almost got bit by a snake.

Richard handed me my bag of berries and said, "Look, let's not tell your Mama about this, OK?"

"OK, but she was sure right about snakes being back here."

Richard managed a smile. He knew Mama was right all along, and I guess he just didn't want to hear her saying, "I told you so."

When we got home, Richard and I never said nothing about that snake that almost jumped up and bit me on the pecker. I ran to the kitchen, sprinkled some sugar in my bag, and ran out quickly to avoid any questions from Mama.

She shouted, "Hey wait up. Tell me how was it? Was it fun?"

I was in a real rush and didn't want to look Mama in the face.

I said, "Yeah, Ma. I had fun, but it's three o'clock, and I'm missing the *Six Million Dollar Man*."

Mama waved her hand, "OK, go ahead."

I ran into my room, turned the *Six Million Dollar Man* on, jumped in my bunk bed, and ate that whole bag of sugary berries. After a while, I forgot all about our li'l forest adventure. Richard came by while I was watching TV. He peeped in and raised his right thumb, meaning that I did the right thing, not telling Mama the whole truth. I just smiled back and sighed relief over my whole forest adventure.

tremOrs

Richard had been living with us for several months when he suddenly had to leave. I was listening outside Mama's bedroom door the night he told her he was leaving. He had applied to be a cook on a cruise ship. (He has always been a good cook.)

Richard said, "Baby, it's gone only be for a couple of months, and I'll be back before you know it."

"But, can't you find another job, one on land rather than going out to sea?" asked Mama.

I stood outside their bedroom door, feeling really sad to hear Richard was leaving. When the conversation ended, I ran to my room and pretended like I was sleeping. I wasn't even in my bed good enough, when I heard our bedroom door open, then the lights come on. It was Richard. He came over, woke Torey and Darrell, and then tapped me on the back. I rolled over still pretending like I was sleeping.

He said, "Look, I just want ya'll to know that I'm leaving early in the morning, but I'll be back in a couple of months."

"Where you going to?" Torey asked.

"Off shore to work on a boat," Richard replied.

"Can't we come?" Darrell asked.

Richard smiled at the question, then rubbed the top of his

head. He explained, "No, li'l man, you can't come, 'cause I want ya'll to stay here and take care of your mama for me."

Torey and Darrell shook their heads yes. I sat in my top bunk trying to act surprised that he was leaving.

"Why you so quiet up there, Cheekie?" he asked.

"No reason—just thinking how I'm going to miss having you around."

Richard grabbed the top of my head. "And I'm going to miss you, too, but I swear I'll be back. Now, why don't ya'll get some sleep, and give me and your mama some time together before I leave."

Torey and Darrell fell straight to sleep. But me, I stayed up all night listening. Richard and Mama made love for hours. I mean they were in that room screaming and yelling, and making up some noise.

It was still dark outside when I heard Richard leaving. I heard him say to Mama, "Take care. I'll call you every chance I get."

Mama shouted out the window as he pulled off in that White Fleet cab, "Goodbye, Richard. Call me. I love you."

That was the last we saw of Richard Cain for what seemed like a long, long time.

After Richard left things seemed so different without him. Mama started cooking again. She changed some, too. Like for instance, she never allowed us to stay outside late any more. And on top of everything, I couldn't dare think about going to pick berries. It was out of the question. There were a lot of things that I missed about Richard. I missed our long talks about making something out my life, him teaching me how to play football, and going fishing on weekends. Things were so different, and everyone was really sad he was gone.

Richard has been gone for only a month or so now, but Mama has started hanging out with Li'l Soul again. As usual, they creep out in the middle of the night, leaving us all alone. We're a little older now, so we enjoy being home alone much more than before. As soon as Mama n'em leave, we wake up. I mean as soon as that door closed shut, our eyes open right up. We creep into the kitchen and make praline candies. We make pralines out of milk and sugar. We add milk and sugar over a pot of burning heat. Then we stir and stir until we have a batch of hard, sugary praline candies.

After making candy, we sit up late watching two of our favorite shows, *Good Times* and *Sanford & Son*. I love *Good Times* the most, though. I love the show because it shows that even families living in the project can have good times—sometimes. But what I love the most is the theme song, "Good Times."

Me, Torey, and Darrell sing right along with the song, "Scratching and surviving, good times. Easy pay a rip off, good times. Ain't we lucky we got'em, good times, yeah, yeah, good times." Boy, we love that song!

Right after we finish watching *Good Times*, Torey and Darrell fall right to sleep, but I stay up and clean that kitchen good, so Mama won't never know we stayed up. Mama goes to Maze to have a good time, but we have good times at home, too. We have the best time being home alone.

Mama hangs out so much at Maze Nightclub, that when Richard finally called a few nights ago, she wasn't home. Torey, Darrell and I were sound asleep when I heard a loud ringing noise that woke me from a deep sleep. It was that telephone ringing and ringing off the hook.

I jumped out of bed, stumbled over Darrell's fire truck, and answered, "Hello."

"Is that you, Cheekie?" asked Richard.

"Yeah, who this?" I asked.

"Oh, you forgot my voice already? This is Richard."

My eyes got real wide when he said his name. I was so happy to hear his voice.

"Richard?" I asked in a real surprise.

"Yeah, Richard. You remember, the man who took you in the woods looking for berries?"

I rubbed my eyes trying to wake up. "Yeah, I remember. I guess I'm still sleepy."

"That's OK, li'l man. Is your mama home?"

I paused right that minute, trying to decide if I should tell Richard that Mama was out at the joint with Li'l Soul.

Richard asked again, "Cheekie, did you hear me? I said is you mama home?"

"No."

"No? Where is she this time a night?"

"Out with Li'l Soul."

Richard shouted, "Dammit! She running the streets with that whore. Look, Cheekie, tell her I called, OK?"

"OK."

"Now take care, and get back in that bed. Oh, and make sure those doors are locked."

"OK."

I hung up and ran in the living room to check both doors. Both doors were locked real tight. Then I ran back to my room, jumped back in bed, and drifted off to sleep.

The following morning, I went straight to Mama's room. She was knocked out sleep. Her clothes were still on. As I got closer, I smelt alcohol on her breath and smoke all in her clothes. I pushed her arm. She didn't move at all. Then, I pushed it again. And she still wasn't moving. I got really forceful then. I pulled and pulled, even shouted out loud. But Mama was out, and there was no waking her up.

I shouted as I pulled her arm again, "Mama wake up! Mama wake up!"

Mama was out so long that I was scared something was wrong with her. After a while, though, she opened one eye, and then the other. Both of her eyes were blood-shot red, too. Mama held her forehead, trying to wake up. Her eyes were wide open, but Mama still acted as if she didn't know who I was or where she was. Mama had what grown folks called a hangover.

When she finally realized it was me, she asked, "Boy, why you waking me up this early in the morning?"

"'Cause Richard called last night."

Mama's eyes got real wide and she sat right up straight.

She said, "Please, tell me you lying!"

I shook my head no.

"What time did he call?" Mama asked.

"Around one o'clock in the morning."

"Damn!" she shouted.

She fell back on the bed real hard and closed her eyes shut. Before I even realized it, Mama was knocked out sleep again.

I took her shoes off, covered her up, turned the lights off, and closed her bedroom door.

Mama not only missed that call from Richard, but a lot of others, too. It seemed that every time he called, Mama wasn't home. She was always running the streets with Li'l

Soul, over a neighbor's house, at the grocery store, just any and everywhere—but never home.

This went on for almost three months before Richard stopped calling altogether. Mama worried herself sick over him not calling. And after weeks had passed and there was still no word from Richard, I thought we were never going to hear from him again.

Yesterday, though, when I came home from school, I opened the back door and saw Richard's things sitting next to the kitchen table. He was home! I dropped my book bag that was hanging loosely off my shoulder, and ran to the back of the house. I knocked on Mama's door and Richard answered. Boy, was I glad to see that smile again.

I grinned, "Hey, Richard! You back?"

"Yeah, I'm back, just like I said I would. What's been up, li'l man?"

"Nothin' much, just going to school."

"That's a good thing. Got to get that education, right, Dr. Cheekie?"

Richard kind of moved the top of my head around in fun. I was smiling hard because I was so glad to see he was home. Mama sat on the edge of her bed listening. By the look on her face though, I could tell her and Richard were in the middle of something really serious.

Richard said, "Look Cheekie, give me and your mama some time to talk. I'll be over in a minute, OK, li'l man?"

I looked over at Mama and she was then rolling her hair with these big pink and blue rollers.

I said, "OK, but can I go down the street to buy me a huckabuck?"

Richard handed me a dollar and said, "Yeah, and buy one for your brothers, too."

"Thanks, Richard."

I closed the door on my way out, but I didn't leave right away. I stood there listening outside the door.

Richard asked, "Now like I was saying, Faye, where were you every time I called? You seeing some other nigger?"

Mama said, "Don't be crazy. You know it's not like that."

"Then what the hell is it then? I send you money, take care of your children, and here you always running the streets with that whore."

Soon as Richard called Li'l Soul a whore, my heart started pumping real fast. I thought about that night Daddy beat Mama for hanging out with Li'l Soul. I felt like something bad was about to happen all over again. I started to feel hot, my stomach was turning over, and I started to sweat—but nothing happened. They talked the rest of that day and into the night.

But then out of the blue that night, something did happen. It came like an earthquake in the middle of the night. Quickly, things started to crumble. While me, Torey and Darrell were sleeping, Mama and Richard woke us. Their voices got real loud, I mean real, real loud. They were arguing. We could hear them because their door was cracked open, and we were right across the hall. Suddenly, Richard slammed the door shut. Their voices grew fainter, but we heard him there, throwing things around and screaming out loud at Mama. I jumped down from my bunk bed. I ran into the hallway and heard him screaming and shouting and tearing that room apart.

I heard him shout, "Bitch, you gone talk back to me like

I'm some nigger off the street?" And then I heard one slap, then another, followed by a real loud fall. My heart was pumping, and my whole body was shaking. I pushed the bedroom door open just a bit. I was peeping and I saw the whole thing. He punched her, and then he took her whole head and slammed it against the dressing room mirror. Glass shattered everywhere. And those pink and blue rollers that were in Mama's head were all scattered over the floor. I mean all over, everywhere. Mama screamed and yelled and shouted, "RICHARD, NO! PLEASE STOP! THE CHIL-DREN!" But he wouldn't stop. He kept beating her for worse, and Torey and Darrell sat up in bed, crying and shak-ing. I just stood there outside the door hoping he wouldn't kill her. I tried to remember how it used to sound when my real Daddy used to beat Mama. This was different. It sound-ed like Richard was trying to kill her!

Then, suddenly, there was silence. The quake was over. I ran to my room, jumped up in my bed, and laid down, praying and hoping Mama wasn't dead. Richard opened the door and screamed out loud, "Shut up in there and go back to bed. Your Mama is fine—just fine. We had a li'l misun-derstanding, but everything is just fine."

But I heard Mama in there crying, and she wasn't just fine. She was lying there on the floor, with blood, blood everywhere. "Poor Mama! What is she going to do now?" I thought as I laid there and tried to sleep after the earth-quake passed. But I couldn't sleep, because the tremors kept coming back, and I kept hearing Mama's voice inside my head, screaming and crying and calling out for help.

running away

"Whatever happened to the old Mama, the one who was strong enough to chase Daddy away with a knife? The sweet, sexy, sixteen year old who was pretty and sassy, with big legs, and big thighs?" These were my thoughts, as I watched Mama in the kitchen preparing supper tonight.

She is fat now, partly because she has had three children, but mainly because she is pregnant again. I can't believe it—Mama is having another baby. She hasn't told me yet, but I can see it. I think Mama is too ashamed to tell anyone she is going to have a baby for a man like Richard.

Her face is different, too. It looks like she has walked into a brick wall. Her eyes are blackened and her nose and lips are swollen. In addition, she has scratch and bite marks all over her body. "This man is a monster," I think to myself as I sit eating at the kitchen table.

Poor Mama. She tries so hard to hide her bruises by covering them with bandages and her blackened eyes with a band of her hair. But she can't hide those marks, because they are too noticeable. My brothers and I aren't stupid. We know what is going on, and we are afraid of what might happen to Mama if Richard keeps beating her. Mama is scared, ashamed, and in pain. She used to be such a high-spirited woman, but now she walks around the house with her head bowed. Her spirit has been broken and she is ashamed of herself.

On the other hand, Richard walks around the house like everything is normal between the two of them. His smile—which I used to love—and his laugh—which I couldn't get enough of—make me sick to the stomach. My love has turned to hate, because of the "earthquakes" that come three and four times a month. I can't believe that what used to be such a nice guy has turned out to be so evil. He reminds me of a vampire: tall and dark, with long finger nails. He bites Mama just like a vampire, too, and scratches her with those long fingernails. The earthquakes just keep coming. I think that all this violence is starting to become a part of me, deep inside, somehow.

Yesterday was Easter Sunday. My Auntie Debbie and her husband, who we call Speedy, came to visit us. Debbie is my daddy's sister, and she lives uptown over on Elysian Fields. She is Torey's Nannan, (that's what we call grandmothers down here in New Orleans).

Mama had us dressed in our finest Sunday's best for church. Easter is the only time we go to church—Mama isn't all that religious. We attended my Grandma Pam's church, New Zion Baptist Church. New Zion is right around the corner from Pam's house.

I was dressed in a three piece, pinned-striped blue suit and a pair of black pointy-toe shoes. I was sharp! And Torey and Darrell were dressed in casual slacks and spring shirts. Boy, we were so excited about Easter! We stayed up all night Saturday eating candy and decorating our Easter baskets. We made our Easter baskets out of shoe boxes. I swear, we used shoe boxes to make Easter baskets. We filled those shoe boxes with green and pink shredded paper, and then filled our boxes with chocolates, Easter eggs and all sorts of Easter favorites.

Anyway, when we got back from church, Debbie and Speedy were already there waiting for us. Richard let them in. He didn't come to church with us. He stayed home to cook dinner. I used to love his cooking, but not any more. I won't even eat when he cooks dinner. I think, "I would rather starve than eat his food." That's just how much I hate him now.

Debbie was so excited to see us. She shouted, "Oh, look at ya'll looking so fine in your nice Sunday clothes. Come here and give Auntie Debbie a hug."

We did, and it was a big hug, too. Debbie hadn't seen us since Mama and Daddy broke up two and a half years ago. She used to stop by often back then, but now she only visits on certain holidays, if at all. Debbie is a tall, slim woman—very pretty too. She is a fashion model, but not a big time model. She does local fashion shows around town. Speedy is a cab driver. Me and Mama often bump into him when we make groceries at Schwegmann's Supermarket. When we do, he always gives us a ride home for free.

Speedy seemed glad to see us too. He asked, "So, how ya'll been, boy?"

"Fine," said Torey who was now sitting on Debbie's lap. She loves Torey, and he loves his Nannan, too.

I was standing by the couch, watching. Mama was trying to keep her smile together, but the truth is she didn't have anything to smile about. Still, she doesn't want anyone to know Richard beats her, especially anyone in the family. As I stood there, I noticed a rabbit in a cage sitting next to the sofa—right beside Debbie's leg.

I asked, "Debbie, who's that rabbit for?"

"Boy, your eyes don't miss nothin', do they?"

I shook my head no.

"I bought this rabbit for all ya'll to play with."

I couldn't believe it! A real rabbit for Easter! I already have a fake white rabbit that Mama bought me, but this was unbelievable.

I reached inside the cage and picked that rabbit up. It's a soft, black rabbit with big ol' ears, and a tiny, little tail. It is the prettiest little rabbit I have ever seen.

Mama said, "Girl, the last thing these children need is a live pet, and a rabbit at that."

"Girl, I think they need a pet around here, give them something to do," Debbie replied.

Mama didn't seem to like us having a rabbit, but we were excited about that black rabbit from the start.

Torey asked, "Can I hold it?"

I held on to that rabbit real tight and didn't want to give it up.

Mama said, "See what you started? They gone be fighting over this damn rabbit."

"Let him hold it, Cheekie. And I see you still cheekie, too, huh?" said Debbie.

I gave it over to Torey, unwillingly. Darrell sat and waited for his turn to hold the rabbit.

I asked, "So what his name?"

"We didn't give it a name yet," Speedy answered.

Darrell shouted out, "Let's call'im Bugs Bunny." Everybody laughed.

I said, "That's a stupid name."

"No it ain't," shouted Darrell.

"Yes, it is," I shouted back.

"OK! OK! That's enough," Mama shouted.

"Why don't we call the rabbit Bugs Bunny, like Darrell said? Because your brother isn't stupid, right, Cheekie?" asked Speedy.

My head was bowed; I felt really bad about calling his suggestion stupid.

I said, "Yeah, you right."

After we talked and played with that rabbit for almost an hour, Mama invited them to stay a little longer.

"Girl, why don't ya'll stay for dinner?"

"Thanks, Faye, but we got to make it over my Mama's house for dinner."

"Can I go, Debbie?" I shouted out with excitement. I just couldn't stand being around Richard, and I didn't want to eat his food. He was in the back room watching TV. He never came around when we had company.

Mama said, "No, Cheekie, you can't go over your grandma's house. You got to go to school tomorrow, anyway."

"But they can bring me back later on."

Speedy said, "Your Mama is right, li'l man. Maybe another time, OK?"

I sighed with disappointment, because I really wanted to leave the house and get away from Richard. After a while, Speedy and Debbie left and I was stuck right there with Richard, anyway.

Over the past week I have become really close to Bugs Bunny. That rabbit has become my closest friend. In fact, it has become *my* rabbit. At first Torey and Darrell were really into Bugs Bunny, but that only lasted for a couple of days. Besides, Easter is over and so is their excitement over rabbits.

Just the other day, me and Bugs Bunny were sitting in Mama's room watching TV. My brothers were outside playing, Mama was cleaning up, and Richard was out somewhere. I was sitting there talking to Bugs Bunny and my fake rabbit (I named her Ginger). I spend a lot of time talking to Ginger and Bugs Bunny. I hold Bugs Bunny in one hand and Ginger in the other.

Bugs Bunny said, "Ginger, why you talking back to me like that."

"Bugs Bunny, it's not what you thinking."

"Don't raise your voice at me," said Bugs Bunny.

"I'm not raising my voice, and stop screaming before the children hear you."

"Oh, now you worrying about your children, but when you running the street with that whore, you not thinking about your children, are you?"

And then I made Bugs Bunny hit Ginger. They were fighting. I mean, I made them really fight. I made them hit, and hit, and hit one another until Bugs Bunny was dead.

I killed Bugs Bunny! I couldn't believe it—he was really dead!

When I realized that I had killed Bugs Bunny, I cried and cried, until Mama came in and found me sitting on the edge of her bed holding that dead rabbit in my hands. Mama asked, "Cheekie, what's wrong with you?"

"I killed him Mama! I killed him! I didn't mean it. It was an accident."

Mama walked over and picked Bugs Bunny up. She shook it a bit, pulled its ears, tried to make it walk; she tried everything. It didn't take Mama long to realize that the rabbit was really dead.

She asked, "Cheekie, how did this happen?"

I cried even louder. "They were fighting and Ginger killed him. It was an accident."

Mama asked, real confused, "They were fighting?"

Then Mama figured out what had happened. She was ashamed, because she knew that I was acting out her and Richard fighting. Mama and Richard fighting is really tearing me up inside, and I guess I took it out on Bugs Bunny and Ginger.

Mama held me in her arms, pressing my head up against her bosom. I cried for a long time. Mama cried, too. She rocked me in her arms while we cried. We cried and cried, until I fell off to sleep.

Now that Bugs Bunny is gone, I feel even more alone than before. I am cracking and breaking inside, and no one knows it but me. I go to the bathroom sometimes, lock the door, and stay in there for hours. I'm trying to figure things out. I ask myself over and over, "Why, Mama? Why do you let'im stay when he keeps beating you like that?"

I can't understand it, and I'm starting to lose respect for Mama. She pretends like everything is fine. She never talks about it. She even went so far as to defend Richard when Ms. Johnson and Gwen ask her about the way he treats her. She says that he is under a lot of pressure, and that's why he hits her. I just can't believe she is making excuses for him. I hate this house, and I want out of this project. But there is really no place for me to go. I am stuck here with no way out. I am living in hell on earth. Next door lives an older boy who sexually abused me, and I'm living in a house with a savage monster who beats my mother whenever he wants. I want out so bad that I ran away to Pam's house the other day. That is the day when Richard went so far as to try to beat me, too.

After I got home from school, I rushed in to my room and turned the TV set on (as usual) to watch my favorite show—*The Six Million Dollar Man*.

I was sitting there on the floor beside the bed when Richard came in, reached over, and turned the TV set off.

He said, "You have time to watch that later, but this room can stand a cleaning now."

I sighed, "Man, please. You ain't my daddy." I turned the TV back on.

He reached over and turned it back off.

He said, "Like I said, clean this damn room up!"

At that moment I started wishing him dead. I even dreamed up ways in my head to kill him. I thought I might stab him, poison him. All sorts of bad things were popping in my mind. As I reached over to turn it back on, he slapped my hand. And I kicked his leg. I kicked the hell out of his leg.

He shouted, "You li'l bastard, come here."

I tried to run for the door, and that's when he grabbed me by the neck. He grabbed me real tight. He squeezed my neck so tight, I thought I was going to choke. I was moving and wiggling, trying to break free. Then, I reached down and bit him on the hand. Mama came in just as Richard was about to punch me in the face.

Mama shouted, "Richard, don't you dare! Don't you dare hit my child!"

He stood over me with his fist balled up, about to swing.

Mama said, "Don't you ever put your hands on my children. Ever! They are not yours to begin with."

I thought he might hit Mama for talking back to him, but he didn't. He just went into the other room and slammed the door shut.

Mama reached over to touch me. I moved away in a hurry.

"Are you all right?" she asked.

I looked at her as if to say, "Of course I'm not all right. You have this monster living with us, who beats you all the time, and you think I'm all right?"

Those were my thoughts, but instead of saying it out loud, I just walked over to the TV set and turned it back on. Mama stood in the doorway watching me for a while, and then she closed the door shut. Soon as she closed that door, I decided it was time to get out of here. I decided to run away to Pam's house. I grabbed a pair of pants, shirt, drawers and my toothbrush and put all of it in a brown Schweggman's bag. Then I ran out so fast, so fast that not even Superman could catch me. I don't remember how I got there, because I cut so many corners and ran so many blocks. But all I know is that in ten minutes, I was standing in front of Pam's house, breathing fast. When I knocked on the door, Pam answered. I fell right in the door, exhausted by my run for freedom.

Pam shouted, "Cheekie, what's wrong with you?"

I tried to catch my breath. "I ran away, Pam. I had to get away from Richard. He beats and bites Mama, just like a vampire!"

She shouted, "What? You mean some man beating on my daughter?"

I shook my head yes.

Pam said, "Come in my room and let's talk."

I sat in a chair next to her bed. The same chair Mama probably sat in years ago when she told Pam she was pregnant. Pam is still in the same house; she moved in back in the forties. Not much about her place has changed since then. But she changed, though. She is a much different person than when Mama was living with her. Pam is still stern and strong, but much more protective of her children and grandchildren. She is now raising four children in the same house she raised Mama.

Pam had children late in life. For example, my Uncle Jerome is only a little older than me. (When Mama was pregnant with me, Pam had just given birth to him.) Of all her fourteen children, I think she loves her youngest daughter, Karen, the most. On the other hand, she seems to like my Auntie Florence the least. Auntie Florence's nickname is Safot.

Pam gives Safot a hard time, all the time. I think it's because she has a different daddy from the rest of her children, and Pam *hates* him. She hates him so much, she takes it out on Safot. I overheard Mama and Annie Mae talking about it one day.

Safot is barely a teenager, but Pam gives her the hardest chores: scrubbing floors, washing dishes, and running errands. Giving her hard work is one thing, but Pam also talks down to Safot, too.

Pam and I were talking about Richard when Safot came in the room and interrupted us. Pam sat on her bed chewing on tobacco. She loves that tobacco, because every time I see her she be chewing it.

"Safot, get in here! I want you to go to Bynum's and get me a newspaper." (Bynum's is the local store right across the street from Pam's house.)

"Yes ma'am. I'm just finishing the last of these dishes," said Safot.

Pam leaned over her bed, spit that tobacco right out in some old newspaper that was laying on the floor next to the bed.

She shouted, "Safot, get in here!"

Safot came running in, then she just stood there, staring at the floor, waiting for the next set of chores to do for her master. Safot looks and acts like a slave, and her own mama is her master. I can see the fear in her eyes, she is so scared when Pam is around.

"Yes ma'am," she said.

"You must be hard of fucking hearing. I said I need that newspaper and I need it now." Pam's eyes got real big, and her voice real strong.

"Yes ma'am, getting right to it," she replied.

I still don't understand how a mother can treat her own child this way. I think of Safot as a ghetto Cinderella and Pam as her evil stepmother, only they are black and live in the Desire Project. Safot is always wearing scarves tied around her head and an old, long dress down to her ankles, looking like Aunt Jemima from the pancakes box. All the children in the project call Safot "Auntie Mama." They tease her all the time.

After Safot ran out the room to go fetch a newspaper, Pam said, "Now, getting back to what we were talking about. You know that is such a shame, you children have to see that kind of stuff. And Faye should be ashamed of herself letting a man like that live with her."

She threw her head way back and sort of chuckled a bit. She always laughed like that, head thrown back while laughing out loud. I kept wondering how she could think that it's wrong for Richard to treat Mama that way, but it's OK for her to treat Safot so mean. Sometimes I just don't understand grown-ups.

She said, "Oh, but it couldn't be me, Cheekie, 'cause you know I would try and kill that nigger dead if he ever raised his hands to hit me."

As soon as she said that, I started crying. I begged Pam to let me stay with her. I cried, "Pam, please let me live here with you. I don't want to go back there."

She explained, "No, Cheekie. Grandma can't let you live here. I barely can feed the ones I got, but what I will do is come over there and set Richard straight. That you can count on."

I wanted Pam to fulfill her promise now—right now. I didn't want to wait another day, because I know if anybody can change things in our house, it is Pam.

I cried and begged to stay, but Pam said no. She handed me a rag for my nose and said, "Here, wipe your face and I'll let you spend the night. You can sleep on the couch in the living room, and Sunday I want you to come and go to church with Grandma, you hear."

I was so relieved that I didn't have to go back home. I was happy to stay, even if it was only for one night.

I looked forward to going to church with Pam, too. I hadn't been to church since Easter Sunday, and I really enjoyed that day in church. Going to church was another thing that was different about Pam. She had been going for a while. She always said, "God is the only person who could make a way out of no way." I just prayed he would make a way for me out of this mess, because I hated living with Richard.

After everyone went to sleep, I sat up on the couch thinking about Richard and the way he treats Mama. I hated the thought of going home in the morning. But I knew I had to.

As I turned over to go to sleep, I noticed this big, giant rat, crawling and jumping around on top of Pam's kitchen table. I was terrified. It looked like the size of a hamster. And then I saw another one running across the living room floor right beside the couch. I thought they might get me— they were just that big. I grabbed my blanket up from the floor, just didn't want one of those giant rats to crawl up my blanket and get me there on the couch. I was so scared that I just sat up most of the night, watching those giant rats jumping and leaping all over the place.

As I sat covered up to my neck, peeping at those rats all night long, I wondered about Mama, about what she was gonna do to me when I got my butt home.

Mama was mad with me when I got home. She was mad because I ran away to Pam's house. Soon as I walked in the door, she asked, "Cheekie, why did you run out of here like that? I was worried sick about you, and I know you was at Pam's house telling her all my business."

"I ran away because I hate Richard, and I'm scared of him."

Mama bowed her head when I said that, turned around and continued washing those dishes there in the sink. She never wanted to face the situation, just went about her chores like it was no big deal. It was then that I really started losing respect for Mama. Soon I started talking back to her and giving her a lot of lip. After she finished washing dishes, she asked me to run an errand.

"Cheekie, I need you to go to Busy B for me." Busy B is a grocery store near our house. I heard her, but I pretended like I didn't.

She shouted again, "Cheekie, you heard me! I want you to come and go to Busy B for me."

I said, "I ain't going to no store. Ask your man, Richard, to go."

Boy, Mama came in my room and slammed the door shut. She was burning hot, so hot she transformed into a ten foot giant, and her voice sounded like Darth Vador from Star Wars. In a voice similar to his, she demanded, "What the hell did you say, Cheekie?"

At that moment, I knew Mama was mad and was ready to beat my tail. So I said nothing, just ran out the door. I jumped under her bed and crawled into a corner, hoping Mama wouldn't come after me. But she did come after me. She was almost nine months pregnant, but she got under that bed, grabbed me and pulled me out. Then she beat me some terrible, so terrible I couldn't sit down afterwards. I cried and shook and pretended like I was dying. I was trying to make her feel guilty for beating me. But it didn't work, because Mama shouted, "Shut up in there, before I come in there and give you some more."

After a while, I fell to sleep so peacefully. Ain't nothing like getting a good beating and then drifting off to sleep. It is the best sleep in the world.

Jesus on the main line

I couldn't wait for Sunday morning to go to church with Pam. I was up at daybreak that morning sitting at the kitchen table eating Apple Jacks. (What else?) Everyone was still sound asleep, but me.

After eating my cereal, I tried to wake Mama up to dress me. I opened her bedroom door and walked over to her side of the bed. Richard was lying with his hands around Mama. I slowly moved his arm from around her. I just hated the sight of him touching my mama. She was lying there on her back, nine months pregnant. She looked like a big balloon lying there asleep.

I pulled her arm, and then I pulled it some more. Mama has always been a heavy sleeper. I don't care how much I pulled and tapped her face, she wouldn't wake up. After about a good five minutes of trying to wake her, I decided to dress myself for church.

I pulled a nice green suit out of my closet, along with a big black bow tie, and the pointy-toe shoes Mama bought me for Easter Sunday. I had never really dressed myself, I mean not like this. I could easily dress myself if I was just going outside to play, but this was different. I had to tie my own tie, comb my hair, and make sure everything matched.

As I sat on the floor beside Torey and Darrell's bunk, Torey woke up. He asked, "Where you going to, Cheekie?"

I turned around and said, "I'm going to church with Pam."

"By yourself?" he asked.

"Yeah. I know how to get there. You remember that time I ran away and got there by myself?"

Torey said nothing else, just sat watching me the whole time I was getting dressed. I sprayed some Stay-Soft-Fro in my head and tried to comb that nappy bush of mine. I like the way Stay-Soft-Fro makes my hair nice 'n shiny and easy to comb.

After combing my hair, I made Torey lock the door behind me. It was around 7:30 in the morning when I left on a walk I'll never forget. That Sunday morning walking to meet Pam, I discovered the horrible reality of life in the Desire Project.

I took Desire Street to Pam's house. Desire Street was the main street and it ran the length of the project. There is this big lump in the middle of Desire Street. It is so lumpy that as cars pass by, they tilt slightly to one side. I don't know how that street got like that. All I know is that it is lumpy from one end of the project to the other.

As I walked along that street, I felt a spiritual closeness with the earth. It was the prettiest Sunday morning. The sun was shining up high, a nice cool winter breeze was blow-ing, and silence hung in the air. I felt good without under-standing why. I couldn't wait to get to church. There is something I like about that church. It could be the singing, or maybe I am amazed at how folks cry and shout all over the place. I don't really know what it is, but nevertheless I couldn't wait.

I got halfway to Pam's house when some woman asked me if I had a dollar to buy her children some food. I just shook my head no, and kept walking. I saw prostitutes standing around on corners, looking to make their next dollar. But what struck me most of all was the children around my age, running around lookin' as if they hadn't been fed or given a bath in days. I felt sorry for them, and it bothers me some to think that I am living in a place like this.

When I finally got to Pam's house, one of her neighbors was hanging out the window. She smiled and asked, "Aren't you Pam's grandson?"

I nodded my head yes.

"Well, you looking mighty sharp this morning. Going to church?"

"Yeah, me and Pam."

"That's nice. You need to keep God in your life, 'cause he will surely make a way for you, you know."

I smiled as if I really understand, but the truth was that I have no idea about nothing. I don't understand who God is, or why people make such a big deal over Him. I like going to church because it makes me feel good.

I knocked on Pam's door and Safot answered. She was happy to see me, and she smiled. "Come in, Cheekie. Pam's getting dressed in the other room."

I walked in and found Karen, Jerome, and Daniel sitting around drinking coffee. Safot was cleaning up, as usual, and preparing Sunday's dinner.

Karen asked, "Cheekie, you going to church with us?"

"Yeah. Pam invited me to go with ya'll."

Safot grabbed hold my shoulder and turned me all around. She said, "Boy, you looking good. Who dressed you?"

"Me," I said proudly.

Jerome said, "No you didn't. Stop lying."

As soon as I was about to tell him I wasn't lying, Pam came in the kitchen and interrupted. She said in her usual mean voice, "OK, Jerome we not gone have that kind of talk in here, you hear me?"

Jerome bowed his head. "Yeah, Ma."

Pam was still in her slip, and she still had a few rollers in her head. She asked, "How you doing this morning, Cheekie?"

"Fine."

"I see you ready to go to church, too. Come here let me fix your pants. Here, tuck this shirt in."

I thought I was looking just fine at first, until Pam found just about everything wrong with my outfit.

"Who dressed you this morning?" she asked, pulling her eye glasses slightly off her nose.

"Me."

She shook her head in disbelief. "Faye should be ashamed of herself, letting her ten year old son dress himself for church. You know I'm gone have to pray for my child, 'cause I just don't understand how a mother would let her child leave the house looking like this."

I bowed my head, almost felt like crying. Pam made Mama seem like the worst Mama in the world, and made me feel like I was looking like a mess.

Safot said as she stood over near the sink washing dishes, "I like his outfit, and his bow tie, too."

Pam looked at Safot as if she couldn't believe what she was hearing. When Pam spoke, it was always final. She didn't like to be questioned by anyone, especially Safot.

Pam walked over near the sink, put one hand on her hip, and then asked, "Safot, are you questioning my judgement?"

Safot's voice cracked. "No, Pam, I was just saying, I mean, I like his outfit."

Pam's voice got real loud, "And what the hell you know about dressing? Look at you, ragged shoes, scarf on your head, and old mammie's dress on. And you talk about dressing. If you know what's best, girl, you better run across the street and get me my morning paper."

Safot dropped that glass she was about to wash, slipped her shoes on, and ran out the door. Boy, was she scared, and so was everyone else. We thought Pam was about to grab Safot and beat her for disagreeing with her.

After Safot ran out, Pam said, "Now have a seat, Cheekie. Boo Boo, fix him a cup of coffee." (That's what we call my Uncle Jerome—Boo Boo.)

I pulled a chair next to the table and sat across from Boo Boo while we drank coffee. Pam and Karen were in the back room getting ready for church, while Pam's other son, Daniel, was in the back room.

Boo Boo handed me some sugar for my coffee and asked, "Man, did you see *The Six Million Dollar Man* yesterday?"

"Yeah I saw it. And Big Foot was beating him up, too. I can't wait until the Bionic Woman show up, 'cause she and the Six Million Dollar Man gone team up against him."

He is just as big a fan as I am. We often talk about the Super Friends and the Six Million Dollar Man. We even play the characters out.

As I sat there drinking my coffee and dipping white bread into it, I wondered about what church was going to be like. I was nervous, but excited at the same time.

We didn't have far to walk to church since New Zion was only a li'l ways from Pam's. Me, Pam, and Karen left around 8:30 a.m., running late for the eight o'clock service. Pam told the others they should come to church, too, but she didn't force them. She didn't even have to force me because I wanted to go. Pam loves my strong desire to go to church. She looked sharp that morning. She wore a pretty velvet skirt and vest set, and a big, black hat to match it. Boy, Pam couldn't wait to get to church to sing, shout, and praise the Lord. She was a member of the choir, too.

Soon as we got to church, boy, we couldn't even sit down. Everyone was shouting, clapping, and dancing all over the place. We joined right in, though, and before I knew it we were praising the Lord up til' the end of the service.

Rev. Owens led the choir and the church in singing all the favorite hymns—"Can't Nobody Do Me Like Jesus," "I'm on the Battle Field for My Lord," and "Jesus on the Mainline." "Jesus on the Mainline" is my favorite.

As the choir sung, "Jesus on the mainline, tell Him what you want. Oh, Jesus on the mainline call Him up, and tell Him what you want," I told Him that I want a new home and Richard gone. I swear I prayed for that the whole time.

As I stood clapping and praying, I watched the whole church shouting and jumping all over the place. I mean all over everywhere. Folks were jumping and falling out so much that ushers and deacons had to catch people and fan them as they passed out. Folks called in the Holy Ghost, and boy it sure was at work that day. I just sat in awe at first as the members of the congregation fell and passed out. Then I joined in clapping and jumping, too. I didn't understand everything, but I enjoyed the music, and the preaching, and the array of folks who were in church that day. I didn't faint though, just clapped and watched everyone else faint.

After that Sunday, I started going to church every week with Pam. In fact, I couldn't wait for Sunday mornings to come. It was a chance for me to get away from Richard. I don't understand everything about God and the power of prayer, but I believe that if I keep praying and asking Him for help in getting rid of Richard, He will find a way to help me. I want him out of our house and I'm not going to stop until he's gone.

Now, even though I am going to church regularly, Mama, Torey, and Darrell don't go. I'm trying to convince Mama to go and to take my brothers, too. Pam put me up to it. She says that I should try to get Mama n'em to go to church, because God will give her the strength to leave Richard. I beg Mama to go to church, but she just won't do it. She always says, "I'll come some day, but not today. You go on Cheekie, and say a prayer for Mama." I've stopped asking now, but I take Torey and Darrell with me. They are eight and seven years old now, and they walk right down Desire Street with me to Pam's house. I am their big brother, and I am determined to save my soul and to help them save their souls, too. I feel like I have to help them. If I don't, who will?

Last Sunday, Torey, Darrell, and I got baptized, and

something wonderful happened. We woke up early that Sunday morning (as usual), got dressed, and ate cereal before we left. As we sat in the kitchen eating, Mama came in dressed and ready for church, too. My eyes lit up with joy. I was so happy to see Mama going to church with us. I thought this was going to help her get away from that monster, Richard.

Mama said, smiling directly at me, "You see, Cheekie, Mama loves God, too. And there is no way I'm going to miss this important day in my children's lives."

We left the house and we walked down Desire Street hand in hand. When we got in front the church, Pam saw us walking up.

She smiled and said to Mama, "I'm glad Cheekie convinced you to come to church. We all need God in our lives, you know, and it's 'bout time you get yourself and your house together. Now, I ain't gone go into detail right here, 'cause this ain't the time nor the place. But we gone talk, you hear what I said?"

Mama shook her head yes. Pam was very stern and strong the way she said that. I knew she meant business, and Mama knew it too.

We were baptized at the end of regular service. First we had to change into white robes, and put white towels around our heads. We walked around inside the whole church dressed like that. As we walked, everyone stood around us singing and holding candles. Mama stood in front the church beside Pam. As soon as we finished walking around the room, we stopped in front the altar. That was where they had this big hole in the middle of the floor. I looked down and saw a pool full of water. I didn't understand how that water got there, because it was right in the middle of the floor. It looked as though they raised the whole floor up, and dumped that water right in. That water was deep, too. So deep that Rev. Owens and one of the deacons had to hold us up so we wouldn't go under.

I went first. I stepped down the stairs that led into the water. The whole church hummed a hymn as Rev. Owens said, "I bless you in the name of the Father, the Son, and the Holy Ghost."

Then he dumped me in that water real quick. I didn't have time to catch my breath, that's how fast it happened. I came up out that water, thinking I might drown or something. I couldn't drown, because Rev. Owens had a rag over my nose so no water could get in. But I was still scared of that deep water, because I couldn't swim.

Anyway, as Rev. Owens finished up with Torey (who went last), Mama was overtaken with so much joy that she fainted right there on the spot. Pam and some others were fanning Mama while humming and singing. I stood in shock that Mama had passed out like that. She was OK after a li'l while though. After the baptism, Pam sang one of my favorite songs, "It Ain't Nothin' but the Holy Ghost":

> It was early one morning, just before
> the break of day, when Jesus came into my
> life, and He washed my sins away. I started
> running and I started shouting. It ain't
> nothin' but the Holy Ghost moving down
> in my feet.

As Pam sang, the whole church rejoiced, shouting and fainting some more. Baptism is not taken lightly in this church. Committing your life to Christ is serious business.

After church was all over, Pam laughed as we were walking home, "Cheekie, we had church today didn't we? I even broke my expensive pair of heels. You know Grandma don't wear no cheap stuff, Cheekie."

When she said that, she sort of threw her head back and laughed out loud. I giggled a bit, thinking how funny Pam was about her clothes and shoes.

"Boy we sure acted like a fool today didn't we, Faye? You fainting and carrying on. But, child, that's OK, because if I'm gone be a fool, I rather be a fool for the Lord."

She laughed some more, and so did we. That's how I remember that day, too. We were a fools for the Lord—me, Pam, my brothers, Mama, and the whole church.

"Thank God and praise His holy name," I thought as I walked home with my Bible in hand and a big bow tie wrapped around my Sunday suit.

bustin loose

It seems like the more time pass, the more things stay the same. Only thing different, though, is that I'm not a little kid any more. At least, that's what I think, 'cause I'm turning eleven. And Mama thought since I was older now, she should give me a big birthday party. And boy do I remember last week, because almost everyone was there! My uncles and aunts on my mother's side of the family were there, some of my daddy's family, but not my daddy. Mama wasn't in touch with my daddy's side of the family often, but that night she decided to "bury the hatchet." So Grandma Emelia, Auntie Sonya, Larry, and even Auntie Selena and her two girls were there. All the neighbors and their children—Ms. Saphena, Ms. Johnson, Gwen, and Sly—were all crammed into our little apartment. Like I said, everyone close to me was there, even Pam.

Mama, now with four kids since my little sister Faye was born a few months earlier, made this day special for me. I wore a short afro, a pair of wide-legged jeans, and a flannel shirt with a collar so big you might have thought I was about to fly away. Everyone was eating and drinking and dancing. Mama cooked our favorites—red beans and rice, and a big pot of gumbo.

My Auntie Annie Mae, who loved dancing with us children, showed us the latest dance, the Bump. The singer cried, "I Ain't Going to Bump No More with that Big Fat Woman," as she bumped us, sometimes knocking us to the floor. We all laughed, as we dropped to the floor one by one. We danced to all the hottest tunes like "Bustin Loose," "Flashlight," and "Loose Booty." I loved to dance.

All the old folks loved to see us children dance, challenging each other. I always pretended to be Michael Jackson. I moonwalked all over the place, sliding and gliding across our wooden floor. And my cousin Tanya sang, trying to out-do me. As she sang, "Why Do Fools Fall in Love?" everybody clapped and cheered her on. We were swinging, singing, dancing, and bringing that place down!

Pam sat and looked, and after a while said, "Cheekie, it's been fun, and I enjoyed myself, but Grandma has to go."

At that moment I remembered the promise that she had made to me that day when I ran away to her house, and asked, "Are you going to stop Richard from beating Mama?"

Even though there had been no earthquakes while Mama was pregnant, I didn't want to take the chance. So, Pam agreed to say something before she left. Richard and Mama were in the bedroom arguing. He hadn't come out all night because he knew no one wanted him there. (They knew he was beating Mama, and I guess he was too ashamed to face them.)

Pam heard them there in the room. Richard was shouting and slapping Mama so loud that Pam heard everything. She grabbed a baseball bat out of our room and knocked on the door. She was just bamming and bamming that bat up against that door real hard.

She demanded, "Faye open this door!"

Mama opened the door, trying to wipe the tears away from her eyes, pretending like everything was all right.

Pam said, "Don't you pretend like nothing's wrong, because I knows what's going on here."

And then she turned to Richard, holding the bat as if she was about to swing. "I can't believe you would have the fucking audacity to hit on my child in the first place, but—while I am in this house? You keep your fucking hands off her, you hear me, or else the next time it's gone be me and this bat that does the hittin'!"

As I stood outside with my ear pressed up against the door, I could tell Pam was mad, and when she got mad there was no stopping her. Her words came out her mouth so fast you barely understood her, but you definitely got the message. Richard said nothing to Pam. He just stood there scared that Pam might swing and hit him in the head.

Pam then turned to Mama, who was standing right behind her and lightly tapped her on the head with that bat. Pam spoke with strength in her voice.

"And you should be ashamed of yourself, letting a two-time loser in your house, beating on you like this, disrespecting you and your children! Faye, this shit has to stop, you hear me? And it is going to stop tonight. Now either you get your act together, or I am going to have every one of these children taken from you."

I cracked the door just a little, so I could see better. Mama stood with that bat hanging over her head and shook her head in disbelief at the threat Pam had made.

"What?" Mama asked in shock.

Pam's eyes got real wide, and she pointed her finger right in Mama's face. "That's right, I am going to tell the authorities what's going on in this house, and if you don't think I'm for true, try me."

Mama started to cry. She was ashamed at what was going on and she was scared that she might lose us. She knew to take Pam seriously.

Mama cried, "Pam, you can't do this. I'm a grown woman."

Pam shouted as she pushed Mama's shoulders real hard, "Well act like one damn it, act like it!"

Richard reached for Pam's shoulder, trying to calm her down.

"Look, Ms. Walker, I'm sorry if I caused any trouble."

Pam turned around with smoke coming from her ears and said, "Don't you put your fucking hands on me."

"Ms. Walker, I was only trying to . . ."

Pam stopped Richard right in the middle of his sentence. "I'm not interested in anything you have to say, because as far as I am concerned, I hope to never have to see your face again."

Mama was still there shaking her head; she just couldn't believe Pam was treating her like a child.

Mama shook her head some more and asked, "Pam, you just won't quit will you? You been interfering in my life since I was a little girl."

Pam shouted, " 'Cause I don't quit **BITCH**! Now I spoke my piece, and I'm leaving, but I'll be watching things back here, and if you don't clean house soon, I will. Now have a good evening."

I ran from the door in a hurry. I didn't want them to know I was listening. But I heard it all along with everyone else at the party. When Pam started shouting everything stopped. I mean everything—music, talking, eating, dancing, and for some, even breathing. But as soon as Pam opened the door, things started right back up again, as if nothing had happened. Me, I was just happy that she told them off.

She came right over and kissed me on the cheeks. She said, "Have a good night, and a happy birthday. I'm sure things are going to be better around here now. That, you can count on."

Pam grabbed her purse and walked out. After a while, Mama came out of the room, still trying to pretend like everything was all right.

"Let's sing happy birthday and cut the cake," she said.

"Are you all right?" asked Li'l Soul.

Mama managed a fake smile, and shook her head yes. "I'm fine. I just want to get this party over with."

I was glad it was almost over with myself, and cutting the cake was my favorite part of the evening. I love vanilla cake and ice cream. I love it so much that I dream about eating cake and ice cream all the time, even owning my own store with cake and ice cream everywhere.

I'm so terrible about it that when I go to other people's birthday parties, I sneak and steal the icing from around the cake a little at a time. Finally, someone always asks, "Who been eating from around the cake?" And everyone shouts, "Cheekie." Boy, I love cake and ice cream.

As everybody started to sing happy birthday, Li'l Soul

interrupted. She said, "Come on let's sing this the black folks' way."

She started singing happy birthday with a li'l more soul in it. "Happy Birthday to you, Happy Birthday to you, Happy Birthday to you, Happy Birthday."

Everyone laughed, and sang that song the way Li'l Soul was singing it, too.

After the song ended, Mama said, "OK, Cheekie. Make a wish."

I closed my eyes shut, and for a moment I escaped into another world. A world somewhere away from Richard, and away from the Desire Project. I dreamed of a nice house, a nice car, money, and free cake and ice cream.

When I opened my eyes, Mama asked, "What did you wish for Cheekie?"

"To go over Grandma Emelia's house tonight."

The reason I said that was because I felt like getting away from this project. Grandma Emelia has a nice house, drives a fine car, and lives in a nice community in St. Rose, Louisiana. (St. Rose is one hour outside of New Orleans.) Mama disappointed me with her response.

"Cheekie, you can't go over Grandma's house. You know she lives too far anyway."

I cried and begged, "Grandma, please let me go, and ya'll could bring me back when my school break is up." (I was out of school for the Christmas holidays.)

Grandma Emelia explained, "Cheekie, your mama is right. Maybe you should wait to the summer, and you can spend the whole summer with Grandma, OK?"

Grandma Emelia only said that because she didn't

want to offend Mama. But me, I was determined to get away from this place.

When everyone started leaving, I screamed out loud, "Please Grandma, let me go, please!"

Mama insisted, "Stop this, Cheekie, and let your grandma go."

I turned around and saw Richard standing in the doorway of Mama's bedroom. He was staring at me, knowing it was him that I was trying to get away from.

After seeing him in the doorway, I was even more determined to get away from this house. I turned to Mama and threatened, "I'll tell them everything, if you won't let me go."

Grandma Emelia asked, "What is he talking about Faye? What is he going to tell us?"

Mama grabbed all their things, and rushed them out of the door.

She explained, "Nothin' Ms. Emelia; he has absolutely nothin' to tell. Now, ya'll take care."

I was about to scream out loud all of Mama's business, but she slammed the door shut.

I ran to the window as they were pulling off. I hung out of the window of our second floor apartment, and I screamed and begged out loud. "Please, Grandma, let me go, please!"

All the neighbors heard me, but I didn't care. With tears pouring down my face and nose running like a water faucet, I screamed, and carried on so much, that Grandma finally told Larry to turn the car around.

When I saw that car turning around, I ran in my room and grabbed a bag with all my clothes in it. (I had packed a bag before they even got there, planning that whole thing all along.)

I got my birthday wish, and for the first time, I was "bustin loose" out of this place I had grown to hate so much. As we pulled off, I saw Mama staring out of the window with a look on her face that seemed to ask, "Why such a big fuss?"

But Mama knew what I knew, and that was why she said nothing else about me leaving with Grandma Emelia.

i'm deep!

"Wow, look at that big mansion. Who lives there, Grandma?"

I was so excited to be driving up to Grandma's house in St. Rose. As we pulled up, a big brick house that covered an entire block towered over the entrance.

Grandma explained, "The Smiths live there. They are nice people, Mr. and Mrs. Smith. They have one son named Ricardo. He is a little older than you, but not much."

I thought, "They must sure be rich to live in a house like that!"

There are two roads that lead into the community—one street called Mockingbird, where my Auntie Selena lives (Selena had recently moved to St. Rose, shortly after Grandma Emelia), and Turtle Creek, where Grandma lived. It is a small community, surrounded by these big old trees. This place is in the middle of nowhere!

Grandma has a nice place, too. It's a brick house with painted gray wood on top. There are five bedrooms, a big back yard, a garage for the Buick, a kitchen, dining room, two bathrooms, and a den which Grandma never allows anyone to go in. She has really nice blue velvet furniture in there with African antiques and pictures on the wall. It is everything our house isn't.

Grandma is a Muslim and goes to the den to say her prayers. Shortly after we arrived, I saw her go in there and kneel down on this African rug she has spread out over the carpet. She goes in there five times a day. I stand outside the glass door, watching her bowing down, chanting things I can't understand.

One day I knocked on the glass door and asked, "Grandma, what are you doing in there and what are you saying?"

"I'm praying to Allah. We Muslims say five prayers a day to Allah," she explained.

Grandma told me about the Muslim religion, the Koran, and the Arabic language that she prayed in, but I was still confused. Grandma told me she had changed her name to Kia. Then she gave me a new name too—Abdul.

She explained, "The names we have were given to us by the white man when they took our ancestors from Africa."

"But why we got to change our names?" I asked, confused.

"You don't have to, but we Muslims believe it is necessary for us to do that. It's part of the process of coming to realize our heritage and the richness of our culture, Cheekie."

Grandma is very knowledgeable about black history and culture. She teaches me about black folks' heritage and culture. Some of it I understand, but to a Baptist, most of it seems strange.

Anyway, Grandma went on and on that day. She finished, "We are the original people, Cheekie. That's right son, we are God's chosen people, you better believe it, and one day the world will acknowledge the greatness and richness of our people. And you know they don't teach ya'll children that in school, but I will because it's information that you need to know. Don't you know Cheekie how deep you are?"

I shook my head no, thinking "deep, what's that mean?"

"Well you are," she said.

Grandma walked over to the other side of the room and pulled a frame off the wall. It was a poem hanging right there on her wall in the den.

She said, "This poem is entitled 'I'm Deep.' It was written by someone at my church. I like it so much that I decided to frame it and put it right here on my wall."

I took that frame out of Grandma's hand and began to read the poem. I understood some of the words, but I don't read well enough yet to pronounce some of the words and to understand what they mean.

Grandma reached for the frame saying, "Give it to me and let me read it for you."

As she held the poem she rose up and began to recite. As she read the poem, she seemed to transform into a totally different person, right before my eyes.

Out of dust I was made
Back in the native land
I am the beginning and the end
I am the son of a slave
I'm Deep.

I am like the top of a peak
Looking over up high
I am like a big wave, rolling, leaping, and creeping.
I'm Deep.

I am sensitive like my mother,
Strong like my father,
And Deep, and Black, and Creative like my people.
I'm Deep.

I am the dream of yesterday
I'm Deep.
I am the hope of today
I'm Deep.
I am the vision for tomorrow
I'm Deep.
I am the world's greatest lover
I'm Deep.
I am the legacy that my ancestors paved
I'm Deep.
I am the richest and the proudest, and the greatest of all
I'm Deep.
I'm Deep.
I'm Deep.

When Grandma Emelia finished reciting she walked over and kissed me on the cheek. She smiled, "So don't you ever forget how deep you are, Cheekie, and don't let anyone tell you that you can't make it in this world. 'Cause you can do and become anything you want to. And don't you forget it."

I smiled back and felt good inside knowing that Grandma believed in me. I felt changed, somehow.

After spending hours talking with Grandma Emelia that day, I decided to spend time with my other grandma, Great-grandma Rose. She lives with Grandma Emelia, but stays in her bedroom most of the time. Going into her room is like entering a different world. Grandma Rose does not share the same views on the Muslim religion. In fact, she is dead-set against it.

She is a devoted Christian, raised in the Baptist church. She resents Grandma Emelia for changing her name and her religion. She doesn't understand Grandma Emelia's strange way of praying.

I tip-toed into Grandma Rose's room. She was sitting on the edge of her bed, looking straight ahead, her purse clutched by her side. She always keeps that purse beside her. She couldn't see me there in her room because she is blind, but she knew I was there.

She asked, "Who there?"

I said nothing, just making fun of her not being able to see me.

After a while, she got even louder, "Now, I knows somebody there. Now who is it?"

I then broke out laughing, I found the whole thing real funny. But Grandma got mad.

She shouted, "Why you scare me like that? You know that's wrong to do that to me, Cheekie."

I felt so bad after scaring her half to death.

I sat down next to her on the bed and said, "I'm sorry, Grandma, for scaring you. I was just playing."

"Well, you shouldn't play like that, Cheekie. You could give me a heart attack or somethin'."

She leaned over and turned the volume on her radio down. She had been listening to gospel music as usual.

"So what can I do for you?"

"Nothin'. I just came by to see you and to talk."

Grandma squeezed a hold of her purse even tighter. She acted as if I was about to steal her money. I had heard from Grandma Emelia that she complains all the time that Rachelle and Tanya steal money out of her purse. To be honest, I thought about taking some of Grandma's money that day. Mostly because I know she has a lot of it and never spends it on nothin'. So, I figured she wouldn't miss a dollar or two. I never did it, just thought about it.

"So, what you and Mella talking about in there?"

"About the Koran and the Muslim religion."

Boy, why did I say that? That burned Grandma Rose up. She sighed and waved both of her hands like she was swatting flies.

"Mella needs to stop talking that shit. When she was a li'l girl, I raised her in the Baptist church, and now she done gone and changed her name call her Kia. Kia my ass. I named her Emelia, and that's what I am going to call her until the day I die. Which will be soon because I'm already old."

She's more than seventy years old. I didn't like Grandma talking about dying.

I said, "Don't say you about to die, Grandma, 'cause you not going to die no time soon."

"Yes I am, too. You know I'm old. But let me not scare you like that, because I'll probably be around to see you graduate. What grade you in now?"

"The sixth grade."

"That's good. You know you got to study hard Cheekie, so you become that doctor I always hear you want to be."

Soon as I was about to ask Grandma for some money, Grandma Emelia walked in and interrupted us.

"It's drop time, Mama."

Even though Grandma Rose is blind, she gets drops in her eyes three times a day. She hates taking those drops, too. She figures she is already blind, so what's the point?

Grandma Rose sighed when Grandma Emelia tried to pull her eyes back to drop those drops in.

"Now, Mama you know this is the doctor's orders, so stop this fussing over nothin'."

"Don't you tell me what to do. I'm your Mama and don't you forget it," she snapped back.

She was trying to pick a fight with Grandma Emelia. But as soon as she dropped that last drop in Grandma Rose's eyes, Grandma Emelia left the room in a hurry.

Grandma Rose leaned over and turned her gospel music back up. "Amazing Grace" began to rise out of the speaker. Grandma Rose smiled because she loved that song the most. She started clapping and singing it out loud. I sat there listening to her clapping and singing the whole time. I even joined in sometimes, and had church right there in her room. At that moment I felt a spiritual closeness with Grandma Rose.

After a while, Grandma Emelia shouted to me, "Come on, Cheekie. Let Mama alone so she can go to sleep."

I leaned over and gave her a kiss on the cheek, turned the lights off, and closed her bedroom door shut.

"Good night, Grandma," I said as I closed the door behind me.

She nodded her head and kept right on singing and humming and clapping out loud to the sweet sounds of her gospel music.

Later that night, I lay in the guest room that Grandma turned into my room thinking about Mama n'em. I thought of them the whole time when I was at Grandma's house, but I never called. I just wanted to forget about that place, about Richard, and everything for a while. While everyone was sleeping, I decided to do something that I thought about all day—stealing some of Grandma Rose's vanilla ice cream. I had seen it there in the freezer earlier during the day and could think of little else.

I tip-toed into the kitchen, carefully pulled a spoon out of the drawer, opened the refrigerator, and took out the carton of Brown Velvet vanilla ice cream. I sat in a chair at the kitchen table and nearly finished the whole half gallon. I divided my time between eating and peeping around in fear of being caught stealing. I tip-toed back and forth all night eating Grandma Rose's ice cream. Each time I only meant to eat just a little, but I couldn't help myself. By morning it was all gone.

When I woke up, though, Grandma Rose was sitting in the kitchen eating. Soon as I walked into the kitchen, she said, "Mella, give me some of my ice cream, and since Cheekie is up now, fix him a cup too."

I felt so bad, because I knew there was none left to eat.

Grandma Emelia opened the refrigerator and shouted, "Child, somebody done ate the whole half-gallon! Now, you know that's a shame, somebody ate all Mama's ice cream."

I bowed my head, and looked like a li'l baby who just got caught doing something he was not supposed to be doing.

Grandma knew it was me, too, but she didn't want to get me in trouble with Grandma Rose. "I'll just run out and get you some more, Mama, but that is such a shame, someone eating all Mama's ice cream like that."

After Grandma left to get some more vanilla ice cream, I sat right in front of Grandma Rose. She just sat there staring out into space. I decided to stand up in front of her and jump up and down. She sat motionless and quiet. Then I made all kinds of ugly faces, waved my hands, anything and everything I could think of. I just wanted to really make sure she couldn't see. I know it sounds stupid, but I really wasn't convinced that Grandma Rose couldn't see me.

After a while she asked, "Cheekie, you still there?"

"Yeah, Grandma. I'm sitting right next to you."

She felt for my hands, and then slowly moved her hands up to my face. She was touching my nose, lips, and mouth. It was like Grandma Rose was trying to see me in her very own way.

She said, "You are a fine young man, aren't you?"

I moved my shoulders up, as if Grandma could really see me.

She smiled, "Look just like your daddy, they tell me."

When she said that, I felt my stomach turning over. I felt funny hearing her talk about my daddy.

"He was a cute li'l boy, too. You know, I was able to see back then."

"Really? So you know what Selena, and Debbie, and my daddy n'em look like?"

"I sure do, and I can feel and tell what you look like, too."

I was so amazed by that, because I thought Grandma Rose had always been blind.

"Grandma, where is my daddy, and why doesn't he come around?"

She explained, "Your daddy is fine, Cheekie. He just always been that way—don't come around family that much. And he has a new girlfriend now. Her name is Vanessa and they have two sons named Zachary and Charles, who we call DooDoo."

"You mean my half brother has the same name as me?" I asked, real confused.

"Yeah, Vanessa wanted her son named after your father."

The phone rang, interrupting our conversation. Grandma Rose stumbled to the phone and answered.

"Hello," she said.

Then she shouted out loud, "Charles, speak of the devil, me and your son, Cheekie, was just sitting here talking about you."

And when Grandma turned around and called out for me, I ran out of the kitchen to Sonya's room. Grandma was just shouting and yelling, trying to get me to talk to Daddy on the phone. I didn't want to talk to him. I did kind of miss him, but I'm still a li'l angry that he left me and never comes around to visit. I feel like he abandoned me and my brothers, and I didn't want to talk to him. Besides, I didn't know what to say to him, anyway.

I found Sonya in her room listening to music. She loves

listening to music, and she loves to sing, too. Sonya is kind of chubby and wears her hair in a jheri curl. She loves to see me dance. She had me in that room dancing to the Michael Jackson song "Off the Wall." She loves how I moonwalk and how I hit all the latest Michael Jackson moves. She loves Michael Jackson so much that she dreamed about what it would be like to meet him. I dream about it, too. We love talking about famous, rich black people. We sat in her room and talked about movie stars and other entertainers.

She asked, "Boy I wonder what it would be like to be rich like Michael Jackson or Diana Ross."

"I know. They must have so much money that they probably can buy anything, huh?"

"I hope to meet Michael Jackson one day," she said.

"Me too, and I would love to meet Diana Ross, too. I want to be rich just like them one day."

"Well, maybe you will, 'cause they were poor once and now look at'em."

We went on and on for hours, dreaming about the life of the rich and famous. In fact, I think about making it big all the time. It's strange, but that is always on my mind, especially when I see Motown specials on TV or something, or when I see Diana Ross and Michael Jackson specials.

Later on, Sonya tried to teach me to sing. I can dance like Michael Jackson, but I sure can't sing like him. Sonya tried to teach me.

"Don't sing through your mouth. Sing through your nose, like this."

Boy, I tried to sing the Michael Jackson song, "Who's Loving You?" but I went flat on the first note. "When I had you, I treated you baaaad." I just kept going flat and Sonya kept laughing out loud at me. I tried to sing, but singing is not one of my divine gifts from God.

After almost two weeks staying with Grandma, I decided to visit my cousins, Rachelle and Tanya. Having spent so much time talking with Grandma Rose and Sonya, it didn't even occur to me that they live just around the corner. I was supposed to leave on the next day, so while Grandma n'em were in the kitchen talking, I tip-toed out the front door.

As I was walking around the corner to Mockingbird Street, I saw these bad children that my grandma had told me about. She said Rachelle was always getting into fights with these children, and that's why she never wanted me to go around Auntie Selena's house by myself. Grandma n'em called those children the fat-ass Snyder kids.

As I got closer to Selena's house, I saw them a li'l ways up the street, and all of a sudden I was scared. Something told me to turn around, but then I thought, "They won't do me nothin'. I don't even know them." Boy was I wrong!

I was two doors from Selena's house when this girl named Tasha walked over and asked, "You Rachelle's cousin, aren't you?"

"Yeah, why?" I asked, trying to be tough.

Before she got a chance to answer my question, her brother, who they called Neck (making fun of the fact that he had a short neck), hit me in the back of the head with a big stick. I felt that hit upside my head, too. I kneeled down in front of him and tried to cover the top of my head. Then her other brother, Tolby, punched me in the stomach. They were double teaming me, and although I tried to fight them off, there were so many of them that I could barely land a punch.

I managed to break away though, and ran until I ended up in front of Selena's house. I bammed and bammed real hard on the door. When Selena opened the door, I fell on the living room floor, screaming and yelling out loud. I was screaming like I had done lost my mind.

She shouted, "Cheekie, what's wrong with you boy?"

They all stood around looking—Tanya, Rachelle, and Popsicle (Selena's new man, who they nicknamed Popsicle because he loved Popsicles).

I was rolled up in a knot, just screaming and yelling. And it seemed the louder Selena shouted, "What's wrong with you?" the louder I cried.

Finally, I said, "Those fat-ass Snyder kids."

At that, Popsicle ran to the next room and came back with his gun, and everybody ran out the door to the Snyders' house. They sure hated those Snyders, especially Rachelle. She and that fat Tasha always fought up a storm.

When Selena knocked on the door, their fat mama answered.

"What now?" she asked with one hand on her hip, puffing on a cigarette.

Selena shouted, "Your fat ass children beat up my nephew, and I'm tired of this shit. Cheekie don't bother no one, and I know they started with him first."

Tasha interrupted, "He started with us first, Mama."

"You lying. Ya'll jumped me for nothin'," I shouted.

Rachelle, who loves to fight anyhow, grabbed a stick and went to hit Tasha with it. She stood over her about to swing, when Tasha's mama threatened, "I wish you would."

Popsicle, who had his gun in hand shouted, "Go ahead Rachelle, hit that fat bitch."

But Selena, who noticed the police coming said, "No Rachelle, put the stick down. Here comes the police."

About time those policemen got down the street, we had already made it inside the house. I was so mad that I just wanted to go back around the corner to Grandma's house. Popsicle drove me back around the corner and talked me to death.

He explained, "Cheekie, man, you have to be tough and not let people take advantage of you like that."

I just stared out of the window, thinking about the fight. I was burning hot; I was still so mad. When we drove up, I jumped right out of his truck and ran inside the house. Didn't even say thanks or goodbye.

Mr. Buggy was sitting in the living room watching TV when I walked in. We children started calling him Mr. Buggy for short, instead of Larry. (Buggage was his last name.)

I asked, "Where's Grandma, Mr. Buggy?"

"She's in there in the den chanting that Muslim shit."

Like Grandma Rose, Mr. Buggy don't care for that religion either. In fact, I don't think Mr. Buggy is religious at all. I looked in the den, and there was Grandma bowing down and chanting, "Allah akhbar, Allah akhbar."

After a while though, Mr. Buggy couldn't take it no more. He was sitting there in the living room, trying to watch a football game. The New Orleans Saints were in the playoffs—a big game that Mr. Buggy was trying to watch.

He shouted, "Mella, now I'm trying to watch this game. Stop that shit for a while."

Grandma simply responded, "OK, Larry."

Mr. Buggy and Grandma reminded me of Edith and Archie Bunker from *All In The Family*. I sat down in the middle of the floor and started watching the football game. I took my shoes off in the living room.

"Boy, get your damn shoes from in the middle of the floor," Mr. Buggy shouted.

"Yours are in the middle of the floor," I said being real sassy.

"I don't care. This is my house, too. Now move'em."

He is a hateful man sometimes, but so am I, and with everything I had been through this was nothing.

We were going back and forth arguing when Grandma Emelia overheard us and interrupted. "Larry, leave my grandson alone. Come here, Cheekie, Grandma has some ice cream for you."

Grandma sure knows my weak spot.

As I walked out of the kitchen, Mr. Buggy warned, "Ya'll might spoil'em rotten, but shit, not me."

I heard him, but I still said nothing. I just sat down at the kitchen table and ate my ice cream. I kept looking at him in the living room, though, just looking, and rolling my eyes, and thinking all sorts of bad things. As I sat there eating, I thought how glad I was that my school break was over since I was starting to hate being around Mr. Buggy.

The next day Mr. Buggy was up early, sitting in the car just waiting to take me home. I couldn't believe he was up so early and that they woke me up so early, too. I knew I was going home, but didn't think it would be that early in the morning. I guess that was just how bad Mr. Buggy wanted me gone.

Anyway, the whole time they drove me home nobody said nothing. But as soon as we drove up to our house, Mr. Buggy turned around and smiled, "OK, boy, this where you get off."

I hated his smile so much that I rolled my eyes and jumped out of the car.

I then leaned over and gave Grandma Emelia a kiss on the cheek.

She said, "Take care, Cheekie. Grandma loves you."

I stood out on the curb as they pulled off. And when they were out of sight, I turned around and saw Torey and Darrell playing marbles. I thought, "I'm sure glad to be away from Mr. Buggy, but coming back home to this place isn't making me too happy."

As I walked upstairs, Torey ran over, shouting and jumping up and down, "Cheekie's home! Cheekie's home!"

I smiled and said, "Yeah. I'm home all right."

"Boy, Mama is waiting for you. She has to tell you about Richard."

"Here we go again. What now?" I thought.

the boogy man

Mama stood in the kitchen stirring a pot of gumbo. She was surprised to find me standing in the doorway.

"Oh, Cheekie, you're home!"

Mama hugged me so tight that I could hardly breathe.

I smiled, "Yeah, I'm home and look what Grandma n'em bought me."

I pulled all my new clothes out of the bag and showed them to Mama one by one. Mama was happy and kind of jealous, too. She was jealous because she felt like Grandma was buying me all the stuff she couldn't buy me.

As we stood there admiring my new clothes, I noticed that the house was bare as if we had been robbed while I was away. I mean there were boxes everywhere.

"Mama, what's going on?"

Mama sat me down in a chair and explained, "Cheekie, a lot has happened over the two weeks since you been gone away. After your birthday party, when everyone left, Richard tried to fight me again. He was pulling my hair. Somehow I broke loose, and we ended up in the hallway. I ran out there 'cause I was scared he was going to kill me. You see, I told him I wanted him out of my house and my life, for good. I just couldn't take it no more. Pam was right. Anyhow, Sly n'em heard us fighting and ran out just in time, because Richard had me by the neck about to throw me over the banister! He was trying to kill me! Sly pulled him off of me, and then they started fighting. Sly beat Richard's ass and told him no real man don't beat up on no woman. Gwen called the police, and they came and took Richard away. As he was leaving, he shouted, 'It ain't over, it ain't over, bitch.'"

I could hardly believe what Mama had told me. She had actually thrown Richard out.

"So, why we leaving then, if Richard is already gone?"

" 'Cause I want to get out of this house. It holds too many bad memories. I put in for another apartment in the front of the project, right around the corner from Annie Mae, down the street from Pam."

I was very happy for so many reasons. Richard was finally gone, and we were leaving this house I hated so much. In fact, I couldn't wait.

"When are we moving Mama?" I asked.

"Soon, Cheekie, I hope really soon, before Richard comes back."

Then the phone rang. Mama looked at the phone as if she knew who it was. She let that phone ring for a long time before she moved her head, signaling for me to answer it.

Before I picked up the phone though, Mama whispered to me, "If that's Richard, tell him I'm not here."

"Hello."

"Cheekie, that's you?" asked Richard.

"Yeah."

"When did you get back?"

"Yesterday, and my Mama ain't here."

I cut him off in the middle of his questions, just didn't want to talk to him.

His voice got real strong, "Don't lie to me, Cheekie. Now put your Mama on the phone."

"Man, I ain't lying to you, and who cares what you think?"

I slammed the phone down real hard. Mama looked in shock that I hung up on Richard. She walked over and hugged me real tight.

"Everything is going to be just fine, you'll see."

I hugged Mama round her waist, smiling at the whole thing. I felt so good hanging up on Richard like that.

Richard called many more times over the next few days. I mean that phone rang day and night. Mama wouldn't answer the phone and was afraid to go outdoors. She was even afraid to send us to school, thinking Richard might come after us. Mama's instincts were right, too.

One day on the playground at school, I was enjoying the day, swinging on the swings and playing on the merry-go-round. Boy, I was so dizzy when I got off that merry-go-round. When my head stopped spinning, I saw Richard. I shook my head, just making sure it was him standing outside the fence. He was dressed in all black with his eyes hidden behind a pair of dark shades. He was the last person I wanted to see, period.

He signaled for me to come over. I was scared at first. Then I thought, "I'm inside the school fence, so he can't get me even if he tried."

I moved closer to the fence. In a mean voice, I asked, "What?"

"How you been?"

"Fine."

"That's good. You know I miss ya'll."

"Man, please."

"It's true Cheekie. Now, I know I've been bad, but I still miss ya'll. Please, tell your Mama I want another chance. Please, Cheekie. I swear I'll be different this time. Would you please do that for me?"

I held my head down, feeling sorry for Richard for a brief moment. He actually sounded sincere. But then I thought back to the times he broke his promises not to hit Mama.

He took out some money and tried to give it to me. I just turned around from the fence and walked away. When I turned back around, Richard was gone.

After he left, I went to the principal's office and called Mama. Boy, Mama was so frightened that she told the principal to send me home from school right away.

When the principal walked me to the school gate, I broke out running. I had this crazy idea that Richard was waiting around somewhere for me. I really thought he was going to hurt me.

I ran upstairs and bammed on our front door as hard as I could. Torey opened the door.

He smiled, "Cheekie, you home from school early."

"Yeah, where's Mama?"

"In the back room folding up some clothes."

Mama heard my voice from the other room and shouted, "Cheekie, come here and tell me what happened."

I walked to the back room and pushed Mama's bedroom door open. I sat on her bed and told her everything about Richard's visit to my school.

I made it out to be more than it really was, trying to make Mama really scared. I just wanted to make sure she wasn't having second thoughts about taking him back.

"And he said, he is coming back, too, 'cause it ain't over. One way or the other, he is coming back."

After telling Mama the whole story, plus a few extra details, I left her in her room folding clothes and thinking what to do next.

The last thing I remember Mama saying was that, "I have to get from around here, before something really bad happens."

Mama was right, because Richard made his move a few days later on one frightful night.

The lights went out in the project. That happened from time to time, leaving the whole project dark. Torey and Darrell were in bed sleeping, but I couldn't sleep. When the lights went out, I was scared that the Boogy Man would come. I don't know where I got that idea from, but nevertheless I was terrified.

Soon as the lights went out, Mama went next door to borrow some candles from Ms. Johnson. It was while she was next door that I heard her bedroom window open. Then I heard footsteps. I was shaking and covered up to my neck with fear.

After a while, I whispered, "Mama is that you?" No one answered.

I shouted out even louder, and still no one answered. Suddenly, Mama appeared in the doorway holding a candle in one hand, and Li'l Faye in the other.

Mama whispered, "Cheekie, what's wrong with you

boy? Stop screaming before you wake them children up."

"But Mama, sounded like I heard someone in your bedroom."

"Maybe this dark got you scared 'cause nobody here but us. The wind blew my bedroom window open, that's all. Now, go to sleep, Cheekie, so you can get up and go to school tomorrow."

Mama cracked the door just a little and left me there in the dark. I still felt like something was strange, so I just sat up in bed listening to Mama in the living room trying to sing Li'l Faye to sleep.

"Hush li'l baby don't say a word, Mama's gonna buy you a mockingbird, and if that mocking bird don't sing, Mama's gonna buy you . . ."

Mama stopped right in the middle of that song. She heard those footsteps in her room, the same ones I had heard. I rose up off the bed, really shaking and trembling inside.

Mama got up off the couch holding a candle in one hand and Li'l Faye in the other hand. Mama wasn't half way to her room when I heard her scream, "Oh, my God! Richard, what in the hell are you doing here? And how did you get in? I'm calling the police."

I couldn't believe it! Richard was in the house. Boy, I was really scared then. I broke out in a cold sweat and my whole body was shaking.

I jumped out of my bed and cracked the door to see what I could see in the dim light.

I saw him pull a gun—a big, black gun—out of his pocket.

He pointed it right in Mama's face and whispered, "No

you ain't calling nobody bitch, 'cause you see I'm going to kill you *and* those children of yours in there."

Mama stood there frozen with fear, not knowing what move to make next. I felt my heart drop to the floor, as my stomach cried out for help.

"Cat got your tongue? So, what are you going to do now? You been hanging the phone up on me, not taking my calls. Bitch are you out of you mind, thinking you can just brush me the fuck off like that?"

Mama started to beg, "Richard! Look, I'm sorry but don't hurt my children. You see, they have nothin' to do with this. This here is between me and you."

"Don't tell me what to do, bitch!" shouted Richard.

Then I heard a slap, and for a moment I couldn't even move. But after a li'l while, I crawled out of my room into Mama's room. I hid there on the floor and tried to find the telephone so I could call 911. I was shaking so bad I thought Richard would surely hear me. But he couldn't see or hear me from out in the living room.

I dialed 911 and whispered, "There's a man in our house with a gun about to shoot my Mama. Please hurry. 3924 Alvar Street. Hurry. Please, hurry!"

I hung up and stayed there on the floor, peeping in on everything. Richard had his hands around Mama's neck, squeezing it tight. He was choking her!

"Give me my baby, bitch! Hand her over to me!"

"Richard! No! Please, not the baby!"

Mama wasn't gonna give him Li'l Faye at first, but Richard threatened, "If you don't give me my baby, I swear I'll shoot all those li'l bastards in there."

Mama handed him the baby, and Richard made a run for the door. Mama ran after him.

"Richard! No! Don't take my baby! Please don't take my baby!"

The police got here too late. Richard was gone and took Li'l Faye with him.

When the police arrived, Mama shouted, "He went out the back door. Catch him, Mr. Policemen. He has my baby!"

All the neighbors were out in the hallway. Everyone was searching for Richard, but he was nowhere in sight.

Torey and Darrell had woke up by then and started crying out loud for Mama. It was such a crazy scene: children crying, Mama screaming, policemen everywhere, but no Richard. He was gone, and Mama was losing her mind.

Two days had passed and there was still no word from Richard. Mama just sat in the kitchen day and night staring out into space. Everyone came by to check on her—Annie Mae, Dorothy, Li'l Soul, and all the neighbors.

Ms. Johnson cooked for us both days because Mama was in no shape to cook. She was losing her mind just thinking that Richard was never coming back with Li'l Faye. The police were looking for Richard and Li'l Faye everywhere, but no one had seen them. It was like he had dropped off the face of the earth.

Later that evening, me, Torey, and Darrell were sitting in the kitchen eating supper when someone knocked on the door. We all looked at Mama wondering if she had heard the knocking. But Mama didn't move at all, just sat there in her own world.

Finally, I got up from the table and opened the door. I

couldn't believe my eyes when I saw Li'l Faye down on the floor, wrapped in a white blanket in front of the door.

I shouted, "Mama, it's Li'l Faye!"

Boy, Mama jumped up from the table, pushed me out the way, and picked Li'l Faye up from off the floor.

"My baby! Oh, thank you, God, for not letting him hurt my baby."

That was the first time Mama had spoken since the police had come in the middle of the night a few days ago. I felt like Li'l Fay and Mama both returned to us that night.

Ms. Johnson and all the neighbors came out in the hall when they heard Mama screaming with joy.

"My baby is back! I don't see no sign of Richard. I guess he ran off before I could see'em."

"Girl, I am so happy for you, Faye. But you best call the police before he comes back and tries this shit again," said Ms. Johnson.

"You right, girl. You are definitely right," said Mama.

Mama closed the door and called the police right away. We all just sat in the kitchen playing with Li'l Faye. I don't know how everyone else was feeling, but I was so happy that she was back. I was sure that Richard had done killed her.

When the police showed up, they warned Mama to be careful, because a man like Richard is capable of anything. They thought Mama would probably hear from him again.

After they had left, Mama said, "You know, I think for some strange reason I am not going to hear from Richard ever again."

But from that time on she was startled whenever our phone rang. We were all looking over our shoulders for weeks later, waiting for Richard to make another move.

One night something did happen, a very peculiar and windy night with dust rising, trees howling, and rain about to come down. The sign of a hurricane on the way. We get those in New Orleans from time to time. But none came like Hurricane Betsy. Mama was a teenager when Betsy hit New Orleans. It killed hundreds of people and left many folks homeless. Mama told me that Betsy hit so hard that the city was declared a disaster area. Well that night, it felt like Hurricane Betsy was coming again. Mama was on the porch playing with Li'l Faye, and Torey and Darrell were riding their bicycles, and singing out loud, "Rain, rain, go away, come back another day." I just hung out of the window looking.

Then a little white Chevrolet pulled up in front our house. Mama stood up as the car rolled to a stop. For a moment I expected Richard to step out. But when the car door opened, a frail, white woman stepped out. I thought it was strange that a white woman was in the Desire Project.

She walked up to the porch and said, "Hi, ma'am. I'm looking for a lady by the name of Faye."

Mama looked puzzled. "I'm Faye. How can I help you?"

"I'm sorry to disturb you, but my name is Ms. Brownstone, and I'm looking for Richard."

"Why is that?" Mama asked.

"Because of this ma'am, because of what that monster did to me," cried Ms. Brownstone.

She showed Mama bite marks and scratches that covered her body. She even had bite marks on the side of her face. They were so deep that we could still see the prints of his teeth on the side of her face.

She cried, "The police are looking for him, too. He beat me up one night, and took all my money with him."

That lady was crying so much her whole face was red. Mama tried to comfort Ms. Brownstone, because nobody understood better than her what she had been through.

"Ma'am, I don't know where Richard is. The police is looking for him 'cause he kidnaped my baby right here one night."

Ms. Brownstone looked up in shock. I could tell she was more terrified than ever.

"He was so nice at first; treated me good. Then one night he just snapped and started beating me up. I was so scared he was going to kill me. I tracked you down through the Project's Housing Office. Richard told me your name and the project you lived in."

"Well, ma'am. I'm sorry I can't be of more help. Hopefully, the police will find his ass soon so you and I both can testify and they could lock him up for a long, long time."

Ms. Brownstone seemed a bit relieved when she left. Mama just stood out near the curb, but as soon as she was out of sight, she got Torey and Darrell inside and locked both our doors extra tight. She was so afraid that something else might happen that night, but it didn't. It just rained all night long. That rain came down, howling and pouring, like Betsy was coming back for more.

A month later, Mama found an envelope in the mailbox from California. It was an obituary. Richard was dead! It stated that he had been shot in the head. Mama couldn't believe it, just couldn't believe he was dead. She was surprised to get mail from Richard's family. She had no idea they knew anything about her. They never were in touch before, and Mama found it real strange to get an envelope in the mail like that. More puzzling, there was no letter explaining the details or nothing. Just an obituary.

Mama worried about it all day long. She even called Li'l Soul and told her what happened. She said, "Child, I won't be surprised if Richard is faking the whole thing, trying to make me think he is dead."

But weeks have gone by and Mama still hasn't heard from him. Finally, I felt like this whole nightmare was behind us. Richard was gone for good, and Mama got word that we could move up-front in the project.

ain't nothin' going on but the rent

"Goodbye, Cheekie! Bye, Torey! Bye Darrell!"

Daphne, Sharrell, Perry, and all the neighbors waved goodbye as we drove off with all our stuff. Annie Mae and her man, Willie Ed, moved us in his truck. Me, Torey, and Darrell just sat in the back of that beat-up truck with all our furniture, just smiling and waving everyone goodbye.

Ms. Saphena, who hung out of the window of her apartment, was waving, too. She shouted, "Keep in touch Faye. Good luck!"

It looked like most of the project had come out to see us off. Gwen and Ms. Johnson were the last faces we saw, 'cause they both stood out on the curb as we pulled away. The last things I saw were their hands waving in the wind and their smiles shining in the sunshine. Mama might keep in touch as time went on, I thought, but me, I planned never to look back.

We moved right up-front on Desire Street, right around the corner from Annie Mae and down the street from Pam. Our place was similar to our old one, except for the two extra bedrooms. Me and Faye had our own rooms, but Torey and Darrell had to share one.

Each time I think about all the stuff that happened to us on Alvar Street, I thank the Lord we finally got away from that place. Stuff like Mama throwing Daddy out, then Mama throwing Richard out, and all the fighting in between. I still remember what Raymond did to me that night, the "invisible man," touching and fondling me. The thought of that night sends chills up and down my spine. Needless to say, I was glad to be up-front in the project.

Our new life up-front is different in many ways from the times spent on Alvar Street. For instance, we are not as close to our neighbors as before. Mama hardly speaks to them at all, and we don't play with the neighborhood children. Since we live around the corner from our cousins, we often play with them.

Another difference can be seen in the way Mama copes with life up-front. She seems to be struggling more than ever before to keep things together. It's been a long time since Mama has had to pay the bills all by herself. She got used to having men around to help out with the bills. Over on Alvar Street, Mama could sometimes rely on her lady friends for help when things got tough financially. But now we are truly on our own and Mama has to find some way to make ends meet.

It didn't take her long to come up with a scheme. She decided to have a neighborhood "supper." "Supper" is simply a fancy way of saying "rent party." Nevertheless, when someone gives a neighborhood supper, everyone helps out in one way or another. Mama spent the whole week preparing for that supper, too. She bought all kinds of food to sell. Folks could choose a chicken plate or fish plate. Side orders included potato salad, macaroni and cheese, peas, bread, and pound cake for dessert. Each plate sold for three dollars and fifty cents. Mama's supper started on Friday evening and lasted until Sunday.

Mama even set up a table in the middle of the living room where Annie Mae hosted a card game. You see, Mama got a cut from the card game, so although she didn't like gambling around us kids, she allowed it that time.

That Friday evening when I got home from school, Mama was sitting in the kitchen brushing her hair and talking on the phone to Li'l Soul.

I heard her saying, "Girl, ain't nothin' going on but the rent, child."

She laughed, and laughed some more. Li'l Soul must have been laughing, too, because Mama said, "Girl, you are so crazy! Now let me get off this phone. See you around five."

I walked in soon as Mama hung up the phone.

"Hi, Cheekie. How was school?"

"Good, Ma. Boy this food smells good!"

"I know. Now, I'm going to fix ya'll a plate, and I want ya'll to stay in that back room and don't disturb me tonight. You hear me, Cheekie?"

I walked over to the stove and lifted the top off one of the pots.

Mama slapped my hand and shouted, "Get out of there! You heard what I said about not disturbing me tonight."

"Yeah, Ma, I heard you."

"Now, Annie Mae is bringing Butterball and Woody over here with her tonight, and ya'll best be on your good behavior."

I walked out, went to my room, and shut the door behind me.

By five o'clock that evening the house was full with people coming to buy suppers. People came from all over the project. Mostly people had heard about the supper by word of mouth, but Mama had posted a few signs here and there, just to make sure everyone knew about her supper.

As Mama stood in the kitchen whipping up her great-tasting meals, I helped out for a li'l while by taking orders, answering the telephone, and making deliveries to the neighborhood folks. All that excitement and work was just the beginning, for it was later that evening when things really got exciting.

Annie Mae started hosting the card game around eight o'clock. It didn't take long for the inside of our house to start looking, sounding, and smelling like a juke-joint—smoke-filled air, loud music and plenty of fun-loving folks. I could hear the sound of Aretha Franklin blasting in the background as Mama took orders and Annie Mae played cards. Like I said before, it was supper time and everybody was having a good time!

We children were in the back room playing around and trying to watch TV. There was so much noise out front that we could barely hear ourselves talking. Woody crept out of the room, disobeying Mama's order to stay out. She came back with a cigarette she had stolen out of her Mama's purse. Woody was always doing stuff like that, stealing ciga-rettes, or drinking alcohol when no grown ups were around. Pam always says Annie Mae better watch over her, because she is too fast for her own good.

As she returned, she proudly held up the cigarette brag-ging, "Look what I got."

"Oh, my Mama gone get you," said Darrell.

"No, she ain't unless you tell her, and if you do I'm gone beat you up."

Woody lit that cigarette and held it between her fingers like she really knew what she was doing. She took a puff or two and blew out these little circles of smoke.

"How did you do that?" I asked in amazement.

"It's easy. Just hold your mouth like this, and it comes out in circles," she said squinting her li'l Chinese eyes and holding her mouth as if she was about to give me a kiss.

I took that cigarette out of her hand and thought about taking a hit off it for a minute.

Darrell said, "You better not, 'cause I'm gone tell Mama."

Woody reached over and punched him in the back real hard.

She said, "You ain't telling on nobody."

Darrell started crying. He fell on the bed, buried his face in the pillow, and cried out at the top of his lungs.

I inhaled some smoke from the cigarette wasting away between my fingers. My lungs caught fire and my eyes got red from the smoke. I coughed out loud at the first puff. Butterball and Torey laughed.

"You can't even smoke, Cheekie," teased Butterball.

"Shut up, 'cause you couldn't either, until I showed you," said Woody.

Soon as I was about to take another puff, Mama knocked on the door. Everyone got real quiet.

"What's going on in here?" asked Mama.

I held my breath, hoping Mama wouldn't smell the smoke.

"Nothin' Mama, just watching TV."

Mama looked around the whole room as if she could tell we were up to something. But luckily Darrell had stopped crying, and she thought the little smoke she smelled was coming from outside, where the party was.

"Well, ya'll be on your best behavior. Now Cheekie, I need you and Woody to go across the street and deliver a supper to Ms. Everlyn."

My heart dropped, and I'm sure Woody's heart dropped, too. All the kids call Ms. Everlyn "The Crazy Lady." They call her that because of this story about how Ms. Everlyn kidnaped a little boy in the neighborhood and he hadn't been seen since. All the kids talk about it. But what is even more frightening about her is that she is always talking to herself while walking up and down Desire Street. She seems to be drunk all the time.

"Ma, I ain't going to that crazy lady's house."

"Boy, stop talking crazy. Ms. Everlyn is not crazy. I have known that woman for years. Now put your shoes on because you going to deliver her supper."

Mama closed the door. Me and Woody were afraid to go to Ms. Everlyn's house, especially at night. I couldn't believe Mama was sending us over there. She doesn't just act crazy, she looks crazy, too, like Ester from *Sanford and Son*.

As me and Woody walked out of the room, Torey n'em teased, "The Crazy Lady gone get ya'll . . . the Crazy Lady gone get ya'll."

Woody was so mad, she slammed the bedroom door behind her.

We walked into the living room where Annie Mae was the life of the party. She sat at the head of the table hosting

the card game. Everybody was so busy shouting and screaming over the card game that they didn't even see us pass.
Mama was standing in the kitchen fixing Ms. Everlyn's
plate. Li'l Soul was sitting at the table brushing her hair and
fixing her make-up in a small mirror she held in her hand.

Li'l Soul smiled, "Hey, Cheekie. Is this Annie Mae's
daughter getting so big?"

Mama turned around to take a look. "Yeah that's her
bad ass all right."

Woody rolled her eyes. "Is the supper ready?"

"Yeah, it's ready. Ya'll better come right back, too, 'cause
I know how you sneak off every time your Mama sends you
to the store. But I don't play that. You hear me, Woody?"

Woody rolled her eyes and said, "Yeah, I hear you."

Mama put the supper in a brown paper bag, and opened
the front door. My Uncle Randy and his friends were playing dice in the hallway outside.

Mama said, "Move out the way, Randy, and let these
children get by."

Randy stood up and stepped aside. "OK, no problem
Faye; no need to get upset."

"I told ya'll to take that somewhere else before my
neighbors call the police. Now, you act like you hard of
hearing."

Randy waved his hand and said, "Girl, we ain't bother-
ing nobody." Then he looked at me. "Ain't that right,
Cheekie?"

I moved my shoulders as if to say "How the hell do I
know? I'm just a kid."

We walked down the stairs leaving Randy and his dice
game behind.

When we got outside, Woody asked, "You scared, Cheekie?"

I tried to pretend like I wasn't. "No, I'm not scared. Are you?"

"Man, I ain't scared of no crazy lady," she said, trying to sound tough.

We crossed the street quickly, but as soon as we got in front of Ms. Everlyn's apartment we both stopped dead in our tracks.

Woody looked at me. "You go first."

"Why I got go first?"

" 'Cause you the boy."

I looked at her as if to say, "Please. That ain't gone *even* work this time."

She grabbed the bag from my hands. "Look give it to me, 'cause you are a sissy anyway."

I grabbed it back and shouted, "I ain't no sissy! I'll go by myself."

She smiled as I walked up the stairs to the Crazy Lady's apartment. She tricked me into going up there by myself.

I knocked on the door real soft. Boy, I could feel my knees shaking and my heart pounding. I was scared to death. I had a vision of being snatched up into the arms of the Crazy Lady, never to be seen again alive—just like the story of the missing boy. I would become a legend myself. People would say, "Stay away from the Crazy Lady! She snatched up Cheekie and ate him instead of the supper!"

Anyway, after a while, I knocked a little harder, and still no one answered. Then I started knocking real hard and pounded three times with my clenched fist.

Then I heard a voice from behind the door. "All right! All right! Don't bam my door down."

It was the creepiest voice I have ever heard. The words seemed to linger in the air like a dense fog. She opened the door wearing a rag around her head and clutching a half-empty bottle of beer in her bony fingers. After lifting the bottle to her lips and taking a long pull of beer, she stared at me for a moment, then asked, "How can I help you?"

"I come to deliver your supper, ma'am."

She was so drunk she barely understood what I was saying. I could tell she was drunk because her eyes were bloodshot and she could hardly stand up, even though she was leaning against the open door.

She said, "Come in, then, and let me get some money."

"I'll wait right here, ma'am."

She turned around and said, "What's wrong with you? You scared to come in here or somethin'?"

I shook my head. "No, I ain't scared."

"Then why do you look so scared?"

"I don't know."

"Look, I know all the kids call me crazy, but I ain't crazy. Now, come in and close the door."

Her voice got real loud as she grew impatient with me. I stood firmly outside thinking, "There's no way in hell I'm going into this drunk woman's house."

She reached for my arm and tried to grab me. I thought she was going to kill me! I dropped that supper of hers and hauled ass out of there. I stumbled and fell down the stairs, got up, and ran outside.

"What happened?" Woody asked.

I grabbed her by the arm and we both started running.

159

We ran halfway up-front by Pam's house, when I stopped to catch my breath.

"What happened?"

"She was trying to get me in her apartment. I mean she was grabbing and pulling me."

"What?"

"Yep, it's true, but I got away. I ran away before she could pay me, so I don't know what I'm going to tell Mama."

Woody pulled four dollars out her pocket. "Here, you can use this."

"Where did you get that from?"

She smiled, "I stole it out of my Mama's purse when I took that cigarette."

I couldn't believe she was actually stealing from her own mama, but at the same time I was relieved I wouldn't have to tell Mama I left without collecting the money. Besides, she wouldn't believe what happened, anyway. She'd say that I was the crazy one for running off without collecting the money.

Anyway, Mama's party lasted all weekend long, and by the time it was all over, Mama raised enough money to not only pay the rent, but buy some new furniture, too.

not the Crazy lady

Summer. Boy, I love these hot, humid, New Orleans summers. What I like most is waking up real early in the morning, eating cereal, and then watching TV. After that, I run down the street to Pam's house.

There, I meet up with my cousin, Woody, and Jerome. We play marbles and hide-and-seek outside, in front of Pam's house. I love playing Super Friends. I always play Superman and Woody is Wonder Woman. Jerome plays the bad guy. We chase him down, running, jumping, and leaping all over the place. Because I'm Superman, I pretend I can fly. Woody likes to jump off the porch with both hands out, like Wonder Woman does.

It be so hot out there, too. But that heat doesn't bother us at all. In fact, when we get real, real hot, that's when we have the most fun.

Like the other day, we were outside playing and jumping around as usual. After playing cops and robbers, and God-knows-what-else, we sat down on Pam's front porch, with sweat running down our faces. All three of us looking like we could use a real thirst quencher.

That was when we looked across the street and saw

these kids playing and taking a shower in the neighborhood fire hydrant. We looked at each other, and before I knew it, we were running across the street to jump in, too. Jerome jumped in first. The water swallowed him up so much that we could barely see him until he came running out.

"Man, ya'll gone get in or what?" he asked.

Woody tied her blouse in front and pulled her hair back in a pony tail. Then she jumped in with Jerome. I just stood on the outside looking in—thinking about jumping in myself. But the truth was I was scared of drowning.

Woody and Jerome realized I was not coming in and decided to take matters into their own hands. They grabbed both of my arms and pulled me in. As they pulled, I screamed and yelled. But once I was in, I turned so that the water would hit me in my back. I felt safer that way. We were having the time of our lives in the fire hydrant, letting the water run all over our bodies and watching everyone jumping up and down as the water poured down their black bodies like a cold drink quenching the throat. They kept trying to turn me around so that the water would hit me in my face, but I kept my back facing that water the whole time.

That was the day I met this girl named Evette. She is so pretty that when I first laid eyes on her, it was love at first sight. Evette has a twin sister, but they are not identical. As a matter of fact, she and her twin look totally different. Evette is fourteen years old, has caramel brown skin, and is short for her age. And she has these big old breasts! Her breasts are much bigger than other girls her age—bigger than some older girls', too. I know she's older than me, but I think that she is the sexiest girl I have ever laid eyes on.

She is a country girl in every sense of the word, stacked like corn bread and made like mean greens.

Now, her sister Angie looks totally different from her. Angie is black and skinny, and much taller than Evette. I couldn't believe they are even twins. But they are.

After taking a shower in the fire hydrant, we played "Hide-and-seek." I was "it," and had to find everyone else. I made sure I found Evette. I found her right in an empty hallway. It seemed she was waiting for me, because as soon as I walked in that hallway, she grabbed me around my neck and started kissing me up and down!

I caught my breath long enough to ask, "What you do that for?"

She looked at me as if to say, "Because I like you, dummy."

But instead she said, "I thought you wanted me too."

"I, I did, but we just met," I said innocently.

"And so what? Stick with me and I'll show you a lot of things on the first date."

She pulled me close and started kissing me some more. We kissed for so long, I forgot all about hide-and-seek. Shoot, I had already found what I wanted. She was real good at kissing, too, like she had done a lot of it.

But I'm not complaining because meeting Evette that day in the fire hydrant changed things for me. Like, when I wake up in the mornings these days, the only thing I can think about is spending time with her. I used to run down the street to play with Jerome and Woody all day. But since I met Evette, I spend all my time with her. Like I said, I was in love from the start. At least that's what I thought.

The other day something really strange happened when

I finally went over to her house. You see, we always met up-front around Pam's house, never at her house. She said her mama was real strict and didn't allow any boys around her house. But one day she called me on the phone and told me to come over her house, because her mama was going away for the weekend to visit a distant relative. I couldn't believe I was finally going to her house. I felt a little strange about the address she gave me when I realized she lived in the same building as the crazy lady.

I thought, "Not the crazy lady."

"Say that address again," I said.

"2416 Benefit Street, right across the street from you in the next court," she said.

I held the phone in my hand; lost for words.

"Cheekie, are you still there?"

"Yeah, I'm here, just shocked about something."

"What?" she asked.

"About the building you live in."

"I guess you are surprised to find out that I live so close to your house, huh?"

"Yeah that too, but mainly that you live in the same building as the Crazy Lady."

She laughed and said, "Child you talking about Ms. Everlyn."

"Yeah, the crazy lady. She is crazy; I know first hand."

"Ms. Everlyn ain't crazy, just always drunk, but not crazy. But enough about her. Come over here right now."

"OK."

I hung up the phone, and I felt my stomach turning over when I thought about having to go back in the same building the crazy lady lived in. I found myself standing in front her building thinking real hard before walking up them stairs. I don't know if I was more scared of the crazy lady because of what the neighborhood kids made her out to be or because of the monster I created in my own head. It's funny how wild the imagination can be when you are afraid of something. I finally got over my nerves and walked up those stairs real calm and real slow. Evette lived upstairs on the right side, across the hall from the crazy lady!

As I was about to knock on the door, I turned around and noticed the crazy lady's door slightly cracked opened. At first I wasn't going to pay it any mind, but there was this voice inside of me saying, "Go on in there and show all of them you ain't no punk."

So, I did just that—pushed her door open and walked in. It was her kitchen I walked in and it was painted in all yellow, with these beautiful yellow and white flower curtains. It smelt good inside her apartment too, like she was burning all kinds of different incense.

As I walked to the back of the house, I felt sweat in the palm of my hand and on my forehead. I still couldn't believe I was actually in the crazy lady's house. And for a brief moment I thought I must have been crazy just for coming in her house like that.

"Ms. Everlyn, are you home?" I called but in a very trembling voice.

I cleared my throat some more and called out again, "Ms. Everlyn, you home? It's Cheekie, Faye's son."

No one answered, but the closer I got to the back room, the stronger I smelt the burning of incense. Then, I heard a soft voice chanting some stuff I couldn't make out. It almost sounded like the stuff Grandma Emelia chants when she be praying to Allah.

I opened Ms. Everlyn's bedroom door and saw her sitting at this small table in her room with the lights off, and candles burning. Cards were spread out on the table. She was sitting there with her eyes closed, chanting. She didn't even know I was in the room.

I took a quick look around the room and saw black dolls and burning incense everywhere. Then, I realized something that terrified me even more—Ms. Everlyn was a voodoo woman! I was so scared that I almost peed all over myself. I tried to slowly back out of the room before she noticed me, but before I could get out, her eyes popped wide open.

"Going somewhere?" she asked.

My voice trembled, and my knees knocked together.

"I'm sorry for disturbing you ma'am. I walked into the wrong house."

She smiled like she didn't believe me. "Is that right?"

I had almost reached the door when it closed suddenly, right before my eyes. I swear that door closed shut all by itself. It was like Ms. Everlyn had special powers or something.

She got up from the table and walked over to the bedroom window and closed it shut.

"That wind is sure getting strong out there."

I figured she only said that because she didn't want me to think she closed that door with her powers. But I couldn't see how the wind blew that door shut. Besides, I didn't even feel no wind blowing by.

"Ma'am, I have to get going. My friend is waiting for me." I tried to sound convincing.

"You are really scared of me, aren't you?"

"No, I ain't scared of you, just got to get going, that's all."

I tried to open the door, but it wouldn't open. Boy, I really was scared then!

"It's probably stuck—gets like that sometimes."

I managed a fake smile. I just knew Ms. Everlyn was going to kill me at that very moment.

She said, "Have a seat Cheekie."

I thought about it for a moment. Then, I figured I better do what she say before she kills me for sure.

I sat down at the same table she was sitting at. She sat across from me and shuffled a deck of cards that was sitting on the table. These weren't the kind of cards that I was used to seeing grownups play with. These cards had what looked like people on the front of them instead of numbers.

"You don't have to be afraid of me, Cheekie. I won't bite."

When she smiled I could see her pearly white teeth and black gums.

"I'm not scared."

"Well, that's good. Give me your hand."

"My hand?"

"Yes, that's what I said."

For a moment I thought she wanted my hand to chop it off or something. There were just so many wild thoughts running through my head about the way she was going to kill me. I slowly moved my hand across the table. She opened it and said, "Interesting."

"What's interesting?"

"You are, Cheekie."

"I am?"

"That's right. I see wonderful things just by looking in the palm of your hand."

I raised my hand and looked at it. I thought maybe she was seeing something I hadn't seen before.

"You won't be able to see what I am talking about unless you have the gift."

"The gift?"

"That's right, the gift of being able to read the future."

"Wow, you can read the future?"

"That's right."

"You a voodoo woman or something?"

She smiled, and I realized I shouldn't have asked her that. But it sort of slipped out of my mouth before I could catch it.

"Well, I don't like to call it voodoo. I see it as a gift from God."

"Well, what do you see in my future?"

"Well, aren't we in a hurry?" she said jokingly.

Then she grabbed hold my hand and started looking at it again. "Well, I see that you are going to achieve great things way beyond this place known as Desire. You are also going to travel to a far off place to pursue your dreams."

I held my mouth open in shock. Of course, I didn't believe a word of it, because I didn't believe that anyone could see the future, not even a crazy voodoo woman.

When she finished reading my palm, I said, "Well, thanks Ms. Everlyn but I really have to get going."

I stood up and walked away from the table.

She smiled, "Well, I'm glad we had this little visit. You know after our last run in, I thought I had scared you off."

"Don't worry about it ma'am. It was nothin', really."

"Well, I'm glad then. Now, you can tell all the kids around here that Ms. Everlyn isn't crazy after all."

I smiled a real smile this time, not fake like before. I wasn't afraid of her anymore. I felt a little closer to her after she predicted my bright future. I still think that she has special powers, though. This time, when I turned the knob, the door opened with no problem. I turned around and smiled again as I walked through the door.

"Have a good evening, Cheekie."

I think I'll always remember my visit with the crazy lady. But when I tell my friends about my visit, they say that I'm crazy myself for believing Ms. Everlyn has powers. Crazy or not Ms. Everlyn taught me a very important lesson about life. Judge a person for yourself, and don't rely on what other folks say.

everybody plays the fool sometimes

"Everybody plays the fool sometimes, and there are no exceptions to the rule," Pam said as I sat in the chair next to her bed with my head bowed and my eyes filled with water. I was feeling a pain in my heart that I had never felt before, because me and Evette had broken up.

It happened about a week after I visited her at her mama's house, the same day when I was over Ms. Everlyn's house. It completely caught me off guard because I thought we were a match made in heaven. I was going to be a doctor one day, and Evette wanted to be a nurse. Besides that we spent all our time together, actually that whole week together before we broke up.

I was over her house every night while her mama was out of town. I would sneak over there late in the evening, and she and her sister Angie would let me in. One day Angie wanted me and Evette to get booty. She was real nasty, because she not only wanted us to get booty, but wanted to watch, too!

I surprised myself a little, because I knew exactly what to do. I guess all that time peeking in on Mama and her men paid off, because I got right on top of Evette (with my clothes on, of course), and started grinding and grinding until I felt my thing getting real hard. All I knew was that it felt good, you know, my thing rubbing up against her.

After a while, Evette shouted, "OK, stop . . . that's enough, Cheekie. Someone might catch us. Come on stop!"

I didn't want to stop, just kept grinding and moving on top of her.

Evette pushed me off of her and shouted, "Get out!"

I couldn't understand why she was so mad with me. For one, I thought she wanted us to do that. But nevertheless I left her house that day confused and hurt at the same time.

Our break up only lasted for a day though, because we got right back together. It didn't last, though, because we broke up again that same week. This break up was more painful than the first.

This time, I caught Evette with another boy.

We were outside in front of Pam's court playing a game of cards on the porch when I noticed this boy named Arnold sneaking stares at her. She was sneaking stares at him, too. I saw the whole thing, but I pretended like I didn't notice. Later on that day, me and Jerome were sitting around talking about it.

He said, "Man, Evette is some fast, and she is cheating on you."

"No she isn't; we are in love."

"Man, you'll see. You'll see for yourself."

He was right too. When I was leaving Pam's house to go home, I saw the two of them going into an empty hallway. The same hallway we had kissed in when we first met. I thought that place was like our special spot. I followed them in there, and I caught them going at it. I stood there in complete shock at the whole thing. They were so busy going at it that they hadn't even noticed me standing there.

After a while though, Arnold looked around and saw me. He turned around and shouted, "Man, what you staring at?"

I said nothing, just ran out the hallway. I was running and running so fast that I felt like I had run from one end of the project to the other end. I was hurt and my heart crushed like never before. I walked around all day before I ended up back in front our house.

When I walked inside, Mama asked, rubbing my head, "Cheekie, where have you been this time a night? You know I don't like you outside this late."

"Nowhere Mama, just walking around, that's all."

"Want me to fix you a plate to eat?"

I shook my head no. I just didn't feel like eating. All I wanted was to get to my room before I burst out crying right in front of Mama. I went right to my room and closed the door. I laid down on the bed, and that was when I let go. I was crying and screaming out loud. That pain was coming from deep down within. I had never cried like that before in my life. I had a lot of pain in my life, but this was a whole new experience for me. Like I said before, I was in love.

Mama must have heard me, because she opened my door and shouted, "Cheekie, what's wrong with you boy?"

I couldn't even get a word out, because I was crying so much.

After a li'l while, I screamed, "Leave me alone, just leave me alone!"

Mama stood there for a moment, and then she closed the door. I cried and cried until I just fell off to sleep. That was why I was at Pam's house with my head bowed and eyes filled with tears. She had heard from Jerome what had happened. I really didn't want to talk about it, but Pam was determined to talk about it anyway.

"So, you got your heart broken? Well, like I said, it happens to the best of us, even happened to me. Now, you gone be OK, right?"

I looked up at her, surprised to hear Pam admit to crying over something, especially a man. I started thinking how long it's been since I saw her with a man in her life. When I was small Jerome and Karen's dad used to be around a lot, but then he stopped.

"That's right," she continued, "I've been hurt quite a few times. Shit, first it was your Mama's dad, who left me with ten children to run off with some younger woman. Then Safot and Daniel's dad. Now that's a nightmare I want to forget. And then there was Karen and Jerome's dad, who I just got sick and tired of being sick and tired of. So you see, I know from experience about losing someone. But you know what? I'm stronger because of it, too. Raising fourteen children by yourself makes you strong. So if I can get through all that, then I'm sure you can get through this. Now, you gone be OK, right?"

I shook my head yes.

"Well, good. 'Cause I don't want you to do nothing stupid over that li'l gal. What's her name again?"

"Evette," I said, wiping the snot that was running from my nose.

"Child, Ms. Lee's daughters, Angie and Evette. Oh, you better off without her anyway. Those two gals are some fast I heard."

I said nothing, just wiped my nose and dried the remaining tears that ran down my face. We must have talked for hours that day. I was really surprised at how Pam was so good at comforting me. It just seemed so funny to me though, talking to my grandma about stuff like that.

As I sat in her bedroom, I realized Pam was still the same, too. She is just as strong and stern since the day I was old enough to remember. Things still haven't changed between Safot and Pam either. In fact, it seems the older Safot gets, the worse Pam treats her. I was watching TV when Safot came in Pam's room after coming back from the neighborhood store.

"I got the beans from Bynum's store, Pam," said Safot, standing there looking like Aunt Jemima.

Pam signaled for her to come closer. Safot handed Pam that brown paper bag with the cans of beans inside. Pam put her glasses on that were sitting next to her bed. She pulled those cans of beans out the bag one by one. For a moment, everything got quiet as Pam looked the cans of beans all over. Then, she dropped her head, moving it from side to side in disgust. Then, Pam got out of her bed and grabbed Safot by the head.

Safot cried out, "What, Pam? What did I do?"

"You can't do shit right, can you? I asked you to bring me white beans and you brought red. I'm tired of this shit. Every time I send you to the store you come back with the wrong thing. It's almost like you doing it on purpose. Are you trying to make me angry, Safot?"

Safot held her hands up against her face, scared Pam was about to punch her. "No, Pam I swear it was a mistake. I swear."

cheekie

Pam grabbed hold her head even tighter, and asked, "Then why you keep bringing the wrong things back, Safot?"

Safot moved her shoulders up, indicating she didn't know why. That made Pam even more mad.

"Oh, so you don't know, dammit. You don't know!"

Pam slammed all three of those cans up against Safot's head one by one.

Safot screamed and begged Pam to stop. But she wouldn't stop, she kept punching her, and then she reached for a stick that was sitting next to the bed. Safot broke loose and made a run for the door. Pam ran after her, but before she could catch her, Safot was out the door and already down the stairs. Boy, Pam was really mad then!

"Oh, she gone run out of my house like that. But that's OK, because you gone stay out, too! You nappy head whore you!" Pam shouted from the living room window.

Pam even started throwing her things out of the window. Me, Karen, and Jerome stood around, shocked that Pam was throwing her out of the house.

Jerome tried to calm Pam down. "Mama, calm down."

Pam pushed him out of the way and ran from the back of the house to the front, throwing Safot's things out of the window. After throwing her last pair of pants out the window, Pam shouted to Safot who was down on the ground outside the window picking up her clothes, "And don't come back either. If you woman enough to run out of here, you woman enough to live on your own."

Pam slammed the window shut, went to her room, and then slammed closed the bedroom door, too. I stood in shock at the whole thing. I just couldn't believe this was the

176

same woman who had just spent hours comforting me over breaking up with Evette. It was like Pam had a real good side, and a real, real bad side. Just too bad for Safot, that she always got the bad side.

Anyway, I left right after Pam went in her room and found Safot outside on Pam's front porch crying.

I tried to comfort her. "Don't cry, Safot, I'll just ask Mama if you can stay with us."

"Help me pick all my clothes up."

Some of the neighbors were standing around watching. Some of the kids even teasing her.

"Auntie Mama got no place to go," they teased.

I felt so bad for Safot that she had gotten kicked out of Pam's house in front of everyone.

After picking up all her clothes, we ran down the street to our house to ask Mama the big question, "Can Safot stay with us?"

We found Mama in her bedroom getting dressed and curling her hair—something I hadn't seen her do in a long, long time.

Mama saw us in the doorway of her room and asked, "What's going on here? Safot, why are you crying?"

"Pam threw her out, and she has no place to go," I said.

"What?" Mama asked in disbelief.

"It's true, Faye. She threw me out and threw all my stuff out of the window."

Mama slipped on her skirt and said, "Child, I know how Pam is. She threw me out one day. And here I thought my mama had done changed."

Safot cried, "Faye, I have never seen her like that before. She went off on me for nothing, and I don't know why she hates me so much. She has always hated me for nothing."

Safot was really crying. Mama felt so sorry for her. I could tell because Mama handed her a tissue for her running nose, and said, "Look, you can stay here for a while, until things cool down. But you can't stay too long, 'cause I can barely feed the ones I got."

"Thank you, Faye. I promise to earn my keep. I promise."

"Well that's good to hear. You can start tonight by minding my children for me, because tonight I am going out for a change. Li'l Soul is singing and she and I have not hung out in a while," she said, putting the finishing touches of her lipstick on.

I was so happy Safot was going to be living with us. It was then that she and I first started to become close. From that moment on, Safot became my favorite aunt. Like her, I knew what it was like to be treated differently by other people.

Mama left us at home with Safot that evening to go out with Li'l Soul. Like Mama said, this was their first night out in a long time. It was also their last, too. Mama told me the next day all about that night she hung out with Li'l Soul.

Mama met up with Li'l Soul at Maze Nightclub around 10:00 p.m. They met up early before the show so that they could have a drink before Li'l Soul went on to sing. Mama told me the whole story while I sat at the kitchen table eating.

"Li'l Soul looked so beautiful last night, with this tight black dress on. You know how much she likes black. Her hair was slicked straight down. We were there a good hour and Li'l Soul was all over this new man she was seeing. His name was Lest. I had never seen her with this man before, but then again, Li'l Soul is not the type of woman to be settled with one man. But this man seemed like he was really into her. And what was even more strange, Li'l Soul seemed to really like him, too. She was sitting all on his lap, drinking, smoking reefer, and being sassy as usual. She seemed unable to get enough of this man, and I seen a glow in her eyes that I have never seen before in my life. Li'l Soul was in love.

"Later that evening, Li'l Soul sang like she had never sung before. She still loves herself some Aretha Franklin and Natalie Cole. And that night, she sang Aretha's songs, 'Jump' and 'Hooked On Your Love.' Li'l Soul was swinging and singing and dancing all over that place."

As I sat eating my cabbage and corn bread, I looked up and noticed Mama started to cry.

"Mama are you all right?"

"Yeah, I'm fine. Just saddens me when I think about what happened last night. Li'l Soul was just so happy, and she even dedicated a song to me. She knew after two failed relationships with your Daddy and Richard, I needed some cheering up. That's why she sung one of my favorite songs, 'I'm Catching Hell.'"

Mama cried some more when she thought about sitting there in the joint as Li'l Soul poured out the lyrics of Natalie Cole's song.

"After she finished singing that song, she came over to the table where I was sitting. She kissed me on the cheek and said, 'Girl, cheer up. Everything is going to get better for you—just wait and see. In fact, come with me because I want to introduce you this man that's a friend of Lest.' That man name was Howard, and he was tall and dark-skinned.

"After Li'l Soul introduced us, we all sat around, Lest, Howard, Li'l Soul, and me, drinking, laughing, and smoking reefer. I was having so much fun being out again and meeting a new man. Then the good times we were having suddenly turned into a nightmare. It started when this woman named Ruby Lee walked over to the table where we all were sitting.

"She shouted, 'So, this is where you been spending your nights, with this high yellow whore.' Everyone got quiet. It didn't take us long to figure out that the lady was shouting at Lest. Li'l Soul, who was sitting on Lest's lap with her back facing the woman, turned around and asked, 'Who in the hell are you?'

"'His, wife, honey, that's who I is!' Ruby Lee shouted.

"Li'l Soul got up off Lest's lap, eyes fiery as ever and smoke coming from her ears.

" 'Look, you didn't tell me you were no married man.'

" 'Look, baby, I'm sorry. I'm really sorry. I meant to tell you but . . .'

"Ruby Lee interrupted him. 'Baby! Nigga you are out of your mind calling this whore your baby.'

" 'Look, lady, I didn't know this was your husband. Now, ain't no need for you to call me no names,' shouted Li'l Soul.

" 'Like a whore like you give a fuck. Everyone knows around here you sleep with any—and everybody's husband. Your reputation precedes you, dear.'"

Mama finished, "The tension was building so thick in that joint that I could have cut it with a knife. And when things really got heated between Ruby Lee and Li'l Soul, Lest stepped in between the two of them and pulled Ruby Lee outside. They were outside in front the joint fighting up a storm. But Li'l Soul, she was devastated like never before. I found her in the bathroom crying.

"She cried, 'You see, Faye. I told you men are nothing but dogs. I thought Lest was different, you know. But he is like all the rest, just see me as some sex object. But you know I got a brain, too, and a heart, just like everyone else. And right now my heart is hurting, hurting like never before, Faye.'

"I had never seen Li'l Soul like that before, broken beyond repair. I tried to comfort her as best I could. I told her what she always tells me when I'm down. There's more fish in the sea, more trees in the forest. It seemed to work, too, because Li'l Soul wiped her tears away, pulled her hair back, and looked into the mirror that was hanging on the bathroom wall.

" 'You are right, Faye. You know I guess everybody plays the fool sometimes, even a bad-ass bitch like me. There are definitely more trees in the forest. And like Millie Jackson once said, 'I got my axe, ready to chop down the first tree I see *babee*.'

"We laughed so much that I was almost on the floor in tears. In fact, we both laughed. And after a while, I thought Li'l Soul was all right. That's why when we got back to the table, I thought the worst of that night was behind us. But that's when Li'l Soul drank her drink that was sitting there on the table and suddenly collapsed. Someone had done put something in her drink!"

My eyes got real wide because up to that moment I had

no idea that the story would end so tragically. I thought if it dealt with Li'l Soul then a man was somehow involved. But not in my wildest dream would I have imagined what Mama had just told me.

"So, what happened, Mama? Is she all right now?"

"Well, they rushed her to Charity Hospital, and took her to the third floor of all places."

"The third floor! That's where the crazy people go."

"I know, and it was such a terrible sight to see when we got to the hospital. It was like Li'l Soul had done gone crazy. And I don't know what they put in her drink. No one claimed to have seen nothing. You know everyone around here minds their own business, 'cause no one wants to get involved in someone else's mess," said Mama, who couldn't take it no more and walked out of the kitchen, went to her room, and closed the door.

I went to my room, too. And I went to bed that night, tossing and turning all night long. It was like a nightmare, and I kept seeing visions while I was asleep of Li'l Soul falling helplessly to the floor after drinking her drink. I hardly got a shut eye in edgewise.

About a week later, when Li'l Soul got out of the hospital, we went over to visit her, me and Mama both. Li'l Soul still lived right around the corner from Pam's house with her mother Ms. Gertrude. That's the first time I remember going to her house, even though I'm sure when I was little Mama took me there many times.

We found Li'l Soul in her bedroom, staring out the window and rocking in a brown wooden chair. She just rocked back and forth, without even realizing we were in the room.

She was wearing a white night gown, and her hair was pulled back in a pony tail. I just couldn't believe that one drink changed her into a completely different person. I mean the woman I saw that day was not the same woman who was always full of spirit and singing the blues.

Mama kneeled down in front of the rocking chair and ran her hands through Li'l Soul's long, pretty hair.

"What's up, Soul? Me and Cheekie come to see how you doing today."

She said nothing back, though, just rocked and stared out of the window.

I walked over and handed her a ceramic bird I had made in my class the week before. I instantly wanted Li'l Soul to have it when I had heard the news of her being sick.

As I set that bird next to her bed, Mama said, "Just like that bird, Li'l Soul, you will fly again girl, I just know you will. 'Cause, like you always tell me, you a bad-ass bitch, girl." Mama laughed in sadness.

Li'l Soul still had nothing to say, and Mama was sickened with grief.

I then reached over and gave her a kiss on the cheek.

Mama said, "Take care of yourself, Soul. We'll be back to visit you tomorrow."

But the truth is that Mama never went back to visit Li'l Soul again. She said it broke her heart too much seeing her best friend like that. It broke my heart, too. And as we walked home after visiting with her, I kept seeing images of Li'l Soul in my mind. The image of her singing in the kitchen that night she and Mama hung out for the first time at Maze Nightclub. Then I saw the image of her rocking in that chair looking aimlessly out of the window.

The Queen of Desire . . . her eyes that once burned with so much hope were now burning hopelessly.

fighting back

Soon after Mama started hanging out at Maze Nightclub, she started dating her new man. His name is Howard, and Mama liked him from the start. I hate the thought of Mama even thinking about dating another man. After all that she—make that *we*—have been through with men, I can't believe she wants another man in her life. But Mama has always been a high-spirited woman who loves having herself a good time.

Last night, Mama thought it was time for all of us to finally meet him. She made such a big deal out of it. She must have said a thousand times before he got there, "Ya'll be on your best behavior, 'cause this is a good man, and I don't want him to think I have bad-ass children."

I thought, "Who cares what he thinks, 'cause there's no way in hell I will ever accept another one of her men friends."

He picked Mama up around eight o'clock. When he drove up towards the building, I was hanging out my bedroom window waiting to get a look at him before he came into the apartment. The truth is that I wasn't interested in meeting him, but I was curious to see for myself what he looked like.

When he stepped out of this pretty red car, he was wearing a nice, dark three-piece suit. He is tall, dark-skinned just
like Mama had said, with broad shoulders and a fake smile
that I hated from the start. I could tell that he liked himself
too much.

Anyway, all the kids playing outside noticed first the
car, then him. They were impressed by a man like that driving a car like that in a neighborhood like Desire. Most
times, when folks saw someone dressed *that* sharp, and driving a car *that* nice they thought, "He must be dealing
drugs."

When he got inside the apartment, I heard Mama out
front introducing him to Safot, Torey, Darrell, and L'il Faye.
I heard it all from my bedroom. I wasn't about to go out
there and meet him for myself.

"And this is my next to the oldest, Torey. Torey, this is
Howard."

"So, where is your oldest son, the one ya'll call
Cheekie?"

Mama got real silent for a moment and then said, "Well,
he's not feeling that good today, but you can meet him next
time."

Mama was lying, but I guess she didn't want me to spoil
her date with Howard. She knew I would ruin it, too. I spent
all day letting her know that I have no interest in meeting
this man she thinks is the "One." I've heard this too many
times before.

As they pulled off in his shiny red car, I watched from
my window, peeping between the curtains. I couldn't help
wondering if Howard is going to be the next nightmare in
Mama's life. I was so scared for Mama, just thinking about

it. At thirteen, I'm starting to feel like a man myself, but I don't want to be like any of the men in Mama's life. I'm starting to think that every man Mama meets is going to be just like all the rest. Ever since I can remember, the men in Mama's life have been physical abusers and two-time losers, just like Pam said.

Soon as Mama n'em left though, I came out of my room. I found Safot in the kitchen cleaning, scrubbing, and cooking dinner. As always, she was doing chores.

As she kneeled down on the floor scrubbing, I asked, "Safot can I go outside and play?"

She looked up and smiled, "Yeah, but don't run off too far, because I don't want to get in any trouble with your Mama, OK?"

I shook my head yes, and ran out the door, with my skates in my hand.

While I was outside skating back and forth in front of the house, I did just what Safot told me not to do—I got into trouble. But it wasn't my fault, I swear. I was minding my own business when these identical twins who lived around our house, pushed me down onto the pavement for nothing. I fell and landed on my knees. I was wearing shorts, so my knees scraped against the rough pavement and started bleeding. I was scared because I saw a lot of blood.

I was down on the ground, staring at my bloody knees, when one of those twins screamed out, "Now tell your Auntie Mama that."

I did too. I ran down the streets and found Safot outside in front the house, hanging up clothes on the clothes line. I ran between the sheets, pants, and shirts and shouted, "Safot! Safot! Look what Lona and Lana did to me."

Safot made me sit still while she examined my knees.

"What they do that for?" she asked.

"For nothing, and they said for me to come and tell you."

Safot was furious. She hated those twins just as much as they hated her. Not because she was hateful, but because those twins teased her all the time, calling her all sorts of names like "picked head," "ugly," and "Auntie Mama." Safot is not ugly, and her head is not picked. But the twins are pretty. They are creole, light-skinned with long-hair. Their clothes always match to a tee. They have things that Safot can only dream about. Anyway, Safot ran down the street after them. I ran right behind her. We found them sitting on their porch, sucking on huckabucks.

"Did ya'll push my nephew down for nothin'?"

Lona said, "Yeah, and what you gone do about it, Auntie Mama?" Then they both laughed out loud.

Safot put one hand on her hip, held her head high and said, "Ya'll think ya'll pretty, don't you? Well, if ya'll so pretty, how come you act so ugly? I know ya'll think I'm ugly, but my beauty is on the inside, where it counts."

They stopped laughing and their smiles turned to frowns; their eyes got real fiery. The twins were mad, and I could tell Safot hit a nerve.

Lana came off the porch and stood in front of Safot, right up in her face, pointed her finger and said, "I would take being ugly on the inside any day, than have a face like yours."

Then Safot slapped her real hard, and real loud. That was the first time I have ever seen Safot fight back. Most of the time, she lets people say and do anything to her, but not this time. Lana grabbed a hold of her face in a real surprise, and before I knew it they were fighting. They both jumped on Safot. But that didn't seemed to bother Safot at all, because she wasn't going to let those twins embarrass her in front of all the neighbors who were outside that day watching.

After all the kicking, scratching, and biting, Ms. Jones, their Mama, ran outside and stopped the whole thing.

She shouted, "Safot, leave my children alone. You around here starting trouble with your nappy head self. Now go on and don't you put your hands on my girls again."

I couldn't believe what I was hearing. Here this woman was taking up for her brats when they started the whole fight. Safot, who was breathing real hard and real fast, tied her scarf back on her head, turned around and walked away.

Safot was mad, too. She was so mad that she made Torey and Darrell go to their room for the rest of the night. When we got inside, I could see scratch and bite marks all over her body. I felt so bad, being the one who got Safot in this mess in the first place. As I sat in the kitchen cleaning the wounds on my knee, Safot stood in front of the living room mirror tending to her wounds. We both were in bad shape.

Not long after Mama got home from her date, Ms. Jones came by to complain about Safot starting the fight. Mama was furious when she left.

She shouted, "Safot! Get out here right now!"

Safot came out holding a towel of ice up against her forehead.

"Why were you outside starting trouble around here?"

"They started with Cheekie first, Faye, and I went down there to try to find out what happened," she said in a trembling voice.

"It's true Mama. They started with me first."

Mama looked down at me as if she didn't really want to hear what I had to say. She was mad that Safot was starting trouble between her and the neighbors.

"Well, I don't care what the reason is, Safot. I am not going to have you around here starting trouble. Now I'm going out of my way having you here in the first place. And don't forget if I put you out, you have no place to go. So just remember that before you think about causing any more trouble."

Then Mama turned and walked out of the kitchen. Safot sat in a chair next to the kitchen table, put her face between her legs, and started crying. She was crying because Mama made her feel like the child nobody wanted. As she sat there crying, I walked over to the kitchen window and saw those twins playing out in front of the house under the street light. I blamed them for the whole thing. Then I turned around and looked Safot right between the eyes. Tears were streaming down her face. As she cried I could almost feel her pain, and for a while, I was drowning in her tears.

I closed the kitchen curtains shut and thought to myself, "Safot is going to show them all one day, especially those twins."

mardi gras mambo

"Cheekie, why don't you give the man a chance? You might find you like him. Please, do it for Mama!"

That's what Mama shouted to me as I ran out of the kitchen. She is trying, once again, to convince me to give this new man of hers a chance. They've only been dating a few weeks and Mama wants to move him in with us. I am so upset! I can't believe that Mama is going to let another man move into our house. I know he isn't Richard, but I just don't trust the men Mama brings home anymore.

I ran across the street to Ms. Everlyn's house. I know that sounds strange—me running over to the crazy lady's house—but I'm really starting to like her, especially when she's sober. I like talking to her when I'm down and out about something. I knocked on her door and as usual she had it cracked slightly. I pushed the door open just a little more and walked in.

"Ms. Everlyn, are you home?"

I walked further towards the back and realized that Ms. Everlyn wasn't home. I found her bedroom door locked, and the whole place empty. I thought, "That's strange. She left her door wide open, and ain't even home."

I was just about to leave when she suddenly appeared. But this time she was drunk. I could tell because she looked dazed and there was a bottle of beer in her hand. When she starts drinking, she can't stop until she goes all the way. I thought, "Oh God, the crazy lady is back."

"What you need today, Cheekie?" she asked, almost falling. She was so drunk that she could barely talk, and her eyes were so red that she looked like she hadn't slept in days.

"Nothing ma'am, just stopped by to talk, but I see you not in the mood today."

She waved her hands signaling me to sit down at the kitchen table.

"Oh, I'm just fine. I had too much of this beer here, but Ms. Everlyn just fine. Now, take a seat and tell me what's the problem."

I sat down right across from her, shaking just a little. I'm not afraid of Ms. Everlyn anymore, except when she is drunk. Grown folks make me nervous when they get drunk because they change into somebody else, somebody I don't want to know. I started to explain to her the problem with me and Mama.

"Well, Mama met this new man named Howard, and she wants to move him in with us. But I don't like him, because he is just like all the rest."

She took a pull of that beer she was holding in her hand and said, "Well, why don't you want to give him a chance? You won't know if he's like the rest until you find out for sure. The only way to find out for sure is to give him a chance, right?"

I thought about that for a moment and then I said, "I gave all of them a chance and they were all the same."

She looked at me puzzled. She had no idea what I was talking about, and she was too drunk to try to figure it out.

"Well, son I don't know about the other ones, but isn't your Mama entitled to a little happiness, too?"

"Yeah, but I don't think Howard will make her happy. Besides she seemed to be doing fine by herself."

She drank some more of that beer, stood up, and stumbled, almost falling. "Look, let me tell you something about women. We all think that we can do just fine without a man, but the truth is we all yearn for the touch of a man every once in a while, even your mother. Now, you can't go around judging people for what someone else did to you. Everyone deserves a fair chance, right?"

I shook my head yes, as if I believed what she was saying. But the truth is that I still don't want Howard to move in with us. I feel deep down inside that Howard is another big mistake. I thought if Ms. Everlyn is a witch or something, maybe she will use her powers to get rid of Howard. That's really why I went over there in the first place.

"Ms. Everlyn can you use your powers to stop him from coming to live with us?"

She stumbled again, then she turned and looked at me like I was crazy.

"Use my powers?"

I shook my head yes and smiled, hoping that she would help me to get rid of him.

"Oh no, Cheekie, Ms. Everlyn don't interfere in people's lives, and besides I only use that stuff to do good. And getting rid of Howard will be doing bad, right?"

I bowed my head in shame for asking her to do that. I

felt so bad that I just wanted to get out of there before I made myself look even dumber.

I got up from the table and said, "Thanks for your time, but I better be getting home."

"Well, you take care, and don't worry. Everything is going to be just fine, you'll see."

The next day Howard moved in. It was right after I got out of school. I was in my room doing my homework when I heard him moving all of his things in. I stayed in my room all night, because I didn't want to have to pretend like I was happy about it. I even missed dinner that evening. I heard everybody else out there eating, talking, and having a good time, but I wasn't one of them. Later that night I was finishing my homework when Howard knocked on my bedroom door.

"Who wizzit?" I asked in a very mean voice.

Howard pushed the door open and walked in my room, uninvited. I couldn't believe he was actually in my room.

I turned around and said in a very cold voice, "Oh, it's you."

I then continued doing those math problems that were giving me hell. But that was no surprise because I always had problems in math. In fact, I wasn't doing so well in any of my classes.

"So, what are you studying?"

I waited a long time before I finally answered, "Math."

"I know math can be a hard subject." He paused. "It used to give me a hard time, too."

I thought to myself, "Who cares, just get out of my room."

"Cheekie, your mama told me why you don't want me around, because of everything you have seen her go through with men. I know that must have been hard to deal with, being so young and growing up around that stuff, but all I can say is that I am nothing like those guys."

I shook my head as if to say, "Yeah right, that's what they all said."

Howard knelt down in front of me and said, "Hey wait, I know you think that is a line or something, but it's true. I'm really truly sorry all that happened to you and your mama. Now, all I am asking is that you give me a chance to prove to you that I am not like that. I know it's a lot to ask, but you will find that I'm different. I really do want to make your mama happy. All I want is a chance to prove it to you and your mama.

After his heart-felt speech, I still had nothing to say. In fact, I changed the subject altogether.

"Do you know how to do this problem?"

He pulled a chair next to mine, and looked that math problem all over.

"I see ya'll are doing fractions. What grade are you in, anyway?" He was happy that I asked for his help.

"Eighth grade, but we just started to really get into fractions," I said defensively, not wanting him to think I was dumb or something.

"Well, that's OK. Besides, it takes time to learn this stuff. But for this problem all you got to do is divide three on this side, and remember to divide three on the other side. And remember that whatever you do on one side of the equation, you have to do it on the other side. So, there you have it, the answer is three."

I was so surprised at how well Howard explained that problem to me. In fact, he was better than my teacher at explaining math. After helping me with my homework the way he did, I thought he was really smart, too.

As we finished my last problem for the night, Mama walked in drinking a glass of brandy and smoking a cigarette. She was happy to see me and Howard getting along so well.

"So, what arc ya'll doing in here?"

"Nothin', Mama. Howard's just helping me do my math homework."

Howard got up from the table, turned to Mama, and said, "Girl, this boy is behind in school, but he catches on fast. But why is he so behind?"

Mama took a puff of that cigarette, moved her shoulders up, indicating to Howard she had no idea. Mama never got past the tenth grade, so she had no idea why I was so behind in school.

Howard, on the other hand, is a high school graduate with two years of college. He is currently working as a bank teller, which explains his nice car and fine clothes.

Mama held that drink in one hand and a cigarette in the other hand. "Child, I don't know nothin' 'bout no school stuff, but Cheekie is a smart child. In fact, he is going to be a doctor one day."

Mama walked over and stood behind me. She smiled rubbing the back of my head, "I am so proud of him, and I just know in my heart that he is going to make somethin' out of hisself. That's right Howard, you are looking at a future doctor here."

"Well, that's good to know. We need more black doctors out there. But for now, we better let this future doctor get some rest."

Mama rubbed my head again and said, "I'm glad you gave Howard a chance. That's all we were asking for."

Howard and Mama left me there, thinking about everything that me and Howard had talked about. Before I went to bed, I decided maybe Howard wouldn't be that bad after all.

Several months have gone by and I am really starting to like Howard. I like how he is just like one of the kids. I mean he likes playing some of the same games we play, he likes going to the movies, everything. But what I like most about him is that he loves parades. It is February—Mardi Gras time in New Orldeans. It seems like we're going to every Mardi Gras parade, which happens every other night.

Mama doesn't go to the parades with us because right after Howard moved in, she found out that she was pregnant. I figured she must have gotten pregnant long before he moved in. But anyway, Mama said she was too tired to be dealing with all those people, so Howard takes me, Torey, Darrell, and Safot right up to Canal Street to catch all the parades.

The celebration starts two weeks before Mardi Gras. You see, Mardi Gras Day actually falls on a Tuesday. During the two weeks leading up to Mardi Gras, we stand out on Canal Street every other night, right there on the corner of Canal and Rampart, right beside Woolworth, and watch those parades come by. The bands, the majorettes, flag girls, came by stepping, dancing, and playing all that Mardi Gras music. Boy, there are people from everywhere—Chicago, New York, California, you name it—they are there! I've never seen so many black folks and white folks together having so much fun. Mardi Gras is the biggest free party in the world! After the bands roll by, come the prettiest floats I have ever seen. Those floats have people on them dressed in all sorts of funny costumes, throwing beads, cups, and all kinds of souvenirs for people to catch.

I'm always amazed at how silly people behave, trying to catch those souvenirs. The way some people act you would think they are throwing gold from those floats. But that just shows how much fun people have at carnival time.

It was so crowded out in front of Woolworth the other night that Howard had to put us on his shoulders one by one, so the men on those floats could see us waving and screaming. And we screamed at the top of our voices as the floats rolled by.

"Throw me somethin' Mister! Throw me somethin' Mister!"

Now, if you think that's exciting, you ain't seen nothin' 'til you see Fat Tuesday for yourself. Now that's somethin' else. Boy, it is really a sight to see!

On Mardi Gras Day we got up early in the morning. We were very excited over what the day would bring. I think we were so excited because before now we've never really had the opportunity to enjoy Mardi Gras Day. Thanks to Howard, this Mardi Gras was one to remember.

As we were getting dressed, Safot came in our rooms and asked, "Are ya'll ready, 'cause your mama n'em are downstairs loading up the food and stuff."

"Yeah, I'm almost ready, but why aren't you ready? I mean, aren't you going too?" I asked.

"No, I'm not feeling that good today. Besides I heard

Pam is going to be hanging out with ya'll, and I'm sure she ain't gone want me hanging around. So you better hurry up now before they leave you," Safot said, just before she closed the door.

I felt so sorry for Safot. Pam wasn't even around much and still was finding a way of getting to her.

We left Safot at home. We loaded all our food and stuff in the back of Howard's car and left around ten o'clock that morning. We were going to meet Annie Mae and the rest of our family right under the Claiborne Street Bridge. That is where most of the blacks hang out. Mama said they hang out there because it is kind of a tradition. Back in the old days, blacks were not allowed to go to Canal Street with the white folks, so they all hung out on Claiborne Street and made their own Mardi Gras Day. Mama told me many times before that even though they weren't allowed on Canal Street, they had the best time right under that Claiborne Street Bridge.

There was one organization in New Orleans known as the Zulu People, who hosted what became known as the black people's parade. Zulu was just like all the other organizations or parades that were in New Orleans, but the difference was that all the Zulus were black. They marched up and down Claiborne Street, just like the Endymion, the Rex, and the other parades that marched on Canal Street. (Endymion and Rex are the names of organizations. The parade is named after the particular organization that sponsors it.)

Mama said that the Zulu people would come marching by with their faces painted black in the original African tradition. The theme of their parade is centered around

African principles. From the form of dress to the style of music, the Zulu People represent a different way for blacks to celebrate Mardi Gras.

As they marched by, they chanted and danced to a beat that became known as the "Mardi Gras Mambo." They chanted, "The Mardi Gras Mambo, mambo, mambo down in New Orleans. It's the place where the blues was born, it takes a cool cat to blow a horn, just listen to the beat of the Mardi Gras Mambo, mambo, mambo, down in New Orleans." And Mama said people would jump and shout and dance the Mardi Gras Mambo beat, and Zulu People would throw souvenirs. One souvenir that is a tradition is the coconut. It's painted in gold and black—the colors of the Zulu Parade—and covered with all sorts of decorations.

Zulu began back in the old days when the horrible Jim Crow laws were still practiced. Things are much different for blacks now. On *this* Mardi Gras Day, we not only went under the Claiborne Street Bridge, but on Canal Street, and everywhere else, too. Now the Zulu Parade is not just considered the "black people's" parade, it is just like any other Mardi Gras parade. They marched all over the city throwing souvenirs, giving local people, as well as tourists, something to remember about Mardi Gras. These days we hang out under Claiborn Street Bridge because we want to, not because we have to. That makes a big difference.

We finally met up with Annie Mae n'em who had already set up a barbecue grill and everything for us.

"About time ya'll got here, child," said Annie Mae when we walked up.

"Well, we got a late start. I was having labor pains and had to wait to see if I was going to be able to come out here today," said Mama who was rubbing her stomach that was slowly growing into a round balloon.

We sat our stuff down and I looked at the many black people lined up along the Claiborne Street. I had never seen so many black folks in one place before in my life! They were dressed in all sorts of costumes, from Indian costumes, to their faces painted in different colors, to wearing almost nothing. We weren't dressed in costumes though. I wore Wrangler jeans, a gator shirt, and All-Star tennis shoes. Mama had her face painted like an Indian, and Howard had a cowboy hat on. Annie Mae and her children were dressed in Indian costumes. The reason why people wear Indian costumes is because there is still a huge population of Indian people right here in New Orleans. During Mardi Gras time they come out in full force. They chant and dance—"second-lining" is what we call it. I don't know how they came to call it that, but as they passed by everyone jumped in and started second-lining too. A second line is nothing more than a group of people getting together chanting music, dancing in the street, and waving handkerchiefs and umbrellas in the air. The second line is a New Orleans tradition.

After second-lining to the popular Mardi Gras song, "It's Carnival Time," Annie Mae and her man, Willie Ed, decided they were going to walk to Canal Street to see the Rex Parade. Canal Street was just a ten-minute walk from where we were, and I couldn't wait to get there and see for myself how wild Canal Street was on Mardi Gras Day.

Mama, who was not feeling that good, didn't want us to go with Annie Mae.

As they were getting ready to leave, Mama said,

"Cheekie, ya'll stay here with me, because it's too many folks up there on Canal Street."

I whined, "Come on, Mama, let us go and see the Rex parade."

"No, Cheekie, and that's final."

Howard took up for me.

"Look, why don't I go, too, so the kids can see the Rex parade. You know when we were kids we would have given anything to see the King of Mardi Gras." (The Rex parade is the longest running organization in New Orleans, and the most well-known parade, too. The Rex is considered the King of Mardi Gras.)

After much discussion, Mama allowed us to go with Annie Mae n'em to Canal Street. And when we got up there I couldn't believe my eyes! That placed didn't look like Canal Street anymore, but more like a crowd of people at a football game. Everyone was gathered around watching the parades go by, drinking and getting drunk all over the place. But what was most unbelievable were the costumes I saw people wearing. I even saw a naked man running up and down the streets and some women without tops on!

But that was nothing compared to what I saw on Bourbon Street. Now, that is a place to remember. It is in the heart of the famous French Quarter, where all of the well-known restaurants and topless bars are located. As we walked along, I saw these women and men up overhead on the balconies doing everything but having sex. As loads of people stood around looking up at the people on the balconies, men on the balconies shouted down, "Show your tits! Show your tits!" And the women shouted up, "Show your dicks! Show your dicks!" Imagine my surprise when I actually saw these people showing their stuff right out there in the middle of the street. I know it sounds wild, but that's all part of Mardi Gras. It's another New Orleans tradition.

As we walked along some more, I even peeped in those topless bars and saw women and men dancing naked. But Annie Mae grabbed me and Woody when we tried to peep. She shouted at us, "Ya'll too young to see that."

I thought, "I see naked people out here on the streets, so what's the big deal?"

Without a doubt, that was the best Mardi Gras ever for me. I sure love me some carnival time! And like the song goes, "If you ever come to New Orleans, you got to go to the Mardi Gras. And when you get to the Mardi Gras, make sure you see the Zulu King, right down there on Rampart and Dumaine."

Et laissez les bon temps roulez!—And let the good times roll!

i can do bad all by myself

"Push Faye. Come on! You are almost there. Push!"

"I can't, it hurts, oh it hurts Pam, please stop the pain, please. I can't take it!"

Mama was having her baby right there in the house because she couldn't make it to the hospital in time. Howard was right there by her side, trying to comfort her the best way he knew how. But it wasn't working, and I have never seen Mama in so much pain.

Pam used to be a nurse's assistant back in her younger days, until she fell down on the job and had an accident. Because of the accident, she was able to collect disability, even though she had no real serious injuries. Needless to say, she knew how to deliver a baby, so when Mama collapsed on the living room floor, I ran down the street to fetch Pam. I ran real hard because I thought Mama was dying or something. I thought that because she was screaming so much.

I fell right inside of Pam's door and shouted, "Pam, hurry! Mama about to have Howard's baby, hurry!"

Pam got there just in the nick of time to deliver the baby.

"It's a boy, Faye, a beautiful, little boy," Pam said when that baby came out of Mama's stomach. When that baby came out screaming and crying, Mama fell back on the floor laughing. She was happy that baby had finally come out of her.

"It's a boy!" Howard shouted with excitement.

Me, Torey, and Darrell stood right behind Pam as she held that little baby in her hand. It was real little too, with all this nasty-looking stuff all over it. But Pam had a big bucket and some towels so she dipped that baby in and cleaned it all up. Before I knew it, the baby was as good as new.

Mama laid out on the floor still trying to catch her breath.

"Here's your little boy, Faye," Pam said as she handed the baby to Mama.

Mama rose up off the floor just a little, and took that baby in her arms.

Howard held Mama's hand and played with the baby at the same time. He was just as excited as Mama. "This here is our little baby boy," he said over and over again.

"What you gone name him?" Darrell asked.

Howard looked at Mama and waited for her to answer. "Well, I think I'm going to name him after his daddy. So, here Howard. Hold your son, Li'l Howard."

Mama handed the baby to Howard and fell back on the floor. Mama sure loved naming her children after the parents. She named me after my daddy, L'il Faye after her, and now L'il Howard after his daddy. Now Mama had five children, four boys and a girl.

After a while, Pam helped Mama to her room. When

Pam laid Mama across the bed, I heard Mama say, "Thanks Pam. Did you see Safot in the other room?"

Pam pulled the covers over Mama and said, "Look Faye, I don't want to talk about Safot. Now you enjoy that precious baby of yours, and make sure you go and check yourself at the hospital as soon as possible, you hear?"

Mama shook her head yes, and she knew not to ask Pam nothing else about Safot. Like I said once before, when Pam speaks, all her children knows it's final.

Anyway, as Pam left I saw Safot peeping from behind the door. She was crying, too. "Poor Safot," I thought, "she has no idea why Pam hates her so much."

The following day, though, Mama went to the hospital just like Pam told her. Me and Howard went with her. I was outside in the lobby when I heard the doctor tell Mama, "Well, Ms. Webb, everything is just fine."

"You sure, doctor?" Mama asked.

"Oh, I'm sure all right. In fact, the both of you are in excellent condition."

"Good. Now doctor I want you to tie my tubes because I don't want to have no more children. This is definitely my last one. In fact, I want you to burn them suckers, because this shit is too painful."

The doctor laughed out loud. That doctor just laughed Mama right out of the hospital. But Mama was serious. She had the doctor schedule her for an appointment to have her tubes burned.

After that baby came, Mama and Howard became even closer. Howard was the proud daddy of his very first child. He acted like he had gone to heaven and back. He called his whole family, who were living in Texas, and told them the news. He called all his old friends and told everyone in the neighborhood. That man told everyone in the project!

He was so excited that he went so far as to ask me, Torey, and Darrell to call him Daddy. I'm not about to. Don't get me wrong. I like Howard a whole lot, but there is no way in hell I am going to call him Daddy. I hate the sound of that word, "Daddy." "I don't have a daddy," I thought to myself as I walked out of the living room. I can't believe he actually wanted us to call him that. I feel like he already has a son, so why not let him call'em Daddy when he is old enough? Mama even tried to convince me to call him Daddy, but I'm stubborn, and once I make up my mind there is no changing it. Come to think of it, I must get that from Pam.

Mama walked over, rubbed the top of my head, and asked, "Cheekie, why don't you want to call Howard Daddy? Hasn't he been like a daddy to ya'll?"

"Yeah, but he still ain't my daddy. I don't have a daddy," I said in a very cold voice.

"Yes, you do. You just mad because he hasn't been around. But that's no reason to take it out on Howard. He is just so excited to have ya'll in his life, and about his new son. So be nice and call him Daddy. Do it for Mama."

I shouted, "Leave me alone! I'm not calling him no Daddy. I don't have a daddy!"

Mama realized that there was no convincing me, and once she saw how upset I was, she just walked out and closed the door.

I laid there in my room crying most of the day. I felt so much resentment that my own daddy had left me that I was taking it out on Howard. But at the time, I had no idea that's what I was actually doing. After crying myself to sleep, I woke up and decided to go down to Pam's house and talk to her about it. I knew if anyone would understand my situation, it would be her.

When I got to her house, she was home all alone. Jerome and Karen were out shopping with their daddy, and Daniel was outside in the court playing football. Pam was sitting in her bed chewing tobacco as usual, and watching TV.

"Oh, Cheekie. Come to see me again today? Have a seat."

"Pam, I want to talk to you about something."

She leaned over and spit that tobacco out in an old newspaper beside the bed. "OK, what about?"

"Howard wants us to call him Daddy, but I don't want to call him that. And besides he's not my real daddy."

I thought Pam was about to give me some real sound advice, but she just broke out laughing. I mean she was there laughing and laughing so hard that I'm sure her insides were hurting. I couldn't believe she thought the whole thing was funny. When I saw she was not going to stop laughing, I got up and walked out.

"Cheekie, don't go. Lordy, I didn't mean to laugh at you. But, it was just so funny."

But even though she didn't mean to laugh, I still heard her laughing at me all the way out the door. I don't know why she thought the whole thing was so funny. Maybe it was how I said it, or maybe it reminded her of something else. I don't know why she laughed, but I thought to myself on the way home, "It's not funny."

A whole month went by, and I still never called Howard Daddy. I thought about it, but I never did. I heard Torey and Darrell calling him Daddy. Since Howard was real cool, I decided to keep the peace, and not call him anything at all. So when I needed him for something, or needed to say something, I would simply say, "Mama wanted to know," or "Can I go down the street?" Never would say the word "Daddy" or never call him by his name. Torey and Darrell knew what I was doing, because every time I did it, they laughed out loud over the whole thing. But I didn't care. I was determined not to say the word "Daddy," and after what happened later, I'm glad I never did.

Mama, who was getting stronger and stronger everyday, decided she and Howard needed some time alone. They both had been real busy ever since L'il Howard was born— late nights, early mornings, and always doing something with us or the new baby. That was why one night they decided to visit their old stomping ground, Maze Nightclub.

Me, Faye, L'il Howard, and Safot were the only ones home that night. Torey and Darrell were spending a night over Annie Mae's house. Me and Safot stayed up most of that night watching TV and playing cards. It was real late when we finally went to bed.

Mama and Howard must have gotten in sometime after three in the morning because when they woke me, the TV was still on but the national anthem was playing, meaning that the station was about to go off for the night. Their voices were real loud and it sounded like they were arguing.

I jumped up in my bed, and at that moment, everything came back to haunt me—Daddy, Richard, all the nightmares. My heart was pounding, almost about to explode. I was scared and didn't know why. All I could think was that something bad was about to happen, *again*.

I got up out of bed and turned the TV off because it was making the most annoying noise and I couldn't hear what they were arguing about. I cracked my bedroom door and I heard everything.

"How could you, dancing all over some man like that, just like a whore or something?"

"I was not dancing like no whore. Besides, Charles was my husband at one time. Shit, we are still legally married anyway!"

I couldn't believe it, Mama and Daddy were dancing together. Boy, I was in shock, and Howard, he was mad as hell.

"So that gives you the right to dance all over him like that, huh, Faye? Answer me, damn it!"

"We were just having a little fun. Now keep your voice down before you wake them children up. I done told you what I have been through with men and I'm not going to go through this shit again. No one controls me, no one. Now, I'm sorry if I upset you. Let's go to bed please, and forget about it," Mama said and closed their bedroom door shut.

Mama sounded like she really didn't want to talk about it anymore, but Howard wasn't finished at all. In fact, I heard him screaming some more once the door was closed. But then I heard a loud fall and I thought my heart would stop. I opened my bedroom door wider then, and heard Mama shouting at the top of her voice, "Get out damn it! I told you if you ever hit me, that was it! Now get the hell out of my house!"

I ran down the hall and opened Safot and L'il Faye's

bedroom door. I walked over to where Safot was sleeping and pushed her arm lightly. She didn't wake up, and when I heard Mama and Howard screaming some more, I pushed her a little harder.

Safot jumped up, and it was like she suddenly realized what was happening before I even had to tell her. She jumped out of bed and asked, "What's going on over there?"

I was breathing so fast, and my heart was pounding even faster. I could barely get my words out. "They arguing about something. Stop it, Safot."

Before we even got out of the room, we heard a glass break against the door and then another one. My heart was racing and pumping so fast that I thought it might explode.

Howard opened the door and ran into the living room. Mama ran out there after him. We ran behind them too. L'il Faye, and Li'l Howard were still sound asleep.

Mama was running from the bedroom to the living room throwing Howard's things out the door. I mean she was throwing all of his stuff out the door—pants, shoes, drawers, everything.

He stood there with blood running down his face, try-ing to catch his clothes before Mama threw them out of the door.

"Look, Faye, let's talk! I'm sorry. I shouldn't have put my hands on you."

"The hell you shouldn't. Now, I want you to get the hell out of my house, because I'll be damned if you gone ever put your hands on me again. I have been through too much shit to ever let a man put his hands on me. Now, I don't want to talk. Just get your shit and get the hell out of my house!" Mama shouted as she ran through the house throwing his things out. I had never seen Mama like this before. She was in control of the situation. It was not the same ol' Mama getting beat and crying out for help. This time it was the man crying, not Mama. He was crying and begging Mama not to throw him out. Me and Safot stood there the whole time, watching this grown man begging and crying out loud.

"Please, Faye. I didn't mean to hit you. I don't know what got into me. Let's not end it this way. Please!" he cried.

Mama was not listening to him, because she kept running back and forth. For a good while, Mama acted as if me and Safot were not even standing there watching. It was like she didn't even notice us. Then, on one of her trips to the bedroom, she shouted to me, "Cheekie, get back in your room! You know you have to go to school tomorrow."

I stood there for a while, wasn't going to move at first. Then Mama shouted again, "Move it I said! Go to your room."

"What about Safot?"

"Safot, help me throw the rest of this stuff out. Cheekie, go to your room."

I walked back to my room and cracked the door so I could still hear what was going on.

By the time Mama and Safot had thrown the last of his things out the door, the police had arrived. I don't know who called the police. Maybe it was a nosey neighbor, but all I know is that they came and took Howard away. He was standing outside in the hallway, looking like a lost puppy, eyes puffy from crying, and all his clothes and things out in the hallway. As the police walked up, he was still trying to convince Mama to give him a second chance.

"Faye, please. Let's talk."

Then I heard the voice of a woman with a deep voice. "Ma'am, what's going on here?" asked a police officer.

"Ma'am, I want this man out of my house. That's all I want!"

"Who's place is this?" asked the other officer.

"It's mine, sir," Mama answered.

"Well, sir, you have to leave like the woman said," replied the woman police officer.

Howard tried one last time to convince Mama to let him stay, "Faye, don't do this. We need to talk."

"We don't have nothing else to talk about. I have gone through this shit too many times, and this is it. Now, if you want to see your child that's one thing, but as far as you and me are concerned, it's over, Howard. So get used to it." Then Mama slammed the door shut.

Soon after the police took Howard away, I laid in bed thinking about what had just happened. I was feeling so bad for Mama. Here she thought Howard was going to be different from the rest, and he turned out to be just like Richard. Well, maybe not as bad as Richard, but still he hit Mama and that's all it took. Mama was determined not to end up living in a situation like that again.

"I'm tired of letting men control my life. Shit, I can do bad all by myself. I'll be damned if I am gone let any man put his hands on me and think he can get away with it."

Safot just sat in silence, listening to Mama talk and cry the rest of the night.

After a while, I drifted off to sleep myself. But the last thing I remember Mama saying was, "I'm not getting back in that type of relationship ever again. Ain't no way in hell

I'm going to take my children through this shit all over again. Ain't no way in hell."

That gave me peace of mind in knowing that Mama was not going to be stupid all over again. That thought brought me so much comfort, I slept like a newborn baby.

Movin' on Up

Li'l Howard is almost two now, and Mama is getting tired of the Desire Project. Desire opened in the early forties, promising better housing opportunities for the poor, but this promise is unmet. The place gets more unlivable everyday. Last year, there were more homicides in the Desire than in the rest of the whole city. Crime and drugs are at an all-time high. Children are often the victims of drugs and violence. That's some of the reasons why Mama wants out.

Already, Torey is attracted to guns and violence. He is only twelve years old, but he hangs around with boys who are almost twice his age. He is always in trouble, either at school or in fights with neighborhood children. Torey is getting out of control, and Mama is afraid of what life in the ghetto is going to do to the rest of us.

Besides, Mama has had a hard life for a long time. She has been living on her own since she was fifteen years old, constantly struggling to make ends meet. She is always reminding us that she wants a better life for her children. It was no surprise to me when I found out that Mama wants out of the Desire.

I became aware of her desire to leave Desire last

Saturday, when I found her turning her bedroom upside down looking for something that she had lost. She was looking through drawers, under the bed, and her closet. She had papers scattered all over the house.

When she started searching through the living room where I was sitting watching TV, I asked, "Mama, what are you doing? What are you looking for?"

She just ignored me and kept searching. I followed her back to her room and saw her looking through a pile of papers sitting on her bed.

I asked again, "Mama, what are you looking for?"

"I'm looking for my welfare papers, ya'll's birth certificates, and stuff like that."

"Why you looking for that stuff?"

"Because I'm going to get ya'll out of this project before something really bad happens. I want out of this damn place, but for the life of me I can't find all the papers they gonna need from me."

"They who, Mama?"

"Look, Cheekie, I don't have time to answer all your questions right now. I got to find these papers and get to the housing office before it's too late."

I was still confused about how Mama plans to get us out of the Desire Project. I know she doesn't have the money to buy a house and she hasn't won the lottery. So, I asked again, "Mama why are you going up to the housing office?"

Mama turned around and looked at me as if to say, "You are really getting on my last nerve." Then she sat on the edge of the bed, pulled her hair back and said, "I didn't mean to yell at you, but it's just that I am getting frustrated looking for all this stuff. You see, I heard from some neighbors that some residents of the Desire Project may be eligible for a program called Section 8 housing."

"Section 8, what's that?"

"It's a program that gives poor folks like us the opportunity to move out of here to a neighborbood with better living conditions. I can move into better housing for the same rent that I pay to live here. And I heard that in some cases, people don't have to pay rent at all."

My eyes lit up. The thought of getting out of the Desire was like a dream come true. I jumped down off that bed and started looking through those papers myself. Mama fell over laughing when she saw my reaction.

"You are so funny, boy," she laughed again.

"Come on now Ma; let's find these papers you looking for."

"Well you're right about that. We better find them and soon because the office opens at nine and it's first come, first serve. So, we better get going."

It took us about thirty minutes to find all the papers. Then me, L'il Howard (who Mama carried on her hip), and Mama headed out around 8:30 a.m. I have never seen this side of Mama before. But then I figure with everything she has gone through, I can surely understand why this is so important to her. She has spent practically her whole life in the Desire and has nothing much to show for it. She even tried to convince Annie Mae and Pam to go sign up, too. But, like most people she talked to, they believed it sounded too good to be true.

When we arrived at the housing office, there were people lined up everywhere. The office wasn't even open yet, but that line was swinging around the corner and down the street. I guess a lot of people wanted out of the Desire. Mama took a spot in line, and we stood out there in the heat and humidity for hours. It was so hot, I thought I could feel my skin burning in the hot sun.

Mama said, "Cheekie, why don't you go and get us some lemonade at Mr. P's truck before I pass out." Mr. P sells candy, sandwiches, and sodas from his truck, just around the corner from our house. I bought lemonade, pig lips, and a bag of barbecue potato chips.

By the time I got back to the line, Mama was already inside the office filling out papers.

"How did you get inside so fast Mama?" I was curious to know how Mama slipped past all those people.

Mama put her hand over her lips telling me to be quiet. Then she grabbed the can of lemonade out of my hand and pulled me to the side.

"Shut up before you get us kicked out of here. Now, I got in because I know the security guard. He lived across the street from me when I was little."

I looked over at the security guard and he raised his right thumb up to us and whispered to Mama, "Good luck."

And luck was exactly what Mama needed. I say that because she had to fill out so many papers. Those people wanted to know our whole family history. There was so much stuff to read that Mama asked me to help her fill out some of the papers. About an hour later, Mama handed her forms to a woman sitting behind a glass window. I don't remember that woman's name, but I do remember that she was a real mean you-know-what. She started asking Mama all these personal questions, with an attitude of course.

"Do you and your husband still live together? Does he pay you any alimony?"

She went on and on with questions. After hours in that heat, and filling out all those papers, the last thing Mama needed was to have to deal with a woman who had an attitude from hell.

"Ma'am, I'm sorry, but I don't think you quite meet the qualifications," the woman said.

Mama couldn't believe it. She put L'il Howard on her other hip, and I knew then that Mama was ready for war.

"What did you say, ma'am?"

"I said you don't meet the qualifications. Now, may I help the next person please?"

"Ma'am, please tell me what I need. You have to help me."

"I said all that I'm going to say. Now, may I please help the next person!" she shouted even louder then before. Her patience was running out with Mama. But Mama wasn't about to give up.

"Where is your supervisor?" asked Mama.

"She's right over there. Now please get out of my line."

Mama walked over and found an older woman sitting behind a desk typing.

"Ma'am, are you the supervisor?"

The woman stood up and extended her hand, "Yes, ma'am. How may I help you, dear?"

Mama was so emotional that she started to cry out loud, "Ma'am, I have been out there in that line all morning, trying to get on Section 8, and now your employee over there says I don't meet the qualifications. I need to get my children out this project. Please help me, ma'am. Please!"

As Mama held L'il Howard in one hand, she stood there in front of that lady, with tears streaming down her face, begging out loud for help. I felt like crying when I saw Mama crying like that. Part of me was embarrassed though, because Mama crying in front of all those people. But it worked, because that supervisor was moved to help us.

She walked over to another worker sitting behind the glass window and said, "Help this lady get Section 8. In fact, make her application one of our priorities."

Mama grabbed hold L'il Howard real tight in excitement and said, "Thank you, ma'am. Thank you so much. I will never forget what you have done for me today."

"That's all right, Ms. Webb. You can thank me by enjoying your new home, OK?"

Mama shook that supervisor's hand in a real hurry, and started taking care of business once again. I turned around and saw that mean you-know-what looking over at us. I was so mad that I felt like breaking that damn window and choking her by the neck. But instead I gave her the middle finger when we walked out of the office. All she did was roll her eyes at me and say, "Next! May I help the next person please?"

After we left the housing office, I ran and told everybody we were moving. I ran to Ms. Everlyn's house, to Annie Mae's house, to Pam's house, I ran everywhere that day! I remember telling Annie Mae about us moving. I ran in her front door, breathing real fast, "We moving! We moving out the project!" I shouted in excitement.

Annie Mae, who was combing Woody's hair when I walked in, didn't believe me at first. She asked, "For true? How ya'll moving?"

"We got Section 8 and Mama is out looking for a place right now."

"That's good. Maybe I should have gone down there after all."

"Where ya'll moving to?" asked Woody.

"I don't know, but now I have to go because I have to tell Pam, too."

I was out the door before they could say "bye." That was just how fast I ran down the street to Pam's house. I saw Jerome playing marbles out front and told him first.

"Man, we moving out the project," I smiled from ear to ear.

"What? When?"

"I don't know, but soon."

"You told my Mama yet?"

"Not yet, but I'm 'bout to tell her now. You coming?"

He shook his head no, and continued playing marbles. I ran upstairs to Pam's house and knocked on the door. Karen answered.

"Where's Pam, Karen? I have to tell her what happened."

"She's in the room watching TV."

I ran in Pam's room and found her watching one of her favorite soap operas, *The Young and the Restless*.

I shouted, "Pam we moving out the project!"

She signaled for me to be quiet because she was in the middle of an important scene. I sat down in a chair next to the TV and started watching, too. It was a scene where these two women were out on the balcony, a young woman and an older woman. The older woman hated the younger woman so much that she jumped off the balcony so everyone would think the younger woman pushed her off. I knew it was only TV but the action was so gripping that I was looking foward to seeing what was going to happen the next day, and then the next day.

When the soap opera finally ended, Pam leaned over, spit her tobacco out in an old newspaper, as usual, and asked, "So, what were you saying?"

"I was telling you that we are moving out of the project."

"How ya'll moving?" she asked in disbelief.

"Well, Mama got on that Section 8 program."

"Yeah? I remember her telling me about that. That's something else how she got it. Well, don't forget your grandma back here, you hear?"

I shook my head no. But as I left her room, I thought, "We are only moving out of the project, not out of the city."

When I finally got back home, I found Safot packing up our stuff and putting everything into boxes.

I ran up behind her scaring her half to death. "We moving, Safot, just like the Jeffersons."

That's when I started singing, "We moving on up to a deluxe apartment in the sky . . . we finally gone get a piece of the pie . . . beans don't burn in the kitchen, greens don't burn on the grill . . . took a whole lot just to get up that hill . . . but now it's you and me baby, and there's no turning back, we moving on up to the sky."

Safot started singing that song with me. We were so excited that we sang all over that house, packing up at the same time.

We were so busy singing and jumping for joy that we didn't even hear Mama come in the door. She must have stood there for a while watching us carry on, because after we finished singing, she clapped her hands. "Well, well! I see I'm not the only one happy we moving."

I jumped up and down, "Mama, you're home! You found a house yet?"

Mama put her purse on the kitchen table and sat down in a chair.

"Yes, Cheekie, I found us a house."

"Where at, Ma? Where at?"

"Calm down and I'll tell you."

I sat in a chair next to the table and Mama explained, "Well, I found a nice place over on St. Claude Street. It's a four-bedroom house with a kitchen, bathroom, and everything."

"Isn't that good news, Mama?" I asked, real confused because I sensed something was wrong in her voice.

"Yeah, that's the good news, but the bad news is that Safot can't come and live with us."

"Why?" I shouted, "Why?"

Safot was still in the back room packing up everything as Mama explained to me why she couldn't come and move with us.

"It's the housing office. They were very strict in giving me Section 8. They say that I can only have me and my children living with me. They even went so far as to say they are going to monitor me on a regular basis. So, you see I have no choice."

I was sad after I heard that news, and so was Mama. I turned around and saw Safot in the living room still humming that song we were singing—just humming and packing. Mama got up from the kitchen table and walked over to

Safot. Safot hadn't even noticed Mama standing in the doorway watching her. But when she did, she turned around, smiling.

"Girl, I know you are so happy to be getting from around here, right?"

"Yeah, that's for true," said Mama with a fake smile. She couldn't smile for real knowing that she had to tell Safot she wasn't coming to stay with us.

"So, Faye, when are we due to move?"

Mama sat down on the bed, grabbed a shirt that was sitting there and started folding it real slow. Mama was trying to hold back as long as she could in telling Safot the truth.

"Faye, what's wrong? You didn't get the place?"

"Yeah, I got the place. But I'm afraid I have some bad news."

Safot stopped what she was doing and sat down on the bed next to Mama.

"Go ahead Faye. Tell me the news."

"Well, because of all the restrictions, you won't be able to come and stay with us. And I am so sorry, girl, because I really don't want to leave you behind."

I stood in the doorway, watching and listening. As Mama told her the news, Torey and Darrell walked in from outside.

"Why Mama crying, Cheekie?" Torey asked.

"Because Safot can't move with us in our new house," I said.

"What? Man that's messed up. But why?" asked Darrell.

I explained to them the same thing that Mama had told me earlier. Torey and Darrell were just as upset as me and Mama. You see, we have really gotten used to Safot living with us. It's like we are losing our big sister.

I thought Safot would start to cry or something, but instead she just continued to fold up those clothes. I could see the hurt in her eyes, but it was like she was trying really hard not to cry.

"So where is she gonna stay, Mama?" asked Torey.

I thought that was a real good question. She couldn't stay with no one else in the family because they all claimed they couldn't afford to take another person in. I thought that was real messed up, that they wouldn't even take their own family in.

"Well, I asked everybody if they can help out. Of course, no one in the family can. And Pam, she flat out said Safot can't come back there. So the only choice I have is to put you in a group home, Safot."

Safot still had nothing to say. She just kept about her work as usual.

"Did you hear me, Safot? I am going to have to put you in a group home."

"Yes, I heard. Now, can I please be alone?"

Mama walked over to her, gave her a big hug, and said, "Everything is going to be all right, girl. Besides, you can always come and visit us. It's not like you going away for good."

Safot managed a fake smile and nodded her head in agreement. After that, we left Safot all alone like she had asked us to do.

Torey and Darrell ran back outside to play, and Mama went down the street to finish taking care of the final details with the housing office. But me, I tip-toed next to the door to hear what Safot was doing in that room all alone. I held my ear up against that bedroom door, and I heard her in there crying out. She was crying like she had been holding that cry in for a long, long time. I walked away from that door feeling the worst I had ever felt in my life. Poor Safot had nowhere to go, and no one seemed to care.

The following week I was hanging out of the living room window and saw a white woman walking up towards the house. It was the social worker coming to take Safot to that group home Mama was talking about. She didn't even have to knock on the door, because by the time she walked up the stairs I already had the door open.

"Mama, the social worker is here!" I shouted to Mama, who was in the back room helping Safot pack up the rest of her clothes.

"How are you?" she asked.

"Not all that good," I said and closed the door behind her.

She looked around the room, then asked, "And why is that, young man?"

"Because Safot has to go away, that's why."

"Ya'll are pretty close, huh?"

"Yeah, you can say that."

"Well let me assure you that Florence is going to be taken good care of in the place where she is going. She won't have to want for anything. And she can always come and visit ya'll on weekends. So, it won't be bad as you think."

I smiled after hearing that Safot was going to a good place. At first, I had all kinds of thoughts running through my head. I imagined Safot going to this old beat up house with a wicked step-mom from hell, who would treat her worse than Pam treated her—if that is possible.

A few minutes later, Mama and Safot joined us.

"Hi, and you must be Ms. Webb?"

Mama extended her hand and said, "That's right, and you must be Mrs. Walker, right?"

"That's right. And this must be Florence."

Safot managed a fake smile and grabbed ahold of her suitcase that was in Mama's hand.

"Well, we better get going. It was nice meeting you, Ms. Webb."

As they were leaving, Mama shouted for Torey and Darrell to come out of the back room and say goodbye. Darrell ran up and gave Safot a hug first, then Torey did the same.

"Well, aren't you going to give me a hug, Cheekie?"

I walked over, gave her a hug, and said, "Take care. Come and visit us soon."

Safot didn't answer, just managed a weak smile. She picked her suitcase off the floor and walked out of the door. She was halfway out the door when she turned around and smiled.

"Don't worry. I'll be back. You'll see. I'll be back."

The way she said it made me feel that in spite of everything, Safot was going to be all right after all.

making the grades

A "shotgun" house, that is what we call our new home. Because you can see straight through from one end of the house to the other. This house is awesome, painted in pink and green with a living room, four bedrooms, kitchen, bathroom, and a huge back yard. I can't believe this is our new home. It all happened so fast, I still haven't gotten used to it, even after a year. It's so big!

Mama and L'il Howard's room is next to the living room. Then comes my room, L'il Faye's room, and Torey and Darrell's room. They share the room next to the kitchen. Mama found it real easy to fix this place up, thanks to her landlord, Ms. Myers. She sold Mama all the furniture for cheap. We have a new living room set, kitchen set, beds—you name it. A new home with new furniture. I'm so excited!

I love our new place so much that I find myself wanting to be at home all the time. I'm in the eighth grade, but I come straight home after school. I seldom play outside with the other kids. Torey and Darrell made new friends, but I just stay to myself. I am afraid to make friends because when I was little, other kids called me all sorts of names. I don't want to go through that all over again.

Staying inside all the time allows me to catch up on my school work. I spend a lot of time studying at the kitchen table. While Torey and Darrell are outside playing or hanging out on the corner with their friends, I'm inside doing my homework. I see education as a way out of poverty. Moving out of the project made me realize that life can get better. Now all I want to do is make something of my life. I don't know if it is our new home or our "new, improved" Mama, or both. As a result of my hard work, I've gone from a 2.5 grade-point average to a 3.5. In fact, before I even realized it, I had the highest grade-point average in the eighth grade.

I found out the news of being at the top of my class one day after school. (I'm still attending Carver Middle School across the street from the Desire Project, because me, Torey, and Darrell were in the middle of a school year when we moved.) I was leaving my social studies class when my teacher, Ms. Stokes, called me.

"Charles, may I speak with you for a moment?"

I walked over to her desk, hung my book bag lightly on my shoulder, and asked, "Am I in trouble or something, Ms. Stokes?"

"No, Charles, it's nothing like that. In fact, it's good news."

"Good news?"

She sat down behind her desk. "Well, first let me say that I am very proud of you. You have excelled these past couple of months, and your grades show it. I have always believed that you could do it. Now, you do know that I am in charge of the awards program, right?"

I shook my head yes.

"And I am the one who selects the king and queen of the awards program, right?"

I started smiling right then, because I knew what she was about to say. I felt my heart pounding with anticipation.

"Well, Charles, because you achieved the highest grade-point average of all the boys this year, you are the king of the awards program."

I was so excited that I jumped up and down. Then I ran behind Ms. Stokes' desk and gave her a big kiss on the cheek.

"Man, I can't believe this!"

"Well, believe it, because it's true. You are the king and Olivia is the queen."

I got even more excited when she said Olivia was going to be queen. She is the most popular girl at Carver Middle, and all the boys want her. She is a soft caramel-brown, with full dark eyes, long hair, medium height, and a butt to write home about.

I left Ms. Stokes' classroom that day feeling very good about myself. For the first time in my life, I realized that I could do anything if I put my mind to it. When I got off the Desire bus that day, I ran home to tell Mama the news. I couldn't wait to see the expression on her face when she heard I was the smartest boy in the whole school.

As I ran up towards the house, I saw Mama standing on the porch talking to Howard. That surprised me because ever since Mama threw him out that night, I hadn't seen much of him. He stops by to see L'il Howard on occasion, but he never stays long. Seeing him and Mama talking made me wonder if they were getting back together. But as I walked up even closer, I realized that Howard was begging Mama to take him back, *again*.

"Come on Faye, give me another chance. I've really gotten myself together since you put me out. I'm working real hard, and even got myself back into church. So, you see, I know things can work out if you just give us a chance, baby."

Mama got up off the porch and said, "Look Howard, I am happy that you have God in your life. I think more black men need to find themselves in church. But that does not change nothin' between me and you. Besides, I am too busy focusing on myself to be getting involved with a man all over again."

Howard shook his head in disbelief when Mama said she was too busy for him. "Busy doing what?"

Mama smiled, "I'm back in school. You see, not only am I getting a GED, but also an associate degree in computer systems."

Howard shook his head as if to say, "Well, you go on then."

"I'm getting myself together and focusing on being a better mother. I made too many mistakes when I was young. But I'm not young anymore, and I have to put my children's needs first. They need a mother that they can look up to, and that's the kind of mother I am determined to be. You see, I gave men control of my life, and they almost destroyed me. But no more. I'm in control, and that's the way it's gonna stay."

Their backs were turned to me, so they didn't even realize I was there listening to the whole conversation.

"Hi, Ma. I'm home," I said, dryly.

Mama turned around and gave me a real big hug.

"Cheekie! How was your day in school?"

"You won't believe what happened today, Ma."

"What?"

"I found out from my social studies teacher that I have the highest GPA in the eighth grade class, and they are going to crown me king of the awards program."

Mama grabbed me real tight, squeezed my shoulders, kissed my chin, and spun me around. "I am so proud of you. I knew you were going to make something of yourself. You see, Howard, I told you that my son is going places."

"Congratulations, man. I'm proud of you, too."

"Thanks," I said in a real cold undertone. I didn't even acknowledge his presence the whole time I was standing there. In fact, my back was facing him, and I didn't look him in the face. I just turned, walked inside and headed straight for the kitchen. I found L'il Faye eating leftover red beans and rice.

"Hi, Cheekie. You want some beans?"

"Nope. I think I'll have me some Apple Jacks, instead."

"You gonna eat corn flakes for dinner?" she asked, squinting her li'l Chinese-like eyes.

I sat across from her and attacked that bowl of Apple Jacks. I may have changed a whole lot since we moved, but I still eat too fast and I still love Apple Jacks.

"Where's Torey n'em?" I asked.

"Down the street at Schwegmann's helping people carry their groceries," Mama answered.

That's their after-school job. It keeps them out of trouble and they make a little pocket change, too.

"My son, the scholar. I knew you were the gifted one." Mama smiled, proudly. She stood over me rubbing the top of my head. Then she gave me another kiss on the cheek.

That's what Mama thinks of me now—I'm gifted. I

don't think I'm gifted. My grades are good because I study hard. I want to make something out of myself. But when a poor black child from the ghetto does well in school, people say he's gifted.

Anyway, I went to bed thinking about that awards program. As I lay there, staring out into the darkness, I screamed with joy deep down inside myself. I had never felt so good before. I slept peacefully all night long.

The following morning I pulled myself out of bed and found Mama sitting in the kitchen reading her textbook. Mama is so determined to keep her promise to herself. No matter how long it takes, she is going to obtain her G.E.D. I feel so proud to see the change in Mama.

"So, you finally up?" she asked, sipping on a cup of coffee.

I went into my regular morning routine. I grabbed a bowl out of the cabinet, poured me some Apple Jacks, and pulled a chair up to the table.

"Cat got your tongue this morning?"

I still didn't have much to say, just shook my head.

"Well that's good to hear. You know I called and told Annie Mae'nem the news."

"Yeah. What they say?"

"They so proud of you. Everybody is coming over here after the awards program."

Mama must have seen the puzzled look on my face, because she interrupted, "That's right, I have already planned a party afterwards. I feel like celebrating."

"So where Torey'nem?" I asked, crunching on a mouth full of Apple Jacks.

"Child you know their Saturday routine. They already down at Schwegman's."

"Where Li'l Faye and Howard?"

"Li'l Faye watching TV in the front room, and Li'l Howard's dad picked him up early this morning while ya'll were still asleep. Anyway, I haven't told you the best part about who's coming to the awards party."

"Who?"

"Well, I got an unexpected call from someone we haven't heard from in a while," she said with a funny smirk on her face.

"Who, Ma?"

"Safot called me and said she'll be coming to the party."

I couldn't believe it. I knew I heard the words come out of Mama's mouth, but I still couldn't believe it was true. Finally, Safot was in touch with us again.

"So, what else did she say? Where has she been the past year? What is she doing with herself?" I asked so many questions at one time that Mama couldn't get a word in edgewise.

"Slow down here. She didn't give me much detail but she said she is doing fine. She was moved to a group home right outside of New Orleans in Metairie. I even spoke to the social worker. She say Safot is making remarkable progress. The changes in her are extraordinary. That's all she said. So I guess we'll have to see for ourselves."

"Wow, I can't wait to see her. I'm glad to hear she's been doing fine."

"Me too, son." Mama squeezed hold my hand real tight. "It will be good to see my li'l sister again. In fact it will be good to see all my sisters and brothers again. We haven't had a family get-together in a while. By the way, I need you to go over Pam's house today and take her this fifty dollars I borrowed from her last week. And while you there, tell her all about the party."

"OK, Ma. But where you going to?"

"I have to run a few errands."

"Where to?"

"It's a surprise. You'll have to wait until tomorrow."

"A surprise?"

"Yeah, that's what I said. Now hurry up and get dressed. You know I don't like ya'll staying back there in that project too late."

Mama rushed out in a hurry, like she always do. She been doing this routine for weeks now—getting all dressed up and sneaking away. It's almost like she done met another man. I'm thinking, I hope not. That's the last thing we need to spoil all this good news. But as I got dressed, I thought, "I guess I'll just have to wait and see tomorrow."

Soon as the Desire bus pulled up to my stop, I jumped off and saw legs and thighs that I hadn't seen in a real long time. They just strutting and walking, just like I remembered. That could only be Ms. Saphena coming through. The men whistled, and cars came to a complete stop. I've never seen anyone stop traffic before. Ms. Saphena not paying them no mind. And boy those men sure have a mouthful to say.

"Girl, you so fine you can catch a fish without a rod," one man said.

"Oh, baby, you so hot you sizzle," another man shouted.

Ms. Saphena just kept on stepping. She dressed in her

usual way, big heels, short dress, and a wig that takes up her whole head and some. She walked by with her head so high in the air, she didn't even see me. I thought about calling out for her, but I was so caught up in all the whistles and hand claps that before I knew it Ms. Saphena stepped right out of sight. She entered a place I been curious about before—Maze Nightclub. It sits diagonal from the Desire bus stop, and right across the street from Busy B Sweet Shop (formerly known as Fletcher's; the place Mama and Daddy first met). It's a small juke-joint, with a big sign on front that's in bright red colors that spells out the word MAZE. For a minute I thought about following Ms. Saphena inside the club to see for myself what she doing in a place like Maze that early in the day. But instead I got an even better idea. I decided to run all the way to Pam's house to get my Uncle Boo Boo to come with me. I knew he would be game to go and see.

I crossed that train track right across the canal that leads to the other side of the project. I hold my nose and walk real slow every time I cross that bridge. I hold my nose because the water in that canal smells like pee and poo all rolled up in one. It's been that way for years. No one comes to clean it out. And I walk real slow because it's an old wooden crosswalk that's leaning to one side. And the wood is all broken up and looking like any moment the whole thing gone collapse and send someone falling in that pile of shit. Not me, I'm thinking, there's no way in hell I'm falling in.

Soon as I crossed the bridge though, I took off running. I ran so fast that I ended up in front of Pam's house in no time. My Uncle Boo Boo and Daniel were playing catch football in the courtyard when I ran up.

"What's up Cheekie, man?" Boo Boo asked, sending the football flying in the air.

"Nothin' much. I came to bring Pam her money back Mama borrowed and to tell her about my party."

"It's your birthday already?" Daniel asked, throwing the ball back to Boo Boo.

"No. Mama giving me a party after my awards program, to celebrate."

"Yeah I heard about that. Keep up the good work man," Daniel responded, throwing the ball to a friend of his across the courtyard.

Boo Boo walked over and I immediately started to tell him about Ms. Saphena.

"Man, I saw this lady who used to live downstairs from us going into Maze. I want to know if you want to go check it out."

"Now how we gone get in Maze Nightclub?" Boo Boo asked, puzzled.

"We can watch from the window. I just want to see."

"Man I can get in trouble for taking my li'l nephew over to some nightclub. Let me think about it for a minute. I'm gone run across the street to Bynum's to play Packman and then we'll see."

As he walked off I thought to myself, "Man he only two years older than me, and he thinking he really said somethin'. If anything we both gone get in trouble for peeping in at Maze."

I continued upstairs and knocked on Pam's door.
"Whozzit?"
"Cheekie," I mumbled real low.
"Who?"

"Cheekie," I yelled.

"Child you better open your mouth if you want to get in my house. You know I don't open my door for anyone," Pam said, letting me in. She meant it too. She don't open that door too lightly. She been that way ever since some man knocked on her door and when she opened he fell right in, dead. I mean he was bleeding, and had a gunshot in his back. The situation freaked Pam out so much that she real paranoid about opening her door for anyone, even family.

She let me in and she headed straight for her bedroom. I took my usual position in the chair next to her bed.

"How you doing Pam?"

"Oh, I making out, Charles."

Pam recently started calling me Charles instead of Cheekie. She say I am getting too old for that nickname. I'm a young man now, and it's time to do away with that childish stuff. I guess she has a say in the matter since she is the one who named me Cheekie in the first place.

"I just come to give you that money back Mama borrowed from you."

Pam leaned over her bed, took the stack of rolled up tens, and put that money right between her titties. She spit some tobacco out and said, "Good, 'cause I can sure use the extra money. You know I'm saving up to move out of this place soon."

"Really!" My face gleamed with excitement.

"That's right. I come into a li'l money from my accident years ago. And now I think I'm gone move out of here. Been back here too long anyway."

Pam hushed me and got real quiet. She was in the middle of her favorite soap, *The Young and the Restless*.

"Child, Ms. Chancellor and that witch Gail done had a fight. It just happened right before you came in."

I was disappointed, because I like nothing more than to see two classy women rolling all over fighting.

"But anyway, I guess we'll have to wait until tomorrow for the rest." Pam turned the volume down and sat back down on the bed. "So what else is going on with you?"

"Nothin' much. Oh I forgot to tell you. Mama having a party after my awards program and she wants you to come."

"Oh Charles, that's great! Grandma real proud of you sugar, real proud. You see you get your smarts from this side of the family," she chuckled.

I chuckled, too.

"It's true, honey. 'Cause you see I ain't no dumb woman. That's right, I went to high school, and college. Became a nurse assistant and worked in a hospital, until I slipped down and had an accident. But, child, I'm going on and on. Would you like something to eat?"

"No ma'am."

"So you ready for the big day?"

"Yeah. Everybody is going to be there."

"Your daddy too?"

I felt a real uneasiness when she mentioned my daddy. I think Pam knew that because she sort of waited on my response.

"I don't think so. We haven't heard from'im in a while. My Grandma Emelia say he called and asked about us, but that's all."

"Child, that's a shame. Charles is such a good man. If only Faye wasn't so young."

It was strange hearing Pam say that my daddy was a

good man, being that she hated him from the very first day she laid eyes on him.

She continued, "I should have realized that from the beginning, that Charles was good for your Mama. But you know your Mama was too busy running the streets with that gal by the name of Li'l Soul. You know she the reason why your daddy and mama broke up in the first place. But don't let me start talking about that poor girl, because I heard she locked up in some crazy house."

Pam reached over and knocked her fist up against the dresser. By knocking on wood, she was wishing nothing like that ever happened to her. Me, I just felt really strange hearing Li'l Soul's name after all this time. Mama never talks about her anymore.

Then I gazed out the window, saw the sun going down, and rose to my feet.

"Well, I better get going, Pam. I have to get home before it gets too late."

"OK then, Charles. Thanks for stopping by, and congratulations on all your success. You must know that Grandma is very proud of you." She grabbed hold my face and gave me a big kiss on the cheek.

"Thanks, Pam. I'll see you on next week."

"I'll be there with bells on, honey. Now before you go, I want to know if ya'll heard from Safot."

"Yeah. Mama say she called yesterday. She coming to my party, too."

"Is that right?" Pam paused for a moment. "Well that's nice."

"You still coming, right?"

"Sure I am. You know I ain't scared to come around no

one. I'm a bold woman you know, and it ain't too much I can't handle," chuckled Pam. "Oh, I'm going to be there all right. I just wanted to know, that's all. Now you take care and be careful out there walking these streets."

I thought as I walked downstairs, "I can't wait to see Pam and Safot in the same room after all this time."

Me and Boo Boo made our way down to Maze right after dusk. Folks started arriving about the same time we got there. They coming from the Florida, St. Bernard, Lafeet—they come from just about every project in New Orleans. Men and women, but mostly men dressed to kill. The music inside jumping, and folks shaking and moving all over the place. I mean they cutting the floor inside that place. I can still hear the song that was playing because it made me laugh so much and think about my birthday party when Annie Mae was doing the bump with us.

"Shake your booty, shake, shake, shake your booty. Yeah, shake your booty."

And boy they sure were shaking booties all over Maze. Me and Boo Boo peeped in from a side window in the alley.

"Man, let's go! That lady you talking 'bout ain't nowhere in sight." Boo Boo jumped up and started to walk away.

I grabbed hold his arm. About that time the music stopped and a man walked up on stage.

We both kneeled down again and listened as the crowd started to cheer. A tall, dark man—had to be over six feet—with a huge Afro was speaking.

"How everybody doing out there tonight?"

Noise and applause and screams came from the crowd.

"That's great. And ladies if you feeling real good, let me hear you say 'hell yeah.'"

"HELL YEAH!" they shouted.

"My, my, my, we got some ladies in the house tonight. Well unfortunately, ladies tonight we got somethin' special just for the fellows. Fellows if you in the house let me hear some barking."

It sounded like a dog pound in there.

"OK. Well get ready fellows 'cause we got that sassy, vivacious lady in the house. Put your hands together for MISS SAPHENA!"

My eyes got real wide. So did Boo Boo's. Then Miss Saphena came from the back wearing almost nothing. She got on red leather boots that came up to her knees, tight-fitted red shorts that sent both her butt cheeks hanging out, and a top that pushed her titties out, smacked dead center.

She made her way to front stage, amidst the barking, and shouting, and screaming from the excited crowd. That's when it really got interesting!

To the sounds of the song "Brick House," Miss Saphena moved around from side to side, shaking this and shaking that, going all down to the floor, taunting and teasing, doing just about everything I never imagined Ms. Saphena could do. And before we knew it, Ms. Saphena was wearing nothing but those red cowgirl boots. By the time we were thrown out of the alley by two bouncers, she was about to ride her way out of those boots as well.

Needless to say, as the Desire bus turned the corner leaving behind the shadow of Maze nightclub, I was completely out of my mind over what me and Boo Boo had just witnessed. And to tell the truth, I don't remember which way my *thing* was pointing—north or south. All I know was that after all these years, the mystery surrounding Miss Saphena was finally solved. She was the hottest act around town.

amaZing grace

With each passing day I thank God for how much things done surely changed. I'm talking about the way Mama has moved on with her life. For the first time since I can remember, Mama is really getting herself together and not relying on men for nothing. I admire her for trying to make things better for us. Finally she is gaining control of her life, and she's doing it all on her own. Mama has always felt like she needed a man around. I think that's why she let all those men move in with us over the years.

The reason I'm thinking about all of this is because it was just yesterday when Li'l Faye and me had the strangest conversation. She made me remember a nightmare that I tried to forget.

After playing a game of Atari, Li'l Faye came in my room and sat next to me. Her li'l Chinese eyes glowed behind her girlish dimples. She is the cutest sister in the whole world. But on this particular day, my li'l sister wanted answers.

"Cheekie?"

"What?" I asked with my eyes glued to the TV set.

"What was my daddy like?"

I turned towards her in shock. Her daddy, Richard, is a subject we never mention in our house. Mama forbids us from even using the name, Richard. But he is Li'l Faye's daddy, and it's no surprise that she wants to know something about 'im.

I tried to explain the situation the best I could. "Well, your daddy loved you very much. In fact, he would do just about anything to make sure no one stood between you and him."

"Really!" she gleamed with excitement over the idea that her daddy loved her that much. I thought that was the best answer I could give her, because when I thought back to that night Richard kidnaped her, I knew I was correct in saying he would do just about anything.

"So my daddy really loved me?"

"That's right."

"Then why don't Mama talk about 'im?"

"Well, maybe Richard's death was hard on her, and she just wants to forget about it. Maybe it's too painful for her to talk about."

"Who are ya'll talking about in my house?" asked Mama, walking into the room. Mama must have heard me say the name Richard because smoke was coming from her ears as her whole face turned red. Mama was mad!

"Nothin' ma, we just talking about the good ole days," my voice trembled in fear.

"Faye, go outside and play with Howard," Mama demanded, with one hand on her hip and the other pointing towards the door.

"Why, Ma?" whined Li'l Faye.

"Because I said so, that's why. Now go!"

Li'l Faye hung her head in confusion over Mama's sudden outburst and dragged her feet out of the room. She knew Mama was mad about something, but not in a million years she would have guessed it was over her very own daddy.

Mama turned towards me and asked, "Why are you discussing that man in this house, Cheekie?"

"I had to say something, Ma. She was the one who asked me about her daddy."

"So what did you tell her?"

"Relax, Ma, I only told her that Richard loved her very much. I didn't even go into all that other stuff."

Mama was relieved to hear that I didn't say much. She walked over to the dresser and sat down.

"So what ya'll been doing today?"

"Nothin' much, just watching TV. I can't wait until my awards program."

"I bet you can't. Have I told you how proud I am?"

"Yeah, Ma. You say it all the time."

"I know I do, but I'm your mother and I'm going to always be proud of you. Oh, I almost forgot—your school principal called me yesterday when you were over Pam's house."

"What he want?" I asked, half frightened.

"He wants to stop by later on today and talk to us about a scholarship for you to attend St. Augustine Catholic High School. I hear it's an all-male school where some of the brightest boys in the city attend."

Even though that was good news, I didn't know how to receive it. For one, I never really thought about leaving all my friends from the Desire Project to attend a new school with strangers. Secondly, I always thought I'd attend Carver Senior High, which is right next to Carver Middle.

Anyway, Mama was real excited about Mr. Freeman's scholarship offer. Me, I wasn't all that sure.

"Ma, why didn't you tell me he was coming today?"

"Because it slipped my mind. You know I'm planning this party and I been__"

Mama stopped dead right in the middle of her sentence. It was like she almost slipped and said something she didn't want me know about.

"What Ma? What were you about to say?"

"Nothin'."

The expression on my face showed I wasn't convinced.

"OK. It's that surprise I was telling you about. But you'll see later on today. For now we have to get this house together because Mr. Freeman will be here shortly."

Mama had us running around that house like worker ants getting everything together. We cleaned the bathroom, the living room, bedrooms, we mopped, and swept, and dusted until we must have gotten every inch of dirt. She even ordered Torey n'em to be on their best behavior. Mama knows that St. Augustine is a really good school and thinks this is the chance of a lifetime for me.

When Mr. Freeman finally arrived, Mama had everything in order, too. But before opening the door, she tugged at her skirt, pushed her titties up a slight, pulled her hair back, and checked the mirror one more time.

"Hi, Mr. Freeman. Come right in and have a seat."

"Thank you, Ms. Webb. I'd like that very much."

Mr. Freeman sat across from me and asked, "How are you making out, Charles?"

"Fine sir, and yourself?"

"Oh, just trying to keep cool. This is our hottest month yet."

"Isn't that for true? Well, then, can I get you something to drink, sir?" asked Mama, holding her hands together. All of a sudden Mama was acting like Dianne Carroll from "Dynasty." She was very lady-like and pronounced every word with confidence. I thought it was funny seeing Mama like this.

"No thanks. I'm fine, ma'am," Mr Freeman responded, taking a long look around the room. He didn't have much to see, either. Besides our two-piece furniture set and a clock on the wall, there wasn't much to look at.

Mr. Freeman was finally about to get to his reason for visiting us when we heard Torey and Darrell fighting in the other room. Mama managed a fake smile and said, "Excuse me for a moment, Mr. Freeman."

Boy I could tell Mama was mad. She went through so much to make the evening just perfect, and now Torey n'em were ruining everything.

I heard Mama whisper from the back room, "Look, are ya'll out of your minds? We are having a very important meeting out there. Now take this shit outside. Go ahead, get out!"

"Man you act like God done come or somethin," responded Torey. He has been annoyed by how Mama has been making over me these past couple of weeks. I think he gets really jealous when he hears Mama say, "Ya'll should be more like your big brother and stop hanging out in them streets all the time."

As I listened to Mama arguing back and forth with

Torey in the back room, I began to wonder why my brothers are so different from me. I mean, we all grew up in the same household, shared the same experiences. But still we are different in so many ways. I am striving for excellence, staying out of trouble, and avoiding situations that cause Mama much worry.

The two of them, on the other hand, always seem to find trouble. They can't see beyond their present situation. They don't embrace the future like I do. It's almost as if they don't think that they are supposed to have a future. Why are they so different? Maybe it's just harder for some kids to overcome growing up in a violent home. Maybe it's the violence and hopelessness in the community. Or maybe not having Daddy around or a real strong male role model to lean on drove them to the street in the first place. Or maybe I am different because I found strength through the eyes of others, like my Grandma Rose, Emelia, Ms. Everlyn and my many teachers at Carver Middle who believe in me. They convinced me that I can have a better life if I want it and work hard to get it. The fact that I am poor and once lived in the worst project in New Orleans doesn't mean that I have to die that way. Pam taught me that through faith in God, I could make something out my life. My grandmamas gave me values that I hold on to.

Torey and Darrell must have gotten their values from somewhere else, because our lives seem at times to be taking completely different paths.

Mama spent almost five minutes trying to explain to Torey why Mr. Freeman's visit was so important. Of course he didn't want to hear of it, and stormed out of the house, mad.

Mama returned to the living room only to face another dilemma. As she entered, she noticed a roach crawling right across the living room wall. I mean that sucker was as big as day, and one of those kind that can fly. I thought to myself, "Those damn roaches always seem to come out when we have company over, never when no one is around."

Mama was still trying to hold that fake smile together, hoping that Mr. Freeman hadn't seen the roach crawling in front of us. I think he did, though, but after a li'l while it crawled right back wherever it came from.

Mama sat down, smiling. "I'm sorry, Mr. Freeman. You know how children can be."

"Yeah, I do know. I have two boys of my own."

Mr. Freeman and Mama spoke back and forth about the ins and outs of raising children. I just sat looking and listening. Mama did most of the talking.

After a while, Mama wanted to get to the real reason Mr. Freeman was visiting us in the first place.

"So getting back to the purpose of your visit, Mr. Freeman, I'm very curious to hear more about this opportunity you spoke about on the phone."

"Well, your son here, as you already know, has done exceptionally well this semester. We at Carver Middle are very proud of him. He scored really high on his CTBS scores and shows real promise of a rewarding future. Now, I know a priest at St. Augustine who wants to offer your son a scholarship."

"This is such good news, and I am sure my son is very interested in attending a school like that."

Mama walked over to where I was sitting, gently caressed my head as if I was a newborn infant or something.

"So what do you think about Mr. Freeman's offer, Cheekie?"

"Well, I guess it's a good offer, but I don't know if I want to attend another school."

Mama stopped caressing my head. Shocked. She really didn't expect me to respond like that.

"What? I can't believe you would say that after Mr. Freeman come way over here to give you this opportunity."

I sat thinking to myself, "Man, she wants this scholarship offer more than me." But of course, I kept my mouth shut and allowed Mama to go on and on about how great of an offer it was.

"Cheekie, don't you know this is a good school? Carver can't begin to prepare you for college like this school can. Besides, it's getting bad at Carver, and I have gone through too much and come too far to let you stay in a place like that."

Thank God Mr. Freeman spoke up on my behalf, because Mama was getting very emotional.

"Ms. Webb, I understand Charles not wanting to leave his friends and all. But son, I think you should take this summer to really think this offer over. Let me tell you why. First of all, Carver Senior is not a bad school, but I think you can really challenge yourself if you go to a school like St. Augustine. Besides, Carver is fighting problems like drugs, lack of equipment, and overcrowding. So, like I said, think it over and let us know at the end of the summer, OK?"

I nodded my head in agreement. Mama rolled her eyes in disbelief.

"Thank you, Mr. Freeman, for coming. I promise you

that we will be getting back to you, so don't give that scholarship away, OK."

"Oh, of course we won't do that, Ms. Webb," he said, heading for the front door. "Charles is a good student, and no matter what he decides he's going far in life."

"Thanks again. Take care and we'll be in touch." Mama closed the door and shook her head from side to side. "I can't believe you turned down an offer like that."

"Ma . . ."

"Don't Ma me. We can finish this discussion later, but for now get some clothes on because we have an errand to run."

"Where to?"

"That surprise I mentioned."

I was in my room almost before she could finish the statement. I could hardly wait to find out where Mama been sneaking off to just about every other day.

Where are we going, Mama?" I asked, as we sat in the back of a yellow cab driving to God knows where.

"You'll see. You'll see real soon," she said, smiling and having fun at my obvious impatience. After twenty minutes, my patience was running out. Finally the car stopped.

"This is it, ma'am," the cab driver said, turning around to collect his five dollars and thirty-two cents that flashed on the meter. I looked around and noticed we were in front of Delgado's Rehabilitation Center.

"A rehabilitation center? Why did she bring me here?" I thought.

"Who's in here Mama? But more importantly, why in the world are we here?"

"Be patient. You'll see in a minute."

We exited the cab and took the elevator straight to the fourth floor. Mama obviously had been to this place before, because she knew exactly where she was going. She walked right over to room 432, peeped in on someone, and asked, "Are you dressed in here, because I have a surprise."

The voice behind the door said, "Yeah, come in, girl."

It was a voice I had heard somewhere before, but it had been so long since I had heard it. That was why when I walked into that hospital room and saw who was sitting there in that bed, I could have fallen over in joy.

"Oh my God, it's Li'l Soul!" I shouted in excitement running over to the bed hugging and rocking her from side to side.

"It's me all right, in the flesh. What you see is what you get and you ain't seen the best of me yet," she said, pushing her hair under and being her usual sassy self.

I couldn't believe how well she looked, especially when I think back to the last time I saw her, rocking in a chair, staring out into space.

She is still pretty, too. Her hair is cut just a little short-er, shoulder length, her eyes still fiery. Li'l Soul is definitely back and it shows all over her face.

"So this is where you been sneaking off to everyday, Ma?"

"That's right. I've been visiting my old girl friend."

"Watch your mouth, girl. I ain't that old, just a little overdue if you know what I mean, but not old," she laughed. I just stood in amazement as she and Mama made fun.

"What's wrong, Cheekie? You act like you done seen a ghost or somethin'."

"I'm fine. Just happy to see you, that's all."

"I'm happy to see you, too. Look at how fine our little Cheekie growing up to be," she said, looking me all over.

"Isn't he handsome, Li'l Soul?" Mama added.

"Yeah, girl, that he is. You know back in my day, he would have been mine."

They both laughed some more. I hadn't seen Mama that happy in a long time. I think she is happier than she has ever been, having her best friend back.

While they were laughing and talking about the good old days, a tall, dark, six-feet, four-inch, black man walked into the room.

"Here's your water, baby," he said, sitting down beside Li'l Soul.

"Thanks, sweetheart," she said, kissing him on the lips.

I wondered who he was and how she had the time to find herself a man in the condition she was in.

"Oh, child, I'm being rude. Fred, this is Faye's son, Cheekie."

Fred reached over and shook my hand real aggressively and asked, "How you doing, son?"

"Fine."

"Me and your dad used to hang out back in the day. I'm the one who introduced your mama and daddy back when they were young and in love. I've heard all about you from your uncle Randy. You know we kick it sometimes together," he said, nodding his head.

Li'l Soul interrupted him, "Cheekie, Li'l Soul is really proud of you, Sugar, and I'm so glad your Mama brought you by to see me. 'Cause I want to thank you."

"Thank me?" I asked, puzzled. "For what?"

Her eyes got real watery, and before long she was almost in tears.

"Thank you for coming to see me that day at my Mama's house. I sensed you were there and that ceramic bird you gave me, I cherish it with all my heart. And it reminds me of the phoenix bird flying high. Just like it, I crashed and burned, but now I'm soaring, honey."

Everyone laughed.

I looked over on the dresser and saw that bird sitting there. I couldn't believe she still has it after all this time. I felt real good, and my heart had never known such joy as the day I saw Li'l Soul in that hospital.

"So how are you doing now? I mean, are you better?"

"Oh, I'm doing just fine, and looking forward to getting out of this place and moving in with my future husband."

"Your future husband?" Mama asked, stunned.

"That's right. Me and Fred here are going to the chapel, honey, and we gonna get married," Li'l Soul sung the tune.

"Girl, it's about time. Ya'll been going together off and on for years now. Shit, ya'll were together when me and Charles met."

I thought that was something special that Li'l Soul was marrying her childhood sweetheart.

"I miss your singing. Do you still sing?" I asked.

"Well, actually I haven't sung in a while. But I'm sure it's still there. Shit, why don't I give ya'll a li'l bit of soul. Something ya'll haven't heard from me before. Since I heard you all into church now, this is especially for you, Cheekie. Amazing Grace, 'cause if it wasn't for God's grace, Honey, I don't know where I'd be."

She hummed a tune and then she started singing out loud

right there in the hospital room. The rhythm of soul ran deep in her veins as she poured out the lyrics of the old gospel spiritual, "Amazing Grace." Li'l Soul sang like never before.

> Amazing Grace, how sweet the sound,
> That saved a wretch like me.
> I once was lost, but now I'm found,
> Was blind, but now I see.

When she finished, we applauded. She can still sing and has that golden voice that dazzles the hearts of everyone who has ever heard her sing.

"So, what did you think?"

"Well, you still got it, Soul," I said, making everyone laugh.

She then leaned over and kissed Fred on the lips and said, "And the next time you hear me sing is going to be at our wedding. Yeah, baby, that was for you, and the best is yet to come."

"All right now, don't start no shit you can't finish," he said tapping the side of her leg.

Me and Mama stood in near tears watching the two of them making over each other. It was the best feeling in the world, seeing how Li'l Soul turned her life around.

"Well, girl, we gonna get going and leave you two love birds alone," said Mama, as the two hugged, tightly.

"OK, Faye. Cheekie, congratulations on your recent accomplishments. Your Mama told me how good you doing in school boy. Keep it up because ain't nothin' out here in these streets child, but trouble. Take it from me, I learned the hard way."

I nodded my head as she stared into my eyes. I had never seen Li'l Soul so serious about anything before. She meant every word she had spoken.

"Yeah, li'l man keep it up. So you can make somethin' out your life and take care of your mama here," Fred added.

"OK girl, we outa here," Mama headed for the door.

"Ya'll be sure to keep in touch now, Faye."

"Of course we will. You are my best friend, child. Even though you always kept me in a heap of trouble, you are still my girl." She and Mama both laughed.

We left her and Fred there in the room making out some more. I thought as we drove home, "Some things just never change no matter what. Li'l Soul can still sing and she is just as sassy as ever."

first born

"Cheekie, hurry your butt up in there!" Mama shouted from her bedroom. I had been in the bathroom for almost two hours. Mainly, I was just sitting in the tub dreaming about the day ahead. I was being crowned king of my school's annual awards program, and the fact that my entire family was coming to celebrate the occasion was exciting! We hadn't been together like this in a long time.

Finally, I dragged myself out of the tub, dried off, and tied a towel around my sleek, frail body.

When I opened the bathroom door, I was suddenly engulfed by the smells of good, down-home New Orleans cooking. Mama had spent the whole night preparing food for the party. And boy she really put her foot in it this time around! I just held myself underneath the festive aroma of greens, pigtails, cornbread, macaroni and cheese, potato salad, not to mention Mama's original sweet potato pies. The scent lingered throughout the house, as I exited the kitchen and found Mama in her bedroom press—combing Li'l Faye's hair.

"It's 'bout time you came out of that bathroom; you know we already running late," Mama said, running the comb back and forth through Li'l Faye's hair as she sat uncomfortably between Mama's legs.

"Girl, keep still before I burn you!" Mama shouted, jerking and pulling Li'l Faye's head. "I'm almost finished."

"But it hurts shu," Li'l Faye whined, squinting her eyes.

I stood in the doorway of the bedroom laughing at the two of them. Neither of them was having fun, but I sure was. It's a scene that I'm very familiar with, though. Mama loves to have Li'l Faye's hair looking its best. But it was all worth it in the end because Mama pressed her hair so good that every nap was straight as a nail. My sister's hair was looking like Shirley Temple's. And as soon as Mama finished, Li'l Faye jumped up off the floor and ran to the other room. She was glad to get away from that hot comb. Her running away like that was so funny, Mama and I both laughed.

"I know what she was going through, because when I was little I used to hate when Pam press-combed my hair. She would leave all sorts of burn marks on the back of my neck," Mama smiled, putting that hot comb through her own hair. "But anyway hurry up and put your suit on. It's lying across the sofa in there. And I need to get dress myself."

Mama sat in front the mirror curling hair, putting lip stick on, and pulling at every part of her body. I slipped in my outfit very easily. Mama rented me a black tuxedo, black shoes, and a bow tie that took up my whole neck and some.

"Cheekie, come in here and let me fix that tie," she shouted when she looked in the other room and saw me struggling with the tie.

She sat on the edge of the bed with one leg crossed over the other. I slid comfortably beside her as she folded and then refolded my tie.

"Child, I always have trouble tying these things. It's times like this when I think about your daddy. Just thinking how it would be easy for him to be doing this kind of stuff."

I felt a nerve jerk through me at the mention of the word "daddy." It was the same feeling I got when Pam mentioned his name. But the fact that Mama was talking about him was even stranger. She rarely ever mentions his name. Pam once said that my daddy was Mama's first love, and no one forgets their first love.

"Ma, you talk to my daddy at all, lately?" I asked, just to see where Mama's head was at concerning my daddy.

"Child the last time I heard, your daddy was seeing some woman over on St. Rock Street. And I even hear he has two li'l boys at that."

"Who told you that?"

"Selena when I called to invite her to the party. She say she was going to tell your daddy to come to the party, too. But you know I wouldn't hold my breath that he'll show up." Mama unfolded the tie for the umpteenth time.

"How you feel about your daddy coming to your party, anyway?"

I hadn't really thought about my daddy lately. I mean I thought about'em from time to time. But never really search my inner thoughts for how I feel. Mama's question struck me like a sharp needle. Instead of giving a verbal answer, I shrugged my shoulders as if to say, "I don't know."

Mama finally got the tie the way she wanted it to be. She called out to make sure Torey and Darrell were getting dressed in the other room and L'il Faye, who was already dressed, was staying out of trouble. Li'l Howard was over his daddy's house, so she didn't have to worry about the routine of dressing an infant. Which was good given the fact that it seemed like it was taking forever for us to pull ourselves together. But then again it was probably me and my anticipation, that time seemed to be moving in slow motion that day.

Anyway, as Mama got herself together I sat on the edge of the bed, watching. She sat in a chair in front the mirror applying the last touches of makeup to her face. She spoke to my reflection in the mirror.

"You know I am so proud of you Cheekie. No, I really mean it. You are the kind of kid that makes a mother proud. Getting a good education is so important. I just wish your brothers in there would let what you got rub off on them. But it's so funny, because when you were born I knew there was going to be somethin' special about you, boy." She gleamed, rubbing her lips together so that the lipstick would smooth out evenly across her lips. She looked up and saw the confused expression across my face. I had no idea what she meant when she said I was special.

"Somethin' special?" I asked.

"That's right. You see there is an old saying in this neck of the woods that if your first born comes out of you smiling, then that child is born with a veil over his face."

"What?" I asked, even more puzzled.

"A veil over your face means that you were going to be somethin' in life. I mean somethin' really special. The doctor even said it when you were born. He say, 'Ms. Webb your son is just smiling; he's going to be famous one day.'"

I smiled, even though I had no faith in what Mama was saying. It was a good story, anyway.

"So how did Torey'nem come out?"

"Screaming, and crying, and raising hell." Mama slipped into her high heel pumps. "That should have told me what was ahead for me right away. But not you, Cheekie. Like I said you were smiling and just so happy. My first-born child, and I couldn't have been more happy. Anyway, we better get going before the program starts without us."

Mama shouted out for the rest of the troops, and without much more said we marched out of the house like a bunch of well-dressed soldiers. Mama was the leader, and I couldn't have been more pleased at that.

I must have imagined this moment in my mind many times before—walking down the aisles of a packed auditorium. I'm on one side of the auditorium, and Olivia is on the other side. We both are stepping in perfect sync with the piano melody as our peers, fellow teachers, and love ones stand on their feet screaming and shouting in overwhelming joy. But the great thing about this particular moment was that it was happening for real.

I couldn't have predicted the pride I would feel on awards day. I was a king—I mean the kind you see on TV or something. I had the crown, the long, curtain around my neck, and a sparkling wand that I waved around the whole place with confidence like a shooting star across the universe. This was a day that I would remember all my life. It's not everyday that someone can say that they were a king. And I know, unlike a royal dynasty where the crown can be worn for months or years, my title was only for a day. But it was that one moment that made me realize that my hard work, studying late nights had finally paid off.

Mama couldn't have been more proud, too, which was evident when I took my seat and glanced out at the cheery faces before me. There sat my entire family in the front row. My brothers, who I always get into fights with, my li'l sister, who asks me the most annoying questions, and yes, Mama. Her smile seemed to stand out far above the rest. Nothing is more heart-warming than a mother's tears of joy.

And the grand entrance was nothing, compared to the rest of the program. By the end of the ceremony, I had more awards and trophies than my hands could carry. I won first place for everything—math, science, English, and social studies! I had never gotten that much attention before in my life. It felt damn good, too.

"Come here sugar and give your auntie a kiss." We could barely squeeze our way in the front door as Annie Mae and the rest of Mama's sisters, brothers, cousins, nephews, and nieces congratulated me. Everyone was there!

"Child, look at our li'l Cheekie," Dorothy commented.

"I see all grown up and smart. Honey, he's gone be a doctor one day," Annie Mae added with one hand on her left hip.

"Well, let them through, Annie Mae, I'm sure they must be hungry," Bob said. He is Mama's oldest brother and rarely comes around anything the family ever gives. So, needless to say, I was surprised to see him.

"Child, you right about that. I am hungry and tied out. I was up all last night cooking and preparing this food." Mama said, walking towards the kitchen. Annie Mae followed.

Uncle Bob walked over, placed both hands firmly on my shoulders and said, "You see ya'll should take notice from li'l Cheekie here. A good education is important. Running round here behind these li'l gals and stuff ain't worth it in the long run."

"Boo Boo." Daniel laughed.

"Man shut up," Boo Boo reacted.

At that moment, Selena, Rachelle, and Tanya walked in the door.

"Hey everybody! I hear there's a party going on in here." Selena smiled.

"Selena? Girl come over here and give me a hug," Bob said. Mama once told me that a long time ago, Bob and Selena had a thing for each other. I could tell by the way they were hugging and kissing all over each other.

"Girl, look at you. Just as fine as the day I laid eyes on you." Bob smiled, spinning her all around.

"You still handsome yourself," Selena said, sassy as ever.

"And these must be your two darling daughters I hear so much about."

Rachelle and Tanya stood silent next to Auntie Selena like a pair of golden angels. But I knew in a li'l while they would be running, jumping and tearing the house down.

"Yeah, these my girls. You know I have two sons, too. But I left those bad ass niggers at home, child." Selena laughed. "But I had to come and congratulate my li'l nephew here."

Selena walked over and kissed me on the cheeks, and then slipped fifty dollars in my hand.

"Keep up the good work." She whispered in my ear.

"I will." I said, smiling all over the place. All the attention and money were steadily rolling in.

"OK, show me to the kitchen 'cause I is hungry." Selena chuckled and headed towards the back of the house.

The grown folks were out of sight as they retreated to the kitchen where Mama and her sisters were continually preparing supper. Us children on the other hand stayed in the living room playing games, watching TV, and clowning around like kids do when grown ups aren't around. But the entire scene was what made this day so special for me. The aroma of good food throughout the house, the laughing sounds of Mama and her brothers and sisters from the kitchen, li'l cousins running back and forth through the house, and good music playing on the stereo. I embraced all of this and took it in because I knew we didn't get together like this often. But with all the excitement, though, there was still one person missing. And as everyone got ready to prepare themselves to eat, we got the surprise of our life.

"Here comes Safot! Here comes Safot!" We heard the li'l kids shouting from the living room. Boy, we all jumped up from the table and ran to the front door. It didn't take long for everybody to gather in the doorway trying to get a good look. I was relieved, myself, because after a while I was beginning to think Safot wasn't coming to my party after all.

Anyway, a cab was parked in front the house. It was definitely a woman inside, but still hard to make out whether or not it was indeed Safot.

She stepped out of the car in a very graceful manner. At last, she stood up straight, and we could get a better look. She wore a loose-fitting casual dress, nice shoes, and a big white hat that hid her face.

Everyone stood silent. Shocked. Amazed. Safot was looking like a whole different person. "Wow! That's Safot?" I wondered, as she stood, then posed for a moment to give everybody a chance to get a real good look. Li'l Faye blurted out loud what I—and probably everybody else—was thinking, "Is that Safot?"

Safot reached down, lifted Li'l Faye's chin, and smiled, "Yeah, it's me all right."

That's when Mama ran out the door, started hugging, kissing and crying all over her. Then all hell broke loose as everybody else joined in.

"We miss you so much sister," Mama cried.

"Me too, girl." Safot said, handing her suitcase over to Bob. "It's only been a little under a year and I am so homesick. And hungry, child."

Everyone laughed. I think we were all filled with joy and amazement to see Safot looking so proud, happy, and beautiful. This is not Auntie Mama that we all knew and pitied. This is not who we expected to see. This is a totally different person. She is a bit taller, with longer hair. She is all smiles, too—not the timid, scared girl who was treated like a dog all her life.

"Girl, come in and take a seat. I know you must be tired out after that bus ride." Mama opened the door to let her in.

"You know I am. Tired and hungry." She stopped dead in her tracks when she caught a glimpse of me standing in the living room. "Boy, you better come over here and give me a kiss."

We must have rocked and hugged for an eternity, because Annie Mae said, "OK, ya'll, there some other folks who trying to get some of that too."

"I'm sorry girl, but I'm just so proud of my nephew here. He's one of the reasons why I came back."

"Look here, Safot, girl, look like you done put some meat on these bones," said Annie Mae.

All the sisters congregated around her to see. They found it real funny to see hips and titties on Safot. She was definitely beginning to fill out, as the grown ups put it.

"Shut up Annie Mae. You still the same—always noticing everything." Safot proceeded to the kitchen, and we followed. It was good seeing everybody, but now it was time to eat.

Mama sat at the head of the table. Everyone was treating Safot like a celebrity or something. But I guess that shows just how happy everyone was to see her. Or maybe Mama n'em were feeling sort of guilty about how they sat around for years and allowed Safot to suffer Pam's humiliation.

Finally, after having everyone fussing and making out over her, Safot removed the huge hat from her head. She used it as a fan, since it was hot as hell in that kitchen.

"Child, it sure is hot in here. But the food smell some good."

"You need a drink of water?" Mama asked.

Safot took a napkin out of her purse and ran it across her face, and then placed the hat on the table top.

"Will ya'll stop treating me like I'm from Mars or something. I'm still the same old Safot."

"We sorry girl, but it just that we haven't seen you in a long time. And to top things off you looking damn good." Annie Mae answered for everyone.

"I know I lookin' li'l different. But ya'll like the new look, right?" Safot asked, pushing her hair under with one hand and slightly bouncing up and down in the chair for effect.

"Girl, you look fabulous. You sure must be doing fine up there in that group home," said Dorothy.

"More than fine. It's been a real good experience. I have been so blessed this past year. The owners of the group home, Mr. and Mrs. Wilcox, are extremely nice to me. They kind of took a liking to me right away. Put me in a good school, got me an after-school job working in a hospital, which is good experience since I plan to go to nursing school. But most importantly, they helped me to love myself for the first time."

Everyone stood silent as Safot explained the transformation she had gone through over the past year. I was really caught up in this story like a tornado churning up the countryside.

"Li'l sista we all very, very happy you didn't let what you went through with Pam destroy you. We all know from personal experience the wrath of our mother, honey. It's no joke." Annie Mae said, shaking her head from side to side. In fact, all Pam's children stood in the amen corner on what Annie Mae had just confessed.

"By the way, how is mother dear?" Safot asked, dryly.

"Child, Pam is still the same. From what I could see she hasn't changed that much at all." Annie Mae answered.

"Not to change the subject, but, sis, I'm sure glad to see you, too. But right now, I just want to eat some of this good food here. It's all right if we eat, sista." Bob said, rubbing his hands together. Everybody was ready to eat.

"Sure. If everyone is ready, let's do this," Mama said, taking her seat. Everyone followed.

"Ma, can I say the grace?" I asked, pulling a chair up next to the table. I was so excited over Safot being home that I just had to thank God myself.

"Sure, go right ahead."

I closed my eyes, bowed my head, and spoke to God from the bottom of my heart. "Bless this food, and our family, Lord. And thank you, Lord, for watching over all of us. Thank you for Mama, for Safot, Lord. Keep us safe in your care, always. We thank you and bless us in the name of your son, Jesus . . ."

"Amen." A strong and familiar voice hung over us as I was completing my prayer.

"Pam! You came." I jumped up from the table, excitedly.

Now, Pam showing up in her Sunday's best was definitely an added surprise that made the whole evening even more interesting.

"Sure, I came. I said I would and I always keep my promise." She smiled, holding her hand underneath my chin. Then she reached in her purse and handed me a white envelope. "This here is for you and all your hard work. Just know that Grandma is real proud of you. You hear?"

I nodded my head. Pam has a way of demanding complete silence when she speaks, and everyone was quiet.

"Now don't let me stop ya'll dinner here. Just carry on like if I was not even here." She chuckled, but didn't mean one word she said.

Bob offered his seat to her, but she declined, claiming that she had already eaten because she couldn't eat Mama's food. "It's too salty," she said. And her blood pressure is already too high. During the whole time, Safot and Pam still hadn't acknowledged each other's presence in the room.

"Anyway, ya'll carry on and I'll just take a seat in the living room." Pam turned away heading towards the front of the house.

"Pam don't be ridiculous. There is an extra seat right here. Please join us." Mama pointed to the vacant seat next to me.

Pam hesitated for a moment, but decided to join us after all. Immediately, the tension in that kitchen rose a notch or two. Everyone was stone quiet. I think we were wondering if Pam and Safot would ever speak to each other. Finally though, Pam broke the silence.

"Grandma is so proud of you Cheekie."

"Thanks again, Pam. You being here means a lot to me."

After much resistance, Safot couldn't take it anymore. She suddenly removed herself out of the frying pan and ran out of the kitchen.

"Pam, ya'll need to talk," said Mama. "Why don't you go back there and talk to her. Regardless of everything, she is still a part of this family. For heaven's sake, Pam, she is your daughter."

Knowing the strong and stern woman Pam is, I thought nothing Mama said would matter to a woman like that. But I guess after much soul-searching and pondering, Pam decided to take Mama's advice. She removed herself from the kitchen table and walked reluctantly to face her past sins. We sat quiet and on the edge of our seats. And we heard everything.

"Safot, we need to talk." Pam cleared her throat.

"About what?" Safot asked, coldly.

" 'Bout this thing that's always been between us."

Safot cried out angrily, "This thing, Pam? What *thing* are

you referring to? You dogged me, your own flesh and blood, since the day I was born. You treated me like a slave. I couldn't *say* anything right. I couldn't *do* anything right. The only time you didn't dog me was when I was asleep, but even then, you invaded my dreams. You never once showed me love, or caring, or understanding. Woman, you made my life a living hell! And now you stand here and say you want to talk about this thing? This thing is my *life*, Pam, and how you tried to make me end it."

"Wait a minute . . ."

"Wait? Wait? No, *you* wait. I've waited long enough to tell you how I feel about our relationship. I've had enough counseling and enough time to think about it, and I know that *I* am not the problem. *I* deserved better. First you dogged me, then you threw me out. You locked the door and threw away the key. I was just a kid!"

There was silence for a few moments, then we heard Pam's voice.

"Safot, I know that what I did to you was wrong, and God in heaven knows that one day I will have to answer for that, but I want to explain."

Safot interrupted.

"Explain? Go ahead, I'm listening."

"Look, I'm still your mother. Listen to me because this is very hard for me, too."

For a few long moments, Safot didn't answer. At last she said, "OK I'm listening."

"When you were born, I was going through a very difficult time in my life. I was injured on my job, had twelve children to raise, bills to pay. I really didn't want another child. And your daddy wasn't shit, and left me for worse. I was mad, so mad that I took my anger and pain out on you all those years. I hated you 'cause every time I looked at you, it reminded me of him. Now, I know I was wrong, and you see I'm woman enough to admit that. I know this don't change what I did to you, and I know it don't change the hell I put you through, but I'm hoping you can find it in your heart to forgive me as I have gone to God for His forgiveness."

"Don't you know, Pam? All I ever wanted was to be loved by my mama. I needed for you to put your arms around me just once, and hold me and hug me and tell me you loved me. That's all I ever wanted Pam. I just wanted my mama's love."

Pam seemed shocked by Safot's tender revelation. She realized, perhaps for the first time, the depth of Safot's pain and the agony she had caused her.

"Just hug me, Pam, and tell me you love me. Please go ahead and hug me right now!" she cried.

There was a long silence. They must be hugging!

"I do love you." We were all amazed to hear the tears in Pam's voice as she spoke tenderly to Safot. "I love you with all my heart, Florence. With all my heart." That was the first time I ever heard Pam cry, and it was also the first time I had ever heard Pam call Safot by her real name.

Mama opened the door joining the kitchen and the room they were standing in. We got a clearer view of the gut-shaking hug between the two of them. It was the best feeling in the world seeing the two of them like that. Mama was crying, too. You know, it doesn't take much to get her crying.

"Now that we have that settled, can we all finally eat?" Mama giggled, at last, giving both Pam and Safot a hug.

Pam was still wiping tears from her eyes as she tried to pull herself back together again. I had never seen her so emotional before. This was a beautiful side of her.

"I think we ready to eat. But I sure hope you went easy on that salt, Faye. I know you can be heavy handed."

Everyone laughed and prepared to eat in good cheer.

Later that evening we kids played out front and left the grown folks inside talking, drinking, and laughing about the good "ole" days. And as Boo Boo and Daniel sent a football flying in the air, me, Rachelle, and Tanya jumped rope. I hadn't jumped rope in a long time. But on this special day, I didn't care about the fact that no boy wasn't suppose to be jumping rope like no girl. In fact, as we played a game of "Oh King Kong was sitting on a fence, trying to make a dollar out of fifteen cents," I jumped, and leaped higher than any of the girls. I guess one day we'll be sitting around like the grown folks inside talking about the good "ole" days and how I used to kick their butts every time we played a game of jump rope.